D0373251

"Of course there are lands!

Brann exclaimed. "What of the Farmy Fields, what of the mountains?"

"You interpret it incorrectly, young man," the Hegman answered. "You begin from the most erroneous premise, that there is an inside and an outside to the city, a city and a planet, I suppose, upon which it rests. All that, of course, is nonsense.

"The eye will fill what is empty, young Brann. If there were lands, there would certainly be folk to fill them, and if such folks then we would have seen them. True?"

"True," Brann answered, reluctantly.
"Have we seen such folk?" asked the Hegman.
"No," said Brann.

"There is the city, there are the mountains and the fields. They are one, and all beyond their unity is only the vision of things and this vision is nothing more than that, for the eye abhors emptiness and will fill it always. When you learn the true answer, you must stop questioning and begin to learn," said the Hegman. "And that is that."

PILGRIMAGE

Drew
Mendelson

DAW Books, Inc.
Donald A. Wollheim,   Publisher

1633 Broadway, New York, N.Y. 10019

PUBLISHED BY
THE NEW AMERICAN LIBRARY
OF CANADA LIMITED

COPYRIGHT ©, 1981, BY DREW MENDELSON

All Rights Reserved.

Cover art by John Pound.

FIRST PRINTING, APRIL 1981

2 3 4 5 6 7 8 9

DAW TRADEMARK REGISTERED
U.S. PAT. OFF. MARCA REGISTRADA,
HECHO EN WINNIPEG, CANADA

PRINTED IN CANADA
COVER PRINTED IN U.S.A.

BOOK ONE

Chapter One

Tailend

On the 37th tier of Tailend, above the Foundations and the Farmy Fields, above the trolley tracks where the engines ran below like minute centipedes, above the valley, at times above the clouds, Brann Adelbran lived. He was a clean-limbed youth of seventeen, brown-haired, hazel-eyed. He was taller than many though shorter than some, and while not stocky he had a large and heavy build that a few years hence, when fully fleshed into that of a man, would make him a powerful and formidable figure. So his brother Grandel was and so his brother Mikla was becoming in so swift a fashion that it frightened Brann and sent him, envious and jealous, to the verge where the empty beams of a dismantled gallery extended beyond his own gallery's edge. There he could watch the Structors work thirty tiers below, like savage rodents gnawing at the base of Tailend. There he could look out across the valley at the Foundations which had supported Tailend before, at their regular stone and concrete impressions, the imprints of the city's bones. They became lost in the haze, and try though he might, he could never find where they began to climb the mountain rampart beyond.

Brann was the third oldest of eight siblings, who along with Grandel and Mikla included in descending age sisters Livna and Sal (twins), Gwenia, brother Thod and baby sister Nam. Grandel no longer lived at home. He occupied a house next to the family plat, but nearer as by custom to the gallery verge where the Structors would begin dismantling tier 37

7

when they came. Grandel had a wife, Mara, and a baby, and he had no pretense of any noble purpose in his life, as did Mikla, or as Brann thought he himself had. Grandel and Mara ran a clothing shop which occupied a space among other shops on a spur of the trans-tier highroad. Their sole aspiration was that when the Structors came again in seven years they should be prosperous and respected enough to be leaders on the Pilgrimage to Frontend.

Mikla had a purpose. When the Structors came again he would join them. By then he would be as brawny as Grandel, seven years older, nearly twenty-six, and a fit candidate for their ranks. Brann could not really understand the single-mindedness which drove his older brother to plan for an event that would occur seven years later, if at all.

"Mikla," he would say, "how do you know that they will take you?"

"I am as strong as any," Mikla would say. "They want brawn. And I'm not stupid either. They want no one stupid. Do you know that one misstep could bring down a whole tier? Do you know that they must calculate the stresses to the finest margin? Can you imagine the mass and heft of the blocks that support this tier? Their structural integrity? They've accepted me into the guild school. That's half of it. They don't accept many. I'll learn what it takes. I'll finish the school; they'll let me join join them."

Often at these times Brann would not listen to Mikla. He was, after all, seventeen; new sensations and emotions were within him. There were feelings that he had never known, so subtle and yet at times so feverish inside him that he would sit on the beam next to Mikla and while Mikla talked (cease-lessly, not noticing that Brann was not listening), he would throw soft bits off the verge, paper and cloth shreds and bits of leaf and stick. He would watch them flutter weightlessly down through currents that always swirled about Tailend. He knew better than to throw anything hard, anything of stone or metal which might gather killing momentum as it plunged past the tiers. What had been law, had grown past law to an ingrained—perhaps hereditary—taboo. Still, he had no com-prehension of the velocity a stone would obtain falling down a mile, down thirty-seven tiers to the Foundations or the Farmy Fields.

The juices in Brann were love; Brann was sick in love with a girl who lived blocks away at the innermost line of the gallery. Every day after school he would run to her house, waiting to see if she was home yet. She was younger than he by nearly a year, a slender, red-haired girl of sixteen. He didn't know that he was in love with her. He only knew that when he tried to study or to work or play, he would catch a whiff that might have been the perfume of her, or he would catch a flash of red that might have been her hair. She lived near the market square and he would traverse this in his travels to see her. Before, even as much as six months earlier, Brann would have thought nothing at all of her. He would have been enthralled only by the market, a place which had fascinated him since childhood.

The market was laid out on a plat a square acre in area. Its rear side abutted the wall dividing Brann's gallery from the one farther in. Between the arches which pierced this wall were the elevators. They were massive things, ten yards wide and deep, half that distance high, with doors that opened vertically like lips covering a great mouth. There were two elevator shafts side by side. In one the cars went only up, in the other only down. It had seemed to Brann in times past that this could not be, that eventually they could rise no farther, that they must come to a stop at the city's roof 113 tiers above the ground.

He had an image of artisans at the roof whose only labor it was to take the cars as they came and tear them down to make room for the following cars (as the Structors endlessly tore down the tail end of the city). He could not imagine that the two shafts were part of the same system, that the cars rose up two more miles to the highest tier, were moved over to the down shaft and dropped. There was one main reason for the down shaft: the Pilgrimage, still seven years off; and not even folk from tier 113 had yet begun their Pilgrimage.

There were other shafts in banks to either side of the large elevators. His mother told him that at one time these shafts also held elevators. These moved no produce, freight or trade goods; they moved people from tier to tier. Brann could not imagine traveling up the tiers other than by foot. Having been up to tier 40 one time at the death of his great aunt

Hela, and down to tier 35 on his own, in direct contravention of his parents' order never to leave his home gallery without permission, he could not really fathom the distances one might travel by elevator up or down.

The smaller shafts were empty, their doors covered over, bricked in and sealed so long ago that it was scarcely understood by anyone that they were actually elevator shafts. One shaft had, until recent times, been accessible. Its door was inside an alley formed by the wall of an ancient houseplat built near the inner face of the gallery. Half a year earlier, the boys with whom Brann played had discovered this sealed elevator door, had found that the mortar of its bricks was loose and crumbling. They had gradually opened a hole into the brick and found that the shaft doors behind it were not closed.

One boy, Halsam, a neighbor of Brann's, more daring than the others, had run home to get a flashlight and bring it back. Then he had wormed his way through the hole and out onto a narrow ledge which occupied three sides of the shaft.

"What do you see, Hals?" Brann asked.

"Nothing," said Hals. "It just goes down. Even with the light I can't see far."

Brann edged out onto the ledge next to Hals, gripping the edge of one of the partly open doors for support. A smell permeated the shaft, powerful and unidentifiable, wet and rancid and old. A cold-air current fell past them.

"Papa says it is always cold on the upper tiers, even in summer. He says that there's snow on the upper galleries all the time," Brann told Hals.

Another boy squeezed through and a fourth, until Brann was pressed to the far right wall of the shaft, to where the ledge was slimy and wet and the handhold slippery. Something fell, perhaps a brick. It plunged down the shaft creating a reverberation that faded into the constant noise inside, a steady deep hum. Below, as if from occasional windows, spots of light picked out gray spaces which gradually blended into a gray blur as the shaft descended. Brann had no concept of the distance down, and here in the dark for the first time he felt a vertigo that never came to him when he perched on the empty beams at the open end of his gallery.

"There is a ladder here," Hals said. "I'm going down."

"No, you can't," one of the other boys told him uncertainly. "How do you know how far the ladder goes?"

Hals shined the light upon it and followed the corroded steps down to where it touched the ledge of the next level, 150 feet below. Then he moved around on the ledge, sliding over slick spots that made Brann hold his breath and say, "Come back, Hals," and then Hals was on the ladder.

He said, "I think I can see an opening. The ladder looks good down that far. I'm going."

This was an enticement that overshadowed danger. On the stairs between levels, adults always asked what reason a boy had for leaving his own level. This was a secret pathway down. The boys delighted in its possibility and forsook fear. Hals stepped down. For a moment he grinned, showing the others how easy it was. The step gave way beneath him. It parted from the ladder with a shrieking noise that was hardly separable from Hals's shriek. He lost his grip on the flashlight which tumbled, spinning, down, and he clung to the ruined ladder, finding purchase for only one foot on the ledge. Hals was transformed instantly from explorer to child, a frightened, crying child who held tight to the metal and begged the other boys to go for aid.

Adults came and after Hals had been brought out safely, his mother, when he was at last pulled free, alternately cried in relief and screamed in anger, beating Hals and holding him in turn. The shaft was sealed again, securely this time, and the boys were forbidden even to go near it.

In the market itself were open stalls of produce: fruits and vegetables and grains that would not grow or for which there was too little room to grow on the open dirt plots of the tiers. (The lights in the ceiling, which was the floor of the tier above, duplicated, Brann knew, the light of the sun in a way that allowed plants to grow within the galleries.) But there was no such profusion of produce cultivated within the city itself. All this was grown in the Farmy Fields which stretched out as far as Brann could see to either side of the Foundations. Farther off toward the mountains the fields merged with the Foundations themselves. Brann had asked his father if there were folk who lived there, too, in the Farmy Fields rather than in the city itself.

But his father, as always when he did not know, said, "It is not to be asked." (So many things were not to be asked.) And Brann asked his cousin, Vill, who was an elevator runner and traveled up and down the great shafts in the cars which carried the produce. Surely his cousin would know. But Vill had said he did not know either. Brann could scarcely believe this of Vill, who in his guild uniform of deep green with gold piping (of the Runners' Guild, older even than the Structors') surely was more widely traveled than anyone he knew. But Vill had said that even he had gone down and up only twenty levels, two days' run by elevator. He had never been all the way down to the bottom, to the ground where the Farmy Fields came up to Tailend and the trolley came to carry folk off on the Pilgrimage.

"Maybe on the Pilgrimage you will find out," Vill told him. "On the Pilgrimage you will see things that I have never seen: the flank of the city where it is said you can see from Frontend to Tailend of the city. On the Pilgrimage you will learn more than you ever will in school."

Cousin Vill said that he personally didn't think people lived outside the city or worked in the Farmy Fields. He told stories of machines, "like the trucks on the highroad," which traveled to and from the fields, with brains like men and women, with arms and hands like them; they never tired or slept. But Brann thought them myths to frighten children— and he was no longer a child—and believed little of what cousin Vill told him. After all, Vill did little more than travel in the cab of the elevator, up two days to the 57th level and down two days to the 17th level, staying in guild houses between. He did bring back marvels at times, intricate mechanical toys from the 44th level that were like humans in miniature, all shiny metal that walked and danced and sat and climbed and needed only the light to revive them when they had tired from their exertion. He brought back cakes and pastries from level 21 that were decorated as if they were galleries in scale with the crowded houseplats and gardenplats seen from a height seemingly impossible. The buildings of the gallery diminished to each side as they must do toward the flanks of the city, 40 miles shrunk to a cake a yard long and a couple of inches wide. Brann had one cake that he had never eaten, stale by now but still a marvel, kept on the shelf above his bed where he could imagine that the cake was actually the gallery in which he lived. He tried to imagine an interminable succession of galleries like this cake, laid side by side, stretching from Tailend to Frontend of the city, each one a tier, and 113 of these layers one on top of the other from ground to roof of the city.

Like Mikla, Brann too had a purpose: he would carry the post. Of all the eighty-odd guilds of Tailend, there was only one Brann wanted to join. It was the Post Guild, and Brann had dreamed of it ever since he knew that there were folk who could move freely from one end of the city to the other, from gallery to gallery through the walls and arches, from level to level; not just two days up and two days down, but days and days beyond into the interior of the city, past galleries that he knew, past galleries that anyone knew (it seemed), to where the city changed, to where there were folk who spoke in ways different from how he spoke and lived in homes that were in no way like the home in which he lived, to places where none had seen the Farmy Fields, or the mountains or the sky in generations. (Perhaps the generations were beyond counting; certainly their number was beyond his understanding.) But the Post Guild moved freely from one end to the other.

Brann had tried without success to discover how one went about joining the Post Guild. The guild house, near its own post elevator (on which none but guild members could travel) between the shafts of the great elevators, was closed to all but men and women of the guild. None had contact with them, save in the stations where the guildspersons dealt with the folk through windows that opened into mysterious paper-cluttered rooms.

"How do I join?" Brann had asked when one day he had gone to retrieve a letter which could not be delivered in person.

"How old are you?" the guildswoman had inquired in turn.

"Seventeen."

"Ah, then you are too young."

"How old must I be?"

"How old do I look?"

"Twenty?"

"Yes," she had laughed just a bit. "And I have been in the guild for five years now."

He was perplexed, and asked how this contradictory answer could be.

"Some are never old enough; some are always old enough." Her voice was strange, a musical accent of tones and odd cadences.

"You are not of this gallery," he said.

"No, I come from farther frontward."

"Is that where I may join the guild?"

"You certainly cannot join it here."

"How do I join?"

"I cannot tell you; you must keep asking."

That had been no answer at all.

He was in love. The girl was Liza, with red hair and with freckles across her nose. He didn't know that he was in love, not really except that things happened inside him when he saw her. He stammered when he saw her though otherwise he was always so swift with his questions and with his words. He blushed when he saw her though usually he was unafraid and unashamed of anything. He was terrified of being with her, but he tried always to be with her, when school was done and when his work in the gardenplat was done and neither Mama nor Papa could find further chores for him to do. She was not sure she wanted it yet; she was no more really woman yet than he was really a man. They were both no longer children and both not quite adults, and he loved her. It did not matter much about this love, for nothing could ever come of it. They could not marry, lovers or no. There were strict rules about it. (Were there an Anthropologists' Guild, it would have been said that the tiers were a set of interlinked exogamous phratries. This had been so since anyone could remember. Had there been anthropologists among the folk, they would have said that this marriage outside the home tier was purposely designed to strengthen the close trade relationships among the galleries. Since there was no such guild, no one said this. They thought not in those terms, but it mattered not, the damage was done.) Liza and Brann, of the same tier, of the same gallery, could not marry—no more than could brother and sister. Of course, nothing prevented them from being together, from spending all their time together, even from engaging in a bit of harmless sex play, which when it became serious enough to be noticed by the adults would only serve to indicate that the children were children no longer and should perhaps begin to look for mates from among the folk of tiers above and below.

"Is there one you would like to marry?" she asked.

"You," he said.

They were in the parkplat. She laughed. "No, really, have you seen any yet that you like?"

"No, of course not. I've only been with my father to the other galleries. I'm not even of age yet for another six months."

A small hillock rose above the flat of the gallery, perhaps a third the height of the ceiling. Here the soil was deep and it supported trees that rose nearly a hundred feet higher, almost to the ceiling. Here the ceaseless motion of air from the inner galleries was screened. The light was diffuse, a shadowless radiation warm both in temperature and hue. He often wondered (with an alien and shivery feeling) if this was the sensation one sitting in such a copse of trees outside the city would experience. There were such wooded spots among the Farmy Fields, much larger (it seemed, for he had no vantage from which to view the exterior of the parkplat) but not so well tended. They were (must be) wild and grew as opportunity presented.

Here was one particularly thick and overgrown spot screened by higher growth on all sides. It was open only to the south where a narrow space between the trees permitted them to see down the hill and along the southern stretch of the high road. Liza sat with her back to a tree, her legs—bare beyond the hem of her short summer dress—stretched out over the mossy earth. She teased at Brann, who—bare-legged and barefooted himself—lay with his head in her lap. Things went through his mind that made him blush, and she teased him, asking why, which only made him blush the more and stammer so that he could not have told her anyway, though she could certainly see and know for herself.

"There is a school one-up that my parents wish me to go to," she told him. "One-up and at the far north of the gallery."

"A guild school?" He felt panic; when would she go?

"Yes. Guild of Health."

The Lord! A long school, the longest. "You won't finish before the Pilgrimage. I won't see you."

"Yes, I will finish, though I will not be signed a Physician before we go to Frontend."

"No," he said, "you can't. Of course, you'll tell them you won't go."

"Why? So that I can remain here with you?"

"It's just that. . . ." He didn't know how to finish it. What he wanted to tell her was that things had to stay just as they were and that if she left and he left, then they would not stay that way (as if, he thought, they ever could).

"My parents want me to go down-two, to tier 35 to the Guild School of Engine Makers, as if there were a reason for it, as if anything I might build or design will be useful at Frontend. We will be so far apart that we will never see each other again. Not until the Pilgrimage. Not until we are with others."

"When do you go?" she asked.

"At the end of the summer; at the beginning of the next term. Possibly three weeks."

"Yes, it's the same for me."

He reached up and touched her cheek, pushing aside the froth of her red hair. This was not what he wanted to do but was absolutely terrified of doing for it would mean an abysmal slide into a passion from which he doubted he could retreat. He wanted to let his arm slide down to rest against her breasts as he touched her. *Others do it, others do it with abandon, so much so that this imagined motion is nothing to what others do.* But others did not love each other the way he loved—thought he loved—Liza. Others could engage and disengage from each other with no more meaning to it than the mechanical description. So he touched her cheek and anyway against his will his arm came onto her breasts, loose inside her light summer shirt, and that was all.

His brother Mikla had been accepted into the Structors' Guild. It was an event. It was more than an event; it was a small miracle; not many had thought Mikla capable. He had turned down offers from other guilds. He had remained an extra two years past the minimum in the gallery general school, doggedly studying for an examination that one in twenty passed. If he failed, he would be too old by a year to

join any of the other prestigious guilds. But Mikla had passed
and it meant a conflict of emotions in the family. He would
be a Structor (if he finished the guild school), a singular
honor for anyone, for any family, but he would not go on
Pilgrimage with the rest of the family.

Of all the folk, only the Structors remained behind. They,
too, journeyed toward Frontend. But their travel was both
inexorable and imperceptible, moving a mile every ten years
as they perpetually tore down Tailend and sent it to the
front. Mikla would be separated from the family sooner than
that. The Structors' school of necessity remained within ten
tiers of where the Structors worked. Now it was on the fifth
tier—the Structors worked this month on the seventh—three
days away by elevator (and at what cost? 190 Paad per person each way, payable in advance, though cousin Vill who
had a pass could travel freely and promised to visit Mikla
whenever he could). Harder than that even was foot travel
between the tiers. The stairs, never meant to be an auxiliary
route for long-distance travel, were haphazardly placed. Even
ten tiers away the folk were as of another nation, with
strange customs, stranger rules. It was said there were border
stations between some tiers where travelers from distant
places were detained. Who knew? Not cousin Vill, whose
knowledge was revealed now to extend little past the market-
plats beyond the elevator doors. What would it be like next
year when the Structors moved to the 113th tier and began
on the galleries directly above? Then they would not see or
hear from Mikla except briefly in the summers when he
would return.

They were in the main room of the Adelbran houseplat.
All the family were there: Brann's seven brothers and sisters,
his papa, his mama, his papa's brothers and sisters, his
mama's family up from tier 36 for the occasion. Brann had
not seen the house so full since Grandel's marriage. The long
table—of oak brought up from the Farmy Fields at Lord
knows what expense generations ago—was covered with the
gold-worked cloth that Brann had also not seen since the
wedding.

His papa and mama occupied the table's head. Past fifty
now, his papa still had the strong build of the Adelbran men;
not so iron hard anymore as his oldest son Grandel, still,

Papa Adelbran was a formidable figure, one Brann could
only marvel at, wondering if he would be so in thirty-some
years. Papa was a bear of a man, a member of the Fire-
fighters' Guild (not so prestigious as some of the others,
though there were always fires in the galleries, in the
houseplats which were old, some of them older than anyone
could guess, dating—as did the Adelbran house—back to the
gallery's original construction). There had been days when
Brann's papa had come home soot-stained and blackened,
smelling of smoke and sweat. At those times he became a
forbidding personage, something quite demonic, who stalked
about singed and reeking, declaring to the Lord above the
city that none of his sons or daughters would have such
work, that all of them would work with their minds, not their
bodies and live not from their muscle but from their wit.

· In the gallery one-tailward (before the Structors had come
to remove it) there had once been a fire which burned for
days. That gallery—older by ten years than the one in which
Brann resided—had not been at all like Brann's in architecture. Some whim of its constructors had given it close-packed
plats with shops and houses intermingled in a single tight unit
from flank to flank and front to back. Instead of the wide
ways and high roads that Brann knew, it had had narrow
crooked pathways and alleys which crawled from the arches
and through the buildings, sometimes overhung by them so
that the ceiling of the gallery was not visible.

In among those structures the fire had caught and traveled.
Fire-fighters from other galleries and even from other tiers
had come. It was said that the plume of smoke from the 37th
tier had stretched eastward from the city for miles and miles
until it merged and became part of the mountains' mist. In
the end Brann's father and the others had controlled and ex-
tinguished the fire. But it had left a swath ten miles wide
from front to back of the gallery, and for months after all
the nearby tiers had smelled terribly of smoke. The folk there
had made no attempt to rebuild a place so soon because of
the coming of the Structors. Where they had gone Brann
didn't know, possibly early to the Pilgrimage, down the elevators to the trolleys. From then on until the following year
when the Structors came the gallery had been a hollow
gaping wound on the face of Tailend.

Forty-three fire-fighters had died controlling that blaze, which had taken three days to extinguish, and each day when their father had gone back to take his shift in the fight, the Adelbran children had wondered if he would return. Then the fire had been put out.

"None of you will do this," Papa had said. "I won't have it. Mine is the worst of all the guilds. I won't have my children numbered among its members."

Of course, Brann until then had thought of following his papa into the Fire-fighters' Guild. But his father said, "You will join the Engine Makers." The man said it so often that Brann began to want it himself and even began to turn his studies toward the Engine Makers' examination.

It was a double celebration really—for Mikla certainly— but also for Brann who had (nearly unnoticed in the excitement over his older brother) passed the exam and would be leaving also. His mama came to him at the end of dinner.

"This is for you, too, you know," she said.

"I know, Mama."

"Then why so sad? Is it because we seem to be favoring Mikla today?"

Brann shook his head. All but he and Mama were near the wide front window of the house which looked along the cross street east to the arches to where, for one short span of ten years, there was sky and even stars. The sun lights were darkened in the gallery roof. (Following the sun—did they darken and brighten so in the city's interior where none had seen the sun for long generations?) They crowded about Mikla, wishing him well, drinking him toasts from tiny glasses that were like the gold-worked tablecloth, special and very old. They drank amber whiskey and said, "Mikla, good luck, Lord preserve."

Her hands were what was so fine about his mama. She was of the Clothiers' Guild, as were Grandel and his wife, a match for his papa in stature and strength. Where the rest of her was thick and strong (she was not ever really pretty), her hands were soft—also they were strong—and supple and dexterous. They could touch and stroke, making whatever hurt, hurt not so much, and they held him now, one hand to each shoulder while she looked at Brann.

"You know it is because he is going so far away. This may

be one of the last times we see Mikla. We won't see him at all after the Pilgrimage. Sure, it is special what he has done. But it is no more than what you can do."

"It's not Mikla, Mama. He's always wanted this. I don't think I've ever heard him speak of anything else. But he is going where he always wanted to go, to the Structors. I . . . Mama, may I ask you this?"

"Of course."

"Is it stupid, is it silly to want to be something you cannot?"

"You will be a fine Engine Maker. Didn't you score higher than most on the examination, so that the marshal of the guild called on you personally to invite you into the guild school? It is what you want, it is what you have always wanted. You will be an Engine Maker, one valued and respected when we leave here and go on the Pilgrimage."

"Mama, I don't know that. I don't know it at all. I don't think anyone here knows it. Where do we go on the Pilgrimage? To Frontend, it is said? We leave here, down the elevators, onto the trolleys and then we are gone. Who has ever returned from it?"

"We have the post."

"Mama, there are letters from them sometimes, brought by the post; but from how far, from where?"

This angered her; they had argued it before.

"So, you still have thoughts that there is a way for you to join the Post Guild? I thought you had outgrown it. No one joins the Post Guild."

"They must."

"Do you know of anyone from this gallery who has? Have you heard of anyone from this tier? From all of Tailend?"

"No, but . . ."

"No, and nothing else. Wherever the Post Guild folk come from, they do not come from here. That is a child's play game, a fantasy that I thought you had outgrown. You will forget it when you go off to school."

"Mama!"

"No more about it. Here is your papa."

He could not talk to his papa about it. They would have had a terrible argument about it once. They had had them repeatedly until it finally became clear to Brann's papa that the

boy was quite serious in his desire to join the Post Guild.
That had been the only time in his life when his papa had
struck him—in a fearful wrath explained only by the fact
that the man wanted all his children to do better than him in
their lives and was terribly afraid of a dream like Brann's
which, he was sure, led nowhere. He had not spoken about
the Post Guild in front of his papa since then.

"Come," his papa said, "your cousins are missing you.
Come and we'll drink a toast to your future."

His sisters were terrors. Now that they knew Brann was
going, they gave him no peace at all. Livna and Sal were
twins, three years younger than he. They conspired against
each other in a ferocious fashion, each trying to convince
Brann that she was the one surely most logical to have his
room when he left. Mikla's room had long since been ceded
to Mama, both as a haven against the children and as a place
where she might work in peace.

First Livna would come to him, brown-eyed and smiling,
saying, "Brann, you have to give me the room. I could put
my chest of drawers here, and my animals over there by the
window, and I could have a place where I wasn't always with
Sal and Gwenia."

He would laugh; she screwed up her face so and crouched
so, begging him, making her voice go high and squeaky. And
he would say, "No, I haven't decided yet," so that she would
bounce down onto Brann's bed, petulant, swearing that it was
a life-or-death matter that she should get the room, that her
sisters were impossible to live with and that Sal was especially
impossible. She couldn't stay in the same room with Sal any
longer and surely he couldn't give the room to Gwenia, who
was "still just a baby, a little girl, really." Though for all their
shapes demonstrated, both Sal and Livna were but girls also.

Then Sal would come, so like Livna that only the leftward
turn of her hair, where Livna's fell more naturally to the
right, and only the eternal pout where Livna had a smile dif-
ferentiated them. They dressed interchangeably and at times
Brann was scarcely certain which had come into his room at
any given time to wheedle and beg. "Livna thinks she should
have it because she's a half hour older."

Then Gwenia would come and she would say, "Brann, I

don't guess I will ever have a room of my own because both of *them* will stay here together and go away together at the same time and that will be a long time from now, so please, Brann, give it to me."

They were at him day and night, incessantly until he was almost willing to go away, even to the Engine Makers' school. In the big house there was no escaping them. He was constantly being trapped on the stairs or accosted as he left the washroom or jabbered at, at the breakfast table until one day his mama shouted, "Enough, I won't hear anymore of it. Brann will decide and that will be the end!" Then all he saw were faces of his sisters mooning at him, which he thought worse than the noise.

His little brother Thod was perplexed by it all. "How come nobody thinks I should get Brann's room?" He made a face. "I have to share my room with the *baby!*" He didn't understand why they laughed.

There was a hideout Brann had. He had discovered it one day while exploring in the maintenance space below the house. Between two great conduits that rose from the house's foundation was an ancient hatchway that predated the house. He had shown it to Halsam, who as Brann's best friend was the only person other than Brann who knew of the place. The hatchway, when freed of corrosion, opened into a forgotten space in the area below the tier.

"It must be hundreds of years old," Brann told Halsam, knowing no such thing, except that Papa had told Brann that there were structures on the tier more than a thousand years old, nearly as old as the tier itself. Brann was not sure what the purpose of the room was. Conduits ten times as massive as those going up to the house pierced the walls of the room and ran transversely, north to south through the gallery. The floor of the room was a truly huge conduit, oriented east/west. It did not seem to have a purpose either. It would echo with an eerie, hollow moaning at times, like the vibration they had heard in the defunct elevator shaft. But nothing seemed to flow through it, nor was there any other sound of motion inside it. Perhaps an entry had once pierced it, sealed now with smoother, newer metal.

"Maybe it goes all the way to Frontend," Halsam speculated one time. "I bet if you got inside it you could walk to the other end of the city."

"I bet you couldn't," said Brann. "There's probably no way out at all."

"There has to be. Why would it be here if there wasn't any reason for it?"

"I don't know."

To the left of the huge conduit was a space which dropped down to a grillwork. It was a space the size of a small closet, barely large enough for the boys together. It was further cramped by a smaller conduit which at some far past time someone had hacked open, exposing a snarled nest of cables, most of which were cut and useless, their copper interiors gone to a greenish fluff which no longer transmitted any messages. The boys did not know the reason for the cables either, but the open conduit with its rotten ruined cables scared them; an acid smell came from it. They left it alone.

The grille was fascinating, though; perhaps as old as the rest of the room, it was not corroded or damaged. Through it they could see a panorama of tier 36 below them. They could look straight down at the spires of a gallery school where boys and girls younger than they would come and go, though not now during the summer. The grille was concave downward, basket-like, so that by hanging head downward with feet supported, Hals or Brann could peer down the long stretch of the lower gallery, over roofs which flattened in perspective north and south. East they could see (upside down) all the way to the gallery verge. West they could see to the dividing wall of the galleries. The streets below were like the streets of their own gallery, and at the same time they were different. The folk were different in dress. The language was all so slightly altered; words that drifted up were shifted or slurred so that even one tier below, the city was strange.

"Cousin Vill says that they are more different even than this when you get farther away from here. He says that twenty tiers down you can hardly understand people at all."

"Are you scared to go to school away from home?" Hals asked. He was not going away. His school, of the Guild of Gardeners, was here on the 37th tier. It occupied a building a mile south on the highroad abutting the parkplat.

"Sometimes I pretend that this is a toy of mine, like the

cake that Vill gave me. All the gallery below is a mechanical toy built just for me so that I can observe it. I pretend that they aren't real people there, that it's only imagination. I imagine that our gallery is the only one that is real and there is nothing else in the city that is real."

"Brann, are you scared? I will miss you, you know. I won't see you for a long time, until next summer. You'll be different then."

"I'm not afraid. Not of going away from here. It's not that it is so far; it isn't far enough."

"You still want to join the Post Guild?" Hals didn't speak of it as if it were impossible.

"Yes," said Brann. He pointed down through the grille. "See there, the power cart. They drive on the cross streets down there. I've seen them go right to the verge."

"Are you going to go?"

"Where? To school?"

"You know."

"To find the Post Guild? To try to join?"

Hals nodded.

"Mama told me that it is a fantasy a lot of children have. They grow from it and become adults, she said. It is just a myth, a story that there is some secret Post school on some faroff tier and gallery."

"But where do they come from, then?"

"I asked her that; she said she didn't know. 'It's not to be asked,' she said."

"Are you going to go, Brann?"

"Maybe. . . ." He was taken with the thought. It had been one and the same as the fantasy before, to be outgrown with it before. "Why not? Why the Lord not?"

"I don't want to hear of it!" Hals objected, frightened. "Don't tell me anything at all."

On the highest tiers above, the Pilgrimage was beginning. Already folk from the roof of the city were on the elevators going down. Daily now the folk from higher tiers moved homeless before the Structors. It would be so from now until the year that the Structors came to Brann's tier, a constant, ceaseless downward motion of folk. Those coming now were strange to Brann, speakers of a language so divorced from his that he could scarcely make out their words or gather much meaning from their inverted syntax. The elevator doors would open upon people in unusual garments, somber as those of Brann's gallery were bright. There were children among them, who, when the doors would rise, stared out, wide-eyed and pale-haired, tugging at the clothing of their parents, asking questions in that singsong language which to Brann was like a chant. They gave Brann the first inkling that—as his papa had said—it was truly cold up above. On the elevators they carried their belongings, crated and packed, the residue of an entire gallery of the city. At times when the elevator doors opened there would be no people at all, except for the elevator runner. The car would be stacked with things incongruous and unnecessary to a long journey, as if the folk traveling down had no concept of the direction and meaning of the Pilgrimage. One such car was filled with cartoned books, packed into the elevator so haphazardly that when the doors closed upon the load, one carton was burst, sending fragile, brittle volumes out onto the marketplat.

Brann had rescued one of the books and showed it to Halsam, opening it carefully so that the crumbling pages remained intact.

Brann read from it: *"Dhegu guer ay leis-lek worad. . . ."*

"It's all like that," he told Hals. "Crates and crates of books like this on the elevator."

Occasionally they would come upon a word with a meaning half clear, sometimes a whole phrase of almost words which did not quite make sense, but should have made sense, and they would puzzle at it before going on. Brann asked his papa, who could not guess at the meaning, and then he took the tattered book to the school, where a master told him, "It is an old version, much changed, of the language we speak."

"Can the up-folk read it, then?" asked Brann.

"I doubt it," said the master. "Their dialect is not so far removed from ours, really. This is very old. I don't think I know of anyone who could read it with understanding."

"Then if it is useless, why do they take it?"

"Because it is their history; our history, too, I suppose. Maybe it could tell us something of the history of the city if we could read it." He read from the first page: *"Dhegu guer,* to burn a mountain; *ay leis-lek,* a road torn; (perceive) *worad,* the branch root, or perhaps network? . . . There is a lifetime of study in this one book, Brann. Can you imagine how many times this book has been carried from back to front of the city?"

Brann thought it useless, but he gave the book to the master. It seemed to please him greatly, and he left the man in the schoolroom leafing through and pondering the book in much the same manner that he and Halsam had.

There were machines going up the elevators. With them were Structors, who—hard-faced and silent—would answer none of a young man's questions, and Brann wished that Mikla were still at home. He could have explained some of the massive machines. Many had been broken apart and went up the elevators in pieces. Car after car carried sections of one; here a great claw with teeth seemingly sharp enough to take a bite out of the tier's supporting beams; here a massive tread, now part of the undercarriage with road wheels set inside a belt; here a console of the sort that Brann had only seen in the postplat (covered there with an immense accumulation of dust, old papers and debris). This one was worn, but obviously functional. A silent Structor stood watch over it. He, like the folk traveling down on their Pilgrimage, was pale-skinned and blond. Unlike the other guilds, the Structors were of diverse types from all the Tiers of Tailend. (Also, Brann realized, the Post Guildspersons were different, more so even, as if none at all had come from nearby.)

Groups of the pilgrims from the upper tier would stop for a few hours or overnight. They camped near the elevators or were offered places in the homes of the folk on Brann's tier. One time a family stayed with the Adelbrans; among them was a boy about Brann's age. They spoke together with much laughing at mistaken and double meanings, with much signing and motion, and mirth.

"Where are you going?" Brann asked the other.

"Eh? Var goin?"

"Yes, where?"

"Ay, te gallry eptied, vey be palgram dawn. Be makna come, alls so var."

"Makna?" Brann pointed to the model of a power cart, the making of which had occupied his weekends for months not long ago. "Machine, you mean, like this? *Makna,* machine?"

"Ay," the boy nodded. *"Makna be machine."*

Gradually Brann gathered a vision of the upper gallery. At its verge, the boy said, snow drifted always and the air was so cold that even the sunlights in the gallery roof gave not enough heat. He learned that the city roof was not solid but was pocked with spaces where one could see the sky and through which snow came so that there was even snow on the cross streets and on the highroad.

"It must be very cold," said Brann.

"Ay, cul'd," answered the boy. He smiled and indicated his heavy clothing. *"Be varm dawn, be hot too mak fer tees."*

The boy's coat was of fur, a lovely black-tipped silver that seemed to be of no animal Brann knew, and he felt a strange disquiet thinking of the deaths which had come before the creation of the coat.

"Fer me, too varm," the boy said and with something approaching solemnity he presented the coat to Brann. Knowing not what else to do, Brann gave him some lighter clothing in exchange.

They had spoken also of the mountains, of what could be seen from the verge of the highest gallery. Could the boy see the mountains from there? *Ay.* And what were they like? Like the face of the city rising again faroff to the east. And could he see the Foundations from there? *Som-time.* Did they truly climb the mountains? *Ay.* Like the track of a snail they were, behind the city, on and on into the mountains. He asked something else he had wondered for a long time. Had the other ever been to the roof of the city? Up onto the roof of his own tier? *Ay, I bain der, I bain alls up.* What was it like? It was snow, and black in patches alternately, a checkered field stretching farther than the mountains' distance in the opposite direction. Could he see the front, Frontend? Could he see the far end of the city? *"Ney."* The boy shook his head. *"Er be lang, er be ney end o'it."*

So far, Brann mused, so far it had no end!

Chapter Two

The Dwarf

In some ways he was a dwarf. He came out of the city's interior galleries frontward, the strangest of them yet. Folk came from the interior from time to time. They were displaced souls, speechless and incoherent. They would come on all manner of conveyance. One had been seen by Brann's grandmother Ebar and she remembered it still and compared the one who had come now with the earlier one who came.

"He was on a wheeled platform, made of metal and wood in no certain shape. It looked as if he had taken bits of wall struts and pieces of metal and woven them into a deck so that it looked more like a nest than something man-made. It was on wheels and there were folk pulling it with ropes. The folk were the same as he was. But they were mute and dumb, with no intelligence in their eyes. They pulled him and he lashed at them with a long metal whip, blood-tipped and sharp."

"You mean no one did anything?" Brann asked. "They pulled him along like the engine of a power cart? Didn't anyone try to stop him?"

"No," Grandmother Ebar said. "We laughed a lot at him and we chased him. I was a child. I was not much older than your brother Thod. The children all followed him, clear through this gallery and all the way to the arches. I remember that they all smelled, a great rotten stench. We threw things at them, trash, stones and garbage, and they just went on as if they didn't notice at all. He lashed out once with the whip at us. I don't know what would have happened if a child had been hit. Maybe we would have mobbed him. Maybe an officer would have tried to stop him. But we were afraid and we just watched the cart move on toward the next gallery tailward. There were seven more tailward from us then, galleries that were gone so long ago it hardly seems possible that they were at all."

"They were completely mute?" Brann inquired. "Didn't they say anything at all?"

"No," said his grandmother. "They were not entirely mute."

It was quiet apparent to Brann that while Ebar's eyes were on him, he was not what she saw. What manner of thing she was seeing he didn't know, except that it must have involved a creaking cart of woven junk and a moving array of folk human only in appearance, all moving tailward from the front verge of the gallery, and all followed by laughing, terrified children.

"They did speak, after a fashion," Ebar said. "It was something of a complex chant, discordant and wordless, a grumble that may one time have been a chant, that may once have had meaning and lost it. Why, who knows how far they had come?"

Grandmother Ebar often spoke in such a way, in concepts and structures that left Brann behind. She had been of the Master's Guild, teaching in the gallery school before Brann was born, and retired from it before then, too. She had not lost one whit of the acuity which had made her such a fine, skilled teacher, and Brann found himself coming to her often with questions. It was not she he resembled, though; her hair was still more blonde than gray, and her light frame had none of the Adelbran stockiness. Her houseplat perched on the tailmost edge of the gallery, in seeming contravention of the rule that the oldest lived farthest to the front. It was a narrow house, hardly one room wide but very deep, shaped so that it seemed to be a wedge pulled back from the gallery's arch itself. She spent her time in a tiny room on the top floor of the houseplat, leaving it less and less in later years (she was past eighty). It was an open, well-lighted room full of green things like a piece of the parkplat transplanted. The room now looked out over the verge of Tailend, so high above the gallery floor as to make it unseen unless Brann looked straight down from the window. It took little for him to pretend that he was suspended there in the room, no gallery, no tier, no city at all above or beneath, while he listened to his grandmother.

The Isocourt was meeting now—one citizen in each hundred chosen randomly from the population of the gallery. They were meeting to discuss the dwarf. In a way he wasn't a dwarf; his stature was that of most other men. He would have measured, had they stood side by side, perhaps an inch taller than Brann. But he was a dwarf nonetheless, long in the torso, short and bowed in his legs, with stubby arms and fingers. Brann's grandmother called it chondrodystrophic dwarfism, which explained precisely nothing to Brann. What it meant, she tried to explain to Brann, was that the stock from which the dwarf had come must have been composed of giants in order that even a dwarf of them would be of ordinary human size. But the dwarf could not say where he had come from. Whether it was that his language diverged so greatly from Brann's folks' or it was that he had lost his language from some accident, or had never had speech at all, he was unable to communicate with anyone on Brann's gallery except to make known one thing. He had come out of the interior of the city Frontward at the greatest speed his bowlegs would carry him. He would have gone right over the gallery verge if he had not been stopped. Though he seemed awed at such a place where the confines of floor and ceiling ended—which he certainly had never seen before (Ebar said)—he still feared it less than whatever he ran from in the city's interior. He wouldn't go Frontward no matter what the compulsion, and when propelled even a few steps in that direction, he grew agitated and then violent so that he was left on the verge where, torn between fear of what was behind him and fear and awe of the void, he squatted at the very edge, a misshapen dwarfed giant whom Brann pitied and about whom he wondered.

Officers had managed to bring the dwarf to the Isocourt, where he squatted most unhappily in the center of the pit. The 100 Magistors seated about the pit's first circumference watched him and talked among themselves. Many were not happy that he had been brought. Brann's sister-in-law, Mara, chosen a Magistor in this year's lotting, was one. It seemed a provocation to many; the dwarf here now. Magistor Sala Tresala (a gardener in other years, he was not particularly a forceful man otherwise and had surprised the folk greatly when he became the most strident voice of this year's court) stalked down into the pit and surveyed them, Magistors and gallery alike, with an angry glance.

"It's not difficult enough, eh?" he asked them. "We must bring this here! I suppose it's an example, a sample, eh? This is what's coming from Frontward. More and more's been coming? Look at it. I talk, it doesn't know; I talk, it watches. Am I worried? Eh! From this? Friend Vardan says I should be. Don't you, Friend Vardan? More and more is coming? Right? More and more, Friend Vardan, your correct words? So we get an exhibition here, an idiot dwarf, a dumb crazy thing, eh? What'd you bring this here for, Friend Vardan, to show us that the interior, Frontward, is not properly pruned, gone to seed? People aren't plants, Vardan, eh, is that not so?"

He walked up to Magistor Vardan and held out a hard hand, pressing one callused finger into the bigger man's shoulder.

"What do you have in mind, Vardan? You want a vote in favor of the Pilgrimage now? I think he does; I think he wants a vote, with the dwarf in the pit and all of you staring at it. Eh? You going to vote that way? You want that, Vardan?"

Brann was not sure of all that was happening. He sat with Halsam and with Liza in the last rank of the spectators gallery. Mara had told him there would be a show today, fireworks and clashes among the Magistors.

"Mara told me there will be a showdown over the dwarf," Brann said. "She told me that there have been more strange folk coming from the interior this past year than anyone ever heard of before. She said Magistor Vardan had a group together that thinks something serious has occurred in the interior, something that's making all the strange ones come out. She said he's going to try to bring up a vote on it."

"A vote for what?" Liza asked.

"A vote to move, to leave early on Pilgrimage, to abandon the gallery."

"Are they afraid of that ugly thing?" Hals asked.

"Not that one exactly. What Mara said was that they think there will be many more of them coming, and that they're building barricades."

"Where?" Liza asked.

"I don't know, somewhere up front. A long way in. She didn't seem to know where."

"Barricades," said Hals. "I never heard of anything like that. What's the point of barricades?"

"Do you really think we're going to leave early?" Liza asked.

The three looked at each other, and they didn't know. This was a change from the usual business of the Isocourt which was often so dull that the Magistors attended only because they were paid for it and barred from any other work during their year's term. The irony—not entirely lost upon Brann—was that business of such mundane nature was carried out in the most splendiferous structure on the gallery. It occupied an area almost as great as the parkplat, just adjacent to it on the inward side of the gallery. Here again were the devices like those Brann saw in the post house, a hundred identical glass and metal desks about the pit, each with a soft chair, each with an array of contacts and lightless, functionless lamp lenses. There was hardly even curiosity anymore as to the reason for such complex devices. Brann wondered at their inert intricacy, at the darkened glassite oblongs in the center of each desk and the identical darkened oblongs of great size which fronted the circle of the first platform. The Isocourt Hall was a dome with the Magistors' circle at the bottom and three successive platforms circling above. Its acoustics were excellent and even without amplification (perhaps a part of the nonfunctional desks), every word said by the Magistors could be heard, while whispers on the platforms carried no distance at all. The color of it awed Brann, something that climbed the spectrum as it did the dome; reds and yellows below to a deepening blue, intensely cobalt at the apex. It seemed to be the color of the night sky, impossibly distant and remote. Brann wondered what it had been like for those who had never seen the real sky, who knew nothing of real distance, to come into the dome.

In the center was the pit, floored with a yielding material which seemed impervious, yet had been worn, especially along its circumference, so that there was a circular depression about it and the remainder undulated where long, used paths had been worn. There was a space beneath this floor through which the folk as children were taken on tours by masters of the gallery school. There was dim light, very green, and the walls leaned away like the bottom of a bowl. They were covered with translucent and dark channels like the network of human veins. Some channels were not dark, sometimes single veins lit with vari-colored pulses, sometimes whole patches were alight. It was, said the masters, a brain of sorts, in which the pulsings were the last vestiges of senile thought. What it thought about no one knew, and the room smelled of the same acid stink that had come from the broken cables beneath Brann's house. The possible thoughts of that brain had been the source of more than a few nightmares for Brann and other children.

All he could understand of it was what Grandmother Ebar said, that the tailend of the city was running down—had been for centuries—and was falling into ruin. "The Structors," she said, "are like scavengers; they save what they can." But he put all this into the same mythical context in which elevators ran up and down the shafts in a blur and folk spoke from house to house and even tier to tier from Frontend to Tailend by devices that operated on something similar to light. The Structors still retained the secret, Ebar said. The Post Guild also (but weren't the devices in the postplat dark like those of the Isocourt?). The tag-ends of such technology—Ebar's word—still created things such as the dancing metallic dolls and the power carts—from the ancient blueprints and materials stocked, Ebar said, not from anything created today. "That is why Tailend is dying, and why the city sloughs it away," Ebar said.

Vardan took Magistor Sala's place in the pit. There were fireworks, as Mara had said.

"Friend Sala speaks with wit," Magistor Vardan began, "but he uses little wisdom. We have reports, Friends. On this tier, seven galleries frontward, the folk are indeed building a great barrier against the strange things of the interior. I didn't bring this creature, this poor thing, here for show. I simply had it brought here as an example. Seven frontward such things are commonplace. Nor are they all so mild and frightened as this one. They are genuine scared seven frontward. We have reports from them, Friends, folk injured, houses, shops damaged, folk dismembered, stranger things still, more horrible. . . ."

"From what source, Vardan?" Magistor Ger Gerebah asked.

"What source, Friend? We have it by post, by letters from there. You have seen them, Ger, as have all the others."

"We are to move because of letters," she said. "Do you all hear that? Because of letters? Who has been there to verify it?"

The Magistor Presiding tapped his wand against a sound board. The note, in the clear acoustics of the chamber, crowned and silenced Magistor Ger. "Friend Ger," he admonished, "Friend Vardan has the pit. Please wait your turn."

Vardan paced the circumference of the pit, staying (perhaps dramatically) away from the dwarf. Though all voices in the dome sounded with equal volume, Vardan's had a timbre, a bass and vibrant quality that made it seem louder than all the others. Brann didn't like Vardan, who as the Secretary of the Guild of Engine Makers, had talked convincingly to Brann's father about Brann's potential as a guildsman.

"He never says what he means," Brann whispered to Hals and Liza. "He won't keep your confidence either. I told him that I was considering not joining the Engine Makers and he went to tell my father immediately."

Liza sneered, "He's such an ugly one. How does a man so skinny have such a big voice? He looks like a little monkler." She chittered and postured, imitating one of the lemuroid animals, the principal denizens of the parkplat. "Yeep, yeep, yeep, yeep, yeep!" she went and she bounced on her seat until another spectator told her to shush. But they all laughed, stifling it only when an officer looked their way.

"Let's go," Hals said. "This is boring."

"If you want, Hals. I'm staying," Brann said. He couldn't

say why. The argument was fierce, but fiercely polite, couched in polite and irritating phrases. But there was something here. Brann wasn't certain he could explain it. It defied an orderly and gradual breakdown of Tailend. It was more intense, a swifter, more substantive breakdown, affecting not just the gallery, but the folk, and folk of galleries frontward—if Vardan was right. Things should be newer as you went frontward, better, stronger, more useful. He became restless listening to this polite debate, edgy and nervous. But he stayed. Liza stayed, too, and Hals, who didn't want to leave alone.

Those who seemed to support Magistor Sala—who stated that he would not vote to go on Pilgrimage early—were a minority. Mara was not in the minority. It angered Brann. He wanted to tell her that she was stupid, wanting to leave. There was a recess for a few minutes while the Isocourt conferred among themselves. Liza and Hals watched Brann as he raced down the ramp and confronted Mara (after all a Magistor) with waving hands and a bewildered look. From there beneath the first platform no voices carried. Mara smiled and shrugged; perhaps she agreed. Brann came back up the ramp and said nothing at all to them, except that he hunkered as Liza had, and he imitated the monkler, pointing at Vardan, or at Mara perhaps, and going, "Yeep!"

There was a group among the Guild of Health which understood the processes of the mind who, if they were put to worry over this problem, could perhaps have said why a people who had resided in one fixed location for 1200 years would plan to leave their home on a minor provocation. But no one asked this question. Well, Brann had asked, but in a circumscribed context; he would never have questioned the concept of the Pilgrimage, only its precipitous application here. The question had not been asked, because no one dreamed of asking it. If there was an answer, it lay with the brittleness of a society that had not been threatened in 1200 years.

What was the matter with them, Brann asked Grandmother Ebar. "Here're some strange folk. This one isn't dangerous. He couldn't hurt anyone. But do you know they all voted, except for Magistor Sala and Magistor Ger Gerebah and maybe four or five others. They all voted for an early Pilgrimage. They're going to put it to a general poll, they said."

Ebar nodded slowly, she rocked slowly, looking out the leaf-framed window. There were streaks of sun on her, spots between the shadows of the leaves, moving as she moved. "Did you ever watch storm clouds build in the mountains?" she asked him. "Have you watched it begin to rain?"

"Uh-huh."

"It's a very strange thing, very unusual. Quite a new concept, the rain."

"But there's always been rain, Grandmother."

"Only for you there has."

"No, Grandmother, for all of us."

"Not true, I never saw rain as a child. It was miles to Tailend then, long ways through galleries very different from the one that burned. Rain was a word in books, a fiction of the Masters in school. Do you know that the folk have lived in this gallery more than twelve centuries? How long do you think they have seen rain?"

Brann didn't know; he hadn't thought about it.

"Ten years. That's no time at all. That's nothing." She squinted into the sunlight. "Only when the rearmost galleries were dismantled and the tailend of the city came here did we see the outside, Farmy Fields, the mountains, rain. I was frightened to death the first time I saw it. My father and I and your great-grandfather, Loez, went to Tailend when I was twelve. We went to the verge and it was raining. There was a storm so that you couldn't see the mountains, and the Farmy Fields were a green-brown blur like a watercolor, and lightning touched Tailend's empty beams. Thunder rattled out over the valley. I became nearly hysterical, screaming at my father to take me back in, away from it."

"It was only a storm," Brann said. "Were you really so afraid?"

"I was. It was different, nothing I had ever experienced before. My father was shaken. I don't think he'd ever seen rain before, either. So he bundled me into his cloak and we ran back inside away from the rain. I've seen it often since in these last few years. It scares me still."

"And it's like that with the strange men?" Brann asked. "Are you saying that the Isocourt Magistors are afraid of

them because they never have seen them before? They want
to run? But isn't the Pilgrimage something different?"

"It's more complex than that, Brann," Ebar said. "The life
here in the gallery is static. It doesn't change. We don't know
how to deal with change. The strange folk are change, one
and the same. Their appearance means that things are breaking down somewhere. It means that it is no longer one single
unchanging city all the way frontward."

"I was thinking that, too, in the Isocourt hall; listening to
them, I was thinking that exactly. But isn't the Pilgrimage
change? We don't know where we're going, we don't know
anything about it at all."

"Certainly we do, Brann. We've always had the Pilgrimage.
It's our refuge, our place of safety. How many have gone before us? How many, like the ones fleeing from the fire, have
chosen early Pilgrimage when threatened with that which
they didn't understand? It's an abstract hope, a thing of
faith."

"You don't believe? You don't think there's anything to it,
do you?" Brann asked her. What his grandmother was saying
was a sort of heresy that surprised and shocked him. He said
nothing and only watched her rocking there in the moving
rays of light. His thoughts were moving like that now, toward
and away from some realization. There was a moist earthy
smell he always associated with this room of his grandmother's house, something that made him think this was the
way it smelled outside, past even the Farmy Fields where it
must all be like the park. He expected strange things when he
came here. Grandmother Ebar seemed fearless, entirely unafraid to say anything she wished. She was notorious for it
(some in the family looked with displeasure on Brann's frequent visits to crazy Ebar), but was this too far; was this
more than she had any right to say? Hadn't he thought the
same things? Hadn't he wondered at the Pilgrimage and the
unalterable necessity for it? Against custom, he wondered
where the pilgrims went. Had they ever been heard from
since? He wondered at their sanguine acceptance of the
Structors' orders to move—which would come here soon if
the precipitous vote to leave early failed. He had expressed
this doubt to no one, keeping it even more secret than his
wish to become one of the Post Guild. He did not know what

would be done to him if he asked of it. There was no precedent, so there was no punishment. The folk did not doubt. The Pilgrimage kept the city alive somehow. All accepted it as something inseparable from life.

He left then abruptly while Ebar rocked. He left then running, down the stairs of her house and out onto the verge onto the reach of a beam, where he sat motionless as the squatting dwarf, contemplating the depth of his grandmother's heresy and wondering if it was as deep as his own.

Hegman Branlee would have known. The church doors were always open for Brann as for anyone who came, so Hegman Branlee. Though not for Brann, certainly for the Hegman it was not difficult to see how the church and the Pilgrimage had become tied into a single unit. Wasn't the Pilgrimage a sort of prophecy? Wasn't it the ultimate extrapolation of a knowledge that there was a final end and a definite beginning to the city?

"It never dies," said the Hegman. "This is the great marvel. As it is broken down so it is built up, as we leave so we return."

Brann made to interrupt.

"Shush, shush," said Branlee. "Do you think the city ends in a mindless, senseless dismantling by the Structors, that we rush off on Pilgrimage into blind oblivion and chaos? That there is a final end and no returning. . . . Thank you, Friend Eza, I believe another chop would go down well with the bread. . . . That there is a far face to the city, a Frontend as some call it? What a most disturbing vision. Then I assume you must postulate an inside and an outside to the city; lands stretching on into lands, far as the eye can see, isn't it, young Brann?"

"But of course there are lands!" Brann exclaimed. What could the Hegman mean? "What of the Farmy Fields, what of the mountains?"

"Ah," said the Hegman, "most disturbing. You interpret it incorrectly, young man. You begin from the most erroneous premise, that there is an inside and an outside to the city, a city and a planet, I suppose, upon which it rests . . . thank you again, Friend Eza, would it be too much trouble to pass the pitcher again? My glass seems to be dry once more . . . and all that of course is nonsense; lands stretching on into lands. The eye will fill what is empty, young Brann. If there were lands, there would certainly be folk to fill them, and if such folk then we would have seen them, true?"

"True," Brann answered reluctantly.

Brann's papa smiled, and his mama nodded agreement, and Brann watched not the Hegman but them instead, wondering all the time if they could truly believe what the man was saying.

"Have we seen such folk, Brann?" asked the Hegman.

"No," said Brann. "But that doesn't mean that they're not there for certain. We know that there are folk up frontward, and we've never seen them either. How do we know they're there? We get letters from them through the Post Guild. No one sees the front folk, no one has talked to them. But we get letters from them, and now there is going to be a poll to see if we move and go on Pilgrimage early, all because of folk we've never met or seen."

"Brann!" his mama said sharply. "How can you speak that way to the Hegman?" She would have said more, would in fact have admonished him sharply, for in matters of the church both she and Brann's papa were of one mind. Brann's words shocked her and surprised his papa greatly.

"Leave it be, Friend Eza," the Hegman told her. "He has a right to question. It is a right inherent in all our teaching. For if he doesn't question, how will he hear the truth? Brann, have some folk of the mountains, or from the other side of the Farmy Fields been writing to you, sending you letters?"

"No," said Brann. "Of course not." His sisters tittered. He turned a mean face upon them and they stifled their noise but tittered silently on.

"Has anyone you know ever received a letter from outside the city?"

"No."

"You've not received some secret communication from them? Some message brought by a bird, or perhaps a monkler has brought you one?" His sisters laughed out loud and Brann gave Sal a look in which death was writ large. But even brother Thod laughed and baby Nam too. He wanted to get up, to run away from the table, but adults did not do such things, and nothing would prove him more childish and incapable of further argument, than to rush away from the house in anger.

"I don't do this to mock you, young man," the Hegman said. "This is not a thing to laugh at." At once his sisters stopped laughing, mirroring the grave faces of Mama and Papa Adelbran. "There is the city, there are the mountains and the fields. They are one, and all beyond their unity is only the vision of things and this vision is nothing more than that, for the eye abhors emptiness and will fill it always. Certainly you may question, for there is nothing learned without it. But when you hear the true answer, you must stop questioning and begin to learn. Do you understand that, young Brann?"

"I suppose so," Brann answered.

"Well then," said the Hegman heartily, "that is that." And he commenced shoveling the potatoes onto his plate with an extravagant gesture.

The times were very turbulent. So Papa Adelbran had invited Hegman Branlee for dinner, as a comfort and a spiritual reaffirmation. There were troubles. Of those on the gallery, a great majority was sure to cast ballots in favor of an early Pilgrimage. There were dissenters, very vocal—Magistor Ger Gerebah most of all—who said that this was a foolish overreaction. It was Ger Gerebah's position that there was as yet no need to abandon homes and businesses on the gallery and run for the elevators in some mindless dash down to safety; she said that the Pilgrimage required planning, at least a year of readiness. So the Structors warned. She enlisted the aid of one of the pilgrims from tier 112, taking him around from meeting to meeting where he told of how much planning and how much preparation were needed before they left on Pilgrimage. But he was a butt of laughter at the meetings, a tall blond man speaking a language so incomprehensible that Ger Gerebah had to translate what he said. And the spectators laughed so loud and jeeringly that finally the man left, traveling down to rejoin his own family on Pilgrimage.

"Do you want to flee like refugees?" Ger Gerebah asked at the meetings then.

"Where is your blond upstairsman, Ger?" one of the folk called out. Others laughed.

"E var to lose it all," another called in garbled imitation of the pilgrim.

But the folk were genuinely frightened and perhaps they laughed because they were afraid of what would be said if they didn't, if it weren't all made into a joke. They were afraid for the same reasons Magistor Ger was: losing their homes and their larger possessions (those that could not be carried by hand in the elevator) and they wished they had time to plan an orderly Pilgrimage. But the letters still came from the city's interior, from some unnamed source, writing, telling of conflict with the strange folk. So the folk were also afraid not to leave, fearing that if they waited until the time of the Pilgrimage they would be able to take nothing, perhaps not even their lives, and that the Pilgrimage would become a disorderly, terrified flight. The thing was—and all the folk knew it—those of this gallery were not fighters; they were not purposely vicious or cruel. It had nothing to do with any hereditary passivity. (This, had there been a geneticists' group among the guilds, might have been their argument, while they searched for a gene locus at which alleles for passivity and aggression competed for expression.)

Grandmother Ebar said that in the city there was only a certain set of prescribed incidents that could take place—prescribed not by law but by the rigid confines of the city itself. Fire there is, she said, and so the Fire-fighters. Disease there is, and so the Guild of Health, she said. But war there is not, she told her grandson, Brann, and there had not been war, so that the word itself was strange, and the probability of war was so infinitesimal in such a rigid social order that there was no Soldiers' Guild, no folk trained in war at all or in defense.

"There are only the officers of the Isocourt," she said, "untrained, unarmed. And the threat of the strange ones becomes the threat of oblivion, against which the unknowns of the Pilgrimage become constant comforts, so long have they been told."

Brann's mama, the gentler of his parents, looked toward this early Pilgrimage with trepidation. Already she was going through their possessions, trying to separate what could be taken from what must be left. She had set aside the gold-worked tablecloth and the book of family portraits, pictures of Adelbrans receding in time to the earliest days of the gallery. Some pictures may even have predated the *last* Pilgrimage and these were of folk whose style of dress had them in tight-fitting garments of an unfamiliar weave and with heads—men and women both—shaved and painted or tattooed. But in one thing they were similar, they had the same heft and weight of bone and feature that characterized folk of this gallery today. Such pictures somehow set in motion in Brann's mind the thoughts of packets of folk, separate islands of humanity traveling always forward in the city, intermingling little except with the tiers one up or down. It was a troubling image. (The nonexistent geneticists would have discussed isolated gene pools and genetic drift and would have found some large significance in the high frequency of blood type A among the folk and its sudden, nearly total absence beginning twelve tiers up.)

Brann's papa poured tea and asked the Hegman what he knew of the mood of the folk. Would they vote to stay or go?

"To go, of course," Branlee said. He sipped his tea, tonged in another sugar lump and seemed satisfied with the result. Branlee said he always prided himself on secular matters. "If the vote indeed is yes, I should think we will begin the Pilgrimage in about ten days."

"So soon?" Mama asked. "Mara says. . . ."

"Our daughter-in-law," Papa interjected, "on the Isocourt this year."

Mama went on, "Mara says that the earliest would not be for another month, maybe two."

Branlee cleared his throat. "Well, in deference to Magistor Mara, it has come to my attention that the Pilgrimage will begin one week precisely after the vote. So Magistor Vardan has communicated to me. I'll not say how I heard this from him but you can trust me that it is true."

"So soon, so soon," whispered Mama. She looked about absently, as if wondering already what she should pack from this room.

Of the children, only Brann had remained in the dining room. The others had been dispatched to bed. He watched Branlee take still another of his mother's iced cakes and engulf it without formalities, chewing, swallowing and drinking the hot tea at the same time. "If we go," he said, his mouth still full, "it is as it should be, the Lord above us knows that. And you, too, Friend Eza, should know that."

"We leave peremptorily?" Mama said bitterly. "Without time or plans, take our children and go? On what? On a word, that there is fighting, there are barricades somewhere . . . galleries frontward, who knows where?"

"Friend Eza, please, it is not just you. We will all go."

"Of course we will," she said. "A gallery full of refugees, fleeing."

"Eza," Papa said, "I've not heard you like this, and to the Hegman."

"And to the Hegman!" Mama said. "That is true, Fral Adelbran. It's quite sufficient that we take to our heels from our home. I need not hear that it is the wish of the Lord above also that we do this, when in truth it is the order of the Isocourt, made not in fulfillment of the commandment to Pilgrimage, but in fear, and they don't even know what they fear."

"I won't hear this," said Papa, standing. "I won't hear you berate the Isocourt and the Hegman this way. If it is to be done, then it is to be done, that's all."

"Wouldn't you battle fire to save this house, this gallery? Haven't you done it before?"

"Fire, I know fire. I know what to do so that it won't burn and injure, temperatures, gases, all that. Oh, I know flames. But I don't know what is happening now. This is the way my mother speaks."

"She does and she has a reason!"

"My mother is old; she doesn't think clearly."

"She thinks more clearly than any of us. She says that she has seen it, growing for years, a weakness in the folk, who would rather flee than protect what is theirs."

"Please, no more argument," said the Hegman. "I think I'll leave now." He massaged the tea mug between his hands; he brought it up two-handed and downed the final swallow. "Yes, thank you. I must be going. Fine evening, fine Friend Eza, Friend Fral, young Brann."

When the Hegman left, there was silence and Brann slipped away to bed.

It was a gray day and the buskers played. Couples strolled

along the verge. Nothing at all seemed different or changed
from what it had always been. In stalls, the vendors sold pas-
try folds of meat and spices, candy and tinted drinks. They
strolled on this path of light commerce along the verge.
Brann tried to envision them close-shaven and tattooed, walking in the same way here when the verge was a far distant
reality to them, without substance. And the couples gawked
at the dwarf. Two buskers played, a fiddle and a horn. The
couples laughed at the dwarf. But the dwarf himself laughed
not at all. He looked only outward, seeking and not finding
any further escape from whatever he fled in the deep insides
of the city. The dwarf had a man's head like that of any of
the folk. It was larger, though, the head of a man perhaps
nine feet tall, the head of a man perhaps four hundred
pounds, the head of a giant with sandy hair in a ragged cut
and eyes which wandered in a nystagmus gaze (whose visions
were of the gallery only incidentally as if an hallucination
twisted his true sight). He shambled back from the couples,
back from the crowd, never allowing them close, but never
allowing himself close to the ultimate limit of the gallery.

"He's dumb, I say. No voice at all," the busker with the
fiddle laughed. The man slouched up beneath the dwarf's
reach. The busker was a dwarf also; it was like father dwarf
and child. He played a few quick bars saying, "Dumb, I say,
doesn't know to dance."

The horn player raised his instrument up and blatted a
short discordant note into the dwarf's face. He wiped his lips
and waved the horn, shouting as a barker, saying come and
see him, the giant dwarf, see the wonder, the brainless fool.
Brann wanted to cry, to shout at them; wanted somehow to
make them stop. But the dwarf took hardly any notice at all.
Only his eyes really moved, here and there, quick, ceaseless,
uncomprehending.

"There is nothing known of where we came from," Grandmother Ebar said. "Folk believe, in fact, that the city is a
timeless thing with no beginning to its history. Which postu-
lates, you understand, that there is no end to it either. Do
you see the flaw in that logic, Brann?"

Brann said that if there was a flaw, he couldn't see it.

"No? You can't see it? Doesn't the city age, doesn't it dete-
riorate year by year?"

"I guess so," answered Brann. "I don't know."

"It does," said Grandmother Ebar. "Look at it, the changes, the decay, the things broken that we cannot fix, the things broken which we do not understand, which just have no function and seem never to have had a function. But they must have been used one day, and if they had a function and we have forgotten it, then somehow the city was once more complex than it is now, and it becomes less complex every day. I believe that when those functionless devices worked, however long ago, there were already devices the uses of which had been lost. I think that we now don't even remember that these things ever existed, much less their uses."

"But it goes in cycles, Hegman Branlee says. Doesn't it, Grandmother? What's old is torn down. New things replace it."

He had brought her pictures, those his mother had saved, because he had wondered just this.

"These are marvelous, Brann," Ebar said. "You can see in here what I mean. The way we live is different. Here the gallery is new." She interpreted the old words for him which someone had written on a picture's back. Even here there was wonder. What was the substance of the photograph that it should survive unchanged so long? "Look close, Brann. Examine the floor of the gallery. Examine the pillars and the archways. What do you see?"

"Nothing different. I see the verge. Some of the houseplats are not the same. They seem to have moved the post house."

"Closely, Brann. Examine it. The new floor of the gallery is already worn. The new pillars are already gouged and scarred and patched. It was already old when it was built." She grew more excited, pointing out where the changes were, what was already old, what things seemed functionless more than a thousand years before.

The picture was wrong. "Grandmother," Brann interjected, "how could the verge be here in this picture, with light coming from behind the elevators? These pictures aren't of this gallery. Tailend is on the wrong side. The sun comes from the wrong place."

His grandmother snatched the pictures from him. Did she cry out just a bit? Was his all-knowing grandmother confused? She held the pictures, in hands that seemed as old, and stared intently at them, going, "Oh my!" She wouldn't answer him, wouldn't say any more at all. She just peered as if myopic at the pictures, exchanging one for another, moving her lips and clucking as old folk sometimes did. She seemed not to notice when Brann left.

Slender as a filament, a gantry extended from the roof of Tailend two miles above on the 113th tier. The Structors who worked there were invisible at that height, even in the brightest sunlight and on the clearest, most cloudless days. Today there were clouds up there, mares' tails of crystalline ice, and below them clouds of thicker substance in layered striation. The sun at noon cast long diffuse shadows down the face of Tailend, and one of these moved in a steady pendulum sweep along the tiers. A block of masonry was moving down. It was a gargantuan segment of the topmost tier. Cables ran to it from below, climbing from anchors in the Foundations. They seemed to appear out of nothing, first as a haze a great distance above the ground, then as a tangle of intersecting lines, finally as a net of distinct cables seemingly close enough to the verge for Brann to reach out and touch them. Above, they dwindled again until the descending segment seemed not anchored by them, but caught instead in an entirely invisible net of force, as a pin suspended by a thread appears to be held magically to a magnet. The great block came down. Soon its scale was apparent. As it descended, Brann could make out the shapes of machines which had gone up piecemeal in the elevators. Now whole and assembled, they seemed like toys, much smaller than insects. He realized their true size and the block exploded in scale; it was city blocks long and wide. It was perhaps the width of an entire gallery, nearly a mile. It traveled down, hardly faster than the pace of the elevators, but steadily, making no stops at all.

On the tiers above, Brann saw folk gathered at the verge of their own galleries so that there was a colorful mottled blur of folk above, diminished and compressed as his view became oblique. Now there was noise. The block came downward.

Brann watched the hunger in the dwarf's eyes. The man, prodded by the increasing crowd of folk, who had come to the verge to watch the first huge chunk of Tailend drop, had found a final refuge on a horizontal beam which projected perhaps thirty feet beyond the verge. He had moved to the very end of the beam and squatted. There was a wind, and the dwarf's sandy hair and his clothes were blown in it. The muscles on his foreshortened arms strained, holding him to the beam as though the wind were a gale. His eyes were fixed on the folk in the crowd, a blank unfocused stare, and he edged slowly back until there was the tiniest segment of beam beneath his feet.

Somehow a sense of purpose communicated itself through the crowd and Brann felt it. Somehow it became a central idea among the watchers that the dwarf himself was to blame for the turmoil in the gallery, that his representation of the trouble became the trouble itself. There came an increasing murmur from the folk, an increasing angry drone which grew and joined with the growing noise from the descending block. It was clear enough—if the dwarf would be ended, so too could the trouble find an end. The dwarf couldn't know what was occurring; he hadn't the words. He couldn't have understood that if there was malice in the folk, it could not find expression.

The dwarfed busker with the fiddle ran out. He bowed his fiddle and perhaps there was a tune. But Brann couldn't hear it over the noise of the crowd. The fiddler capered a bit, a miniature version of the giant dwarf, and if it was possible, the dwarf seemed to Brann to draw back still farther on the end of the beam. He was making a noise at last, a muted nasal "Un!" which grew in intensity until the noise increased above the collective sounds of the crowd, surpassed and dominated it.

No one there could comprehend the possibility that the dwarf might jump. The fact of pushing or causing the dwarf to fall from the beam was so far from their comprehension that they knew of no real action to take. The leap caught them by surprise. Focused on the dwarf, oblivious to the outside activity, virtually none of the folk had been aware that the huge block of masonry from the top of the city was now abreast of their gallery. It moved there, creaking downward some twenty feet beyond the beam end where the dwarf squatted. He made a frog-like leap, kicking out toward the ragged face of the block, and in the silence that came after the jump, Brann could hear the dwarf's nails scratching at the masonry.

"He's falling!" someone cried.

The dwarf's voice was now gigantic, "Un! Un! Un!" and an odor of broken stone blew in from that block. When they knew he would fall, he didn't. He held on somehow and found a grip on a stone projection. They knew how strong he was then. With one arm he pulled himself up, and with the other he found a cable. Then he was up along that face and up onto the top of the block and he swung out there, secure on a supporting cable.

His eyes again began to move and he watched the crowd as the block of masonry and houses creaked downward. Finally, he was gone.

Chapter Three

The Shaking

It was darkness and it was the Sabbath, but the darkness brought no quiet. Voices of the folk came through the dark, along the highroad and through the marketplat. It was the Sabbath and still it made no difference. They moved as if there were no prescript against such motion on the day of the Lord above. Power carts moved through the night in streams from the verge and from the far flanks of the gallery. The elevators filled and moved away, down and down. They were too slow and the folk crowded toward them. The open mouths of the elevators gaped, the doors slid up and down. Packed, the cars went down carrying folk away.

Brann watched from the hill of the parkplat. Somewhere his mama and papa had joined those leaving. Somewhere his sisters and his brothers huddled close about his parents. They waited for an elevator car to carry them down.

He heard a noise in the trees and the noise came closer, up the hill. It became a voice.

"Brann? Are you here?"

"Liza!"

"Are you there, Brann?"

Brann shined his flashlight out into the trees and he saw Liza's red hair. The light flashed over her for an instant, bare legs and arms moving. He took her arm.

"They're mad ones going this way," she said. "There's no order in it at all."

"I know," said Brann. He watched the lights of the power

49

carts on the highroad. The noise of the folk moving and of the power carts and the other machines was a strange thing in the Sabbath night. "What did you bring?" he asked her.

She slung a satchel from her back and dropped it to the ground. "Give me your light," she told him. She opened the satchel and showed him its contents. "A blanket, clothes, cooking things, food." She held up a thin-bladed knife. "I brought this, too, Brann." She looked at him. "What if there are more like that dwarf? My mama said there might be."

Brann took the knife from her. "Could you use that?" he asked. "Could you protect yourself with that?"

She was quiet and packed the knife away again. "I don't know," she finally said. "We'll find out maybe."

"I brought one, too," Brann said.

As she replaced things in the satchel, Brann saw that she had brought one of the silver dancing dolls that he had given her (and he almost smiled about it, knowing that it meant something special).

She shined the light on his satchel. "What did you bring?"

"The same as you," he answered. He showed her. She came to the coat given Brann by the boy from the 113th tier. "Oh, that's beautiful," she said. "Will you need it?"

"I don't know what we'll need. It's cold at the roof of the city. It could be we'll go there. The boy who gave me this said it's cold there, that there's snow even inside of the city, not just on the gallery verge."

Liza surveyed her own light clothing. "I have nothing like that," she told him.

He clicked his tongue and put the coat away. "It may be that I won't need it." He took out his blanket and tied the satchel tight.

She helped him spread the blanket.

"I brought 200 Paad," Brann told her. "Did you bring any money?"

"860 Paad," she said. She opened her belt pouch to display a sheaf of orange-red crinkled bills.

"So much!"

"It was school money. I got it out of deposit yesterday." Her voice was wistful. "I don't suppose I'll have that chance now."

They smoothed the blanket and spread hers on top.

"Have you heard from Hals?" she asked him. "Is he coming?"

Brann shrugged. "He said so. I don't know. I was by there this morning and they were already gone."

"From here, do you think he went down already? He has no brothers or sisters. They keep a close watch on him."

"Hals is my best friend," Brann said. "We all said we'd go together, you, me and Hals. I think he'll come."

Brann was afraid in a way and it had only partly to do with the turmoil of the folk below. He was going to spend the night with Liza. They had planned it. They had decided to hide here in the parkplat and wait until the gallery cleared. They had planned it very carefully. Brann would come here first and Hals would come and Liza.

"The streets will be filled with folk and there will be officers. When they've decided, they won't let us stay behind, and our parents won't, surely," Hals had said.

"We'll hide from them," Brann had told them, "in our place at the parkplat."

But Hals had not come; he'd said it would be difficult to get away from his parents. "I'll do it though," he'd assured them. "We will all three stay together."

It was dark there and very still in the trees. Brann wanted to take Liza's hand and he was afraid to do even that. The wind from Frontward had stopped blowing two days ago. It had stopped with the shaking that had come then. The shaking was responsible for it all. It had been dark then, too, and Brann's family had been at their meal. Then the tiny vibration had begun. The dishes had rattled in the cupboard and fallen. There had come a distant humming noise like that which Brann and Hals had heard in the closed elevator shaft. Then for one sharp instant the house shook as if the plat below them had been lifted. The rest of the dishes had sprung completely from the cupboard, shattering with a great noise on the floor. Little Thod had cried out at it. Brann had wanted to and had not, looking instead to his mother and father for strength. Baby Nam had wailed. They hadn't known what it was.

In the streets a house here and there had collapsed. In one place the street itself had caved in, exposing great conduits like those in the secret room below Brann's house. Another shake had come, smaller than the one before, and after that others still less violent. But the winds from Frontward had stopped abruptly and it had become so quiet for an instant that the gallery seemed dead.

Then the folk had fled without voting, without the poll which would have said whether they would go or not. The most frightened of the folk had crowded the elevators from the first instant after the shaking. Folk from the south flank of the gallery had come north. One of them said that the elevator there would not run, that cars hung without motion and that folk had to be helped out. Not even the Magistors or the school Masters had known what had happened.

Brann and Liza and Hals had talked before about what they would do when the folk went on Pilgrimage.

"I'm not going with them," Brann had said. He'd told them of Grandmother Ebar's pictures and of Hegman Branlee's confusing argument for the rightness of the Pilgrimage.

"Everybody goes on Pilgrimage," he'd said, "and none is ever heard from again. I want to go to Frontend myself. Everything has changed. Now we're no longer going in an orderly way. We're running away headlong. Nobody knows why. They say it's all one thing, the dwarf, the shaking. Mara says that the Isocourt doesn't know, either."

Brann had been surprised. He'd thought that Liza would perhaps go with him. He'd not been all that sure and her decision to come had unnerved him. It was what scared him now that he was alone with her. He didn't even move past that to any concept of her loving him. He'd been surprised when she had said that she would come and that she had said it without any hesitation, as if her promises to her parents and her plans to join the Healers' Guild were nothing, and he was much more than nothing to her. But Halsam, who had always scoffed at Brann's notion (secretly held and secretly confided to Hals), to look for that place where he might join the Post Guild, had said that he also was coming.

"Aren't you afraid, Hals?" Liza had asked him. "Didn't you always say the safe route was best?"

"Yes," Hals had answered, "I think maybe I'm ashamed of that now. Besides, doesn't the shaking change it all?" He stood with Brann and Liza and looked at the great hole in the floor of the gallery and all the cables and conduits exposed. "What do you think happened?" he had asked.

"I think the Structors did it," Liza had said. "From there, maybe a block broke loose up above somewhere and it crashed down into the lower tiers of the city."

Brann hadn't told them that Grandmother Ebar had thought it much worse. "There has been some immense happening," she'd told him. "From here, maybe the city itself is finally down."

Of this he'd said nothing to Halsam or Liza.

Now they waited on the hilltop, and Brann felt Liza's fingers come between his hands. He sat with his arms encircling his knees, and she sat next to him so that their bare legs touched. They'd done this so many times before and nothing had come of it but now the same touching terrified Brann. Where was Hals? Liza laid her head on Brann's knees. Their fingers played.

"We'll stay here the night, won't we, Brann?" she asked.

He knew then that Halsam was not coming that night (he was sure of it). He thought at once that it didn't make any difference. Liza was coming with him. The touches that had been sufficient before were not so now. The things he had feared before were not terrifying now. Her face was hot. He kissed it. "Your face is all warm," Liza said. (His also? That surprised him.) They kissed again and he pulled away. An orange light had sprung up among the buildings on the highroad farthest south.

"It's a fire," Brann said, "in the houseplats nearest the flank."

"Maybe someone set it," Liza answered. "They are all so crazy tonight."

"I wonder if Papa will go to fight it?"

"They won't; they're running. They won't come back."

Liza seemed to know how it should be. Their bare legs were against each other's and that was not enough now and they played with snaps until they were almost unclothed. And almost unclothed, they moved against each other, lost thoughts of the flight in progress, lost fear that Halsam would find them. He wondered if he should enter her, perhaps tried and did not, the motion—silky, effortless—was enough. She moved beneath him, they lost the outside entirely, moved very swiftly and things were done.

"I was so scared," she said. He lay on top of her, his arms around her bare shoulders.

"I was too," he said.

They pulled the rest of their clothing off, burrowed into the blankets and slept.

There was another shaking in the night. It was slighter than the others but it lasted a long time. The smell of smoke drifted up on air currents that had a directionless and fitful quality now that the breeze from frontward had ceased. South in the darkness they could see the fire and its orange reflection from the roof of the tier, blended. They didn't sleep much, the noise was ceaseless, and it grew after the last shake. It became panicked and strident. The traffic on the highroad grew. From time to time there would come metallic sounds from the highroad, as of vehicles colliding—where none had ever gone faster than a walker's pace before. And from the market square there was the noise of a crowd gathered and the eternal opening and closing of the elevator doors.

After the shaking, Brann heard noises in the parkplat: the voice of one of the folk, a man calling, "Treena, come!" and a woman's which was indistinct. There were more voices in the parkplat that night and Brann found his knife and had it ready next to their blankets. But none of those in the park came to the top of their hill. Another shaking, the worst yet, came.

Brann heard Liza take a breath and hold it. When the shaking stopped and the noise of the branches falling and of houses somewhere coming apart stopped, she breathed out again. "Is the city falling?" she asked Brann.

"I don't know," he said. This time he told her of Grandmother Ebar's thoughts.

"I have read of where this occurred before," Ebar had told him. "It was a time perhaps two hundred years ago and it was much worse than this. It was written that smoke came on the wind from Frontward for weeks and that there was no water in the conduits so that the folk almost perished for thirst. It was written that the Structors came here from Tailend, right into the heart of the city and tore into the streets so that the water came again. The crematorium burned the dead with a constant flame for five days and nights. They said that was when the small elevator shafts were closed and the cars never ran again . . . you know the broken arch near south crossroad 81?"

Brann had nodded, recalling the pillar that had somehow been torn free of the ceiling and lay toppled across the crossroad, a section cut through it at some time past so that traffic could flow.

"It is written that the shaking did that," Ebar had said, "and that some had feared the tier over would buckle and fall onto ours. There are other scars from that shaking if you look for them. There is the small motion of the highroad where it jogs past the parkplat. There is the row of sunlights above the school that darken out of sequence from all the rest."

And Brann thought of the conduits in the secret room beneath his houseplat, of their hollow sound and the rotten cable and its smell.

"It is said among some," Ebar had told him, "that the city itself is too heavy, that the Foundations cannot support it here, that they are giving away, year by year."

"What will happen, Grandmother?"

"I don't know, Brann. Perhaps the city will fall, perhaps the Foundations will crumble."

"You're not frightened of it, Grandmother?"

"The city is of an age beyond knowing, Brann. So old that the twelve hundred years of this gallery are only a small fraction of that time. If it has lasted so long, it will last a bit longer. It will outlast me, maybe it will outlast you."

A shaking then had rattled the pots of her green-planted room and sent one ivy-like growth to the floor where its pot burst with a dull noise.

All that night and into the next morning Brann and Liza stayed in their hiding place in the parkplat. The sunlights grew brighter and the noise of the crowd did not diminish. There was an awful crying in the bushes below them. They could hear a muffled scream and the sounds of a fight. There was an inhuman cry of pain and the noise of someone running headlong down through the bushes. The cry subsided and Brann went to see. He held his knife and he crept down on hands and knees through the low growing shrubs. Liza followed. There was a clear spot in the trees and the two moved up to it belly down on the wet grass.

"Do you see anything?" Liza asked.

"I see a man," said Brann. He wondered how someone could lie so still. The grass was torn until the bare dirt showed, dark and steaming in the cool morning.

"I think I see blood," said Brann. Liza came up next to him; together they stared at the form.

"Is he dead, Brann?"

"Let's see." Brann moved out in a crouch and knelt over the man. "Lord above, Liza, look at this."

She came out. "Someone's cut him, cut his throat," and she went to her knees then, puking into the wet grass. Brann felt the same way and wished he could let himself go, also. There was a tight heaving in his stomach but it quelled and he stood up. Liza wiped her mouth with a handful of grass and stood, too.

"He was robbed," she said. "Somone has cut all his pockets open."

"And his satchel," said Brann, nudging the torn thing with his foot. "Why would they do that, Liza?"

"I don't know. They're all crazy now, all running away."

Could they just leave him, Brann wondered? "We'll take him somewhere," he said.

"No we won't," said Liza. "We'll go back up onto the hill and wait until they're all gone. This could happen to us."

They hid again and listened to the sounds of flight throughout the day. One time there was the ululation of fire carts moving south, and Brann wondered if his father was among those who must be going at last to fight the fire. But the fire sirens did not come again, and the smell of smoke grew heavier.

"I think they've given up," he said to Liza. As the sunlights faded into night, they could see the glow of the fire closer, yellow now behind the farthest buildings, and the dark ragged skyline southward in sharp silhouette. This night they saw few lights on the highroad and the crowd noise was gone from the marketplat. Only the intermittent sounds of the elevators coming gave evidence that some still waited to leave.

They hid in the blankets again, had each other almost completely again and did not even hear when the noises ceased entirely outside and the elevator doors closed for the final time.

"Brann?" they heard. "Liza?" Someone was shaking them through the blankets. Brann came awake to silence and pushed the covers from his face to see a sharp-faced boy with gray eyes and dark hair which was tousled and speckled with dust and soot.

"Halsam!" Brann cried. He reached for the other boy and wrestled him to the ground with happy laughter. "You came!"

"I came," said Halsam. "It took me a while to get away from my parents." He saw the girl's red hair and sleepy face emerge from the blankets. "Hello, Liza."

"Hello, Hals."

"What happened?" Brann asked. He crawled out from the blankets and then felt inside them for his shirt and shorts. Halsam reddened perceptibly at Brann's nakedness. Liza crawled out, too, and turned her back to dress.

"My papa wouldn't let me out of his sight," Halsam said. "Do you know from here what I had to carry? Tools—garden tools! Papa said that those had been in the Orbenn family for generations and that he wasn't going to leave them for any reason. We got down to the marketplat two days ago, just at sunlight . . . Lord above, Brann, there were folk everywhere all crying and shouting. They had bundles and people couldn't find each other and babies were getting lost. Every time an elevator car came, they just pushed on, maybe a hundred at a time. I don't know how they breathed in there. The drivers were running them so fast I thought maybe one would come apart. I never saw it like that before."

"Did you see Vill?" Brann asked.

"I think so," answered Halsam, "but I couldn't get close enough to talk to him." He sat on the rumpled blankets. "Do you have anything to eat? I didn't eat since yesterday morning."

Brann dug into his satchel and came out with a chunk of bread. They split it three ways. Hals resumed his tale, punctuating it with bites of bread and sips of water from Liza's bottle.

"They just kept crushing onto the elevator," he said. "Sometimes the cars were already part full from up above. I think the whole gallery up and down on Tailend might be moving. Anyway, we pushed into a car, Mama and Papa and me, and somehow they got the doors closed. . . . Then we started down. There were so many folk on the car I could hardly move; I almost couldn't breathe. It smelled awful, like the cars had been running for a long time without cleaning. So we got down one level without any problem. But when we got two down, there was a fight. A whole crowd of folk was waiting for the car, and as soon as the doors opened, folk started pulling us out of the car. I don't even know why the runner opened the doors because the car was so full no one else could have even gotten inside. Then a man took hold of my arm and started to drag me out. Papa shouted at him, saying, 'Bastard, leave off of my son,' and Papa jabbed a pruning shears at the man. There was a terrible fight and someone pulled the elevator runner out of his cage. I didn't see Mama and Papa anymore. I got shoved out of the elevator entirely and I lost everything I was carrying except my satchel. I went over by a pillar out of the crowd and saw the doors of the car close again somehow. I guess Mama and Papa were on it. The car went on down. I didn't know what was happening then and I thought that I would try to come back up here and see if you had gone yet.

"The up elevators were closed entirely; they weren't even stopping for folk. I went to the stairs. The shaking was as bad two down as here. Folk were coming down the stairs, too, not even waiting for the elevators. It will take them forever that way from here but I don't think they care. I kept going south trying to find a stairway that wasn't full of folk coming down. All of them were full, with folk falling over the rails and people being carried without knowing what was happening. Ten miles south I came to a main staircase up and it was empty. I started climbing up the stairs. There was stuff everywhere, people's belongings, clothes. I saw a woman dead. She looked like she'd been trampled." He made a face of disgust. "I didn't stop to look at her. It was pretty ugly. I found out why no one was on the stairs. There was a fire. Ev-

erything from the highroad blocks around all the way to the
verge was burning. I had to wait all day for the fire to burn
down enough so that I could go up. The stairs to this tier
were empty, too. I guess because all the folk saw fire below
and took another way down. There were already some starting to come down those stairs when I went up. . . .".

"That was two nights ago?" asked Brann.

Halsam nodded.

"Just when we got here," said Liza.

"If you came to this tier two nights ago," Brann asked,
"how come it took you so long to get here?"

"Lord above," said Halsam, "didn't you see at all? They
were all going crazy up here. The worst of any place. I don't
know why. Folk were crowded on the highroad, running into
each other's carts, and I saw people fighting. I hid out in an
empty house all night and all day yesterday. I was afraid to
go out onto the street. Finally it got quiet last night but I
waited until morning to try to find you."

Halsam finished his bread and brushed crumbs away. "I
bet that below it's still like that, everybody from all up here
piled up for the elevators and all jammed on the stairs. We
aren't going to go down, are we?"

"I don't know," said Brann. In fact he had no idea where
to go from here. Halsam's story had surprised him entirely.

They came down from the park into the marketplat. Brann
could hardly believe the enormity of the change. For the first
time that he could recall, the stone counters of the stalls were
empty and not a noise or motion altered the stillness. The
open flag floor of the market was littered with baggage discarded in flight and as he had before in the time when the
blond folk had come down on Pilgrimage, Brann wondered at
the strange whims of the folk, the items they had chosen to
carry away with them. Where the parkplat merged into the
market, a trunk had broken open. Dishware had spilled from
it, and mugs and glasses. Pieces of utensils lay scattered
where they had been dropped. Farther along lay a rug, half
unrolled and trampled with dirt.

"Who'd take a rug along?" Brann wondered. The design
was worn, something of trees and mountains, fading into
threadbare emptiness in the center. Satchels lay where folk

had dropped them. Books lay scattered and the filthy flag-stones were unlike the clean-swept floor that Brann had al-ways known here.

They came to a food stall, that of old Marka Zoll, whose fruits somehow, though they had come from the same Farmy Fields and up the same elevator as those of the other mer-chants, seemed fresher and riper, more tempting than any of the others'. Nothing remained but fruit rinds here now and juices smeared down the front of the stall. Squashed oranges and trampled plums stained the flags bright purple and orange. There was blood on the stones of the stall, and the three peered inside but there was no other sign of the old woman—if it was her blood after all. Brann prayed it was not. Marka Zoll was gone. Closer to the elevator cages the disorder was vast. Though he couldn't imagine how it had been accomplished, Brann examined a massive stone stall which had been overturned. Bolts of cloth like bright streamers were tangled and snarled about it. Something had been battered against the elevator doors until they didn't close completely, and blood smears were on the half-open lips.

Brann shined his flashlight through the opening in the doors. He looked up and down the immense shaft, trying to catch sight of a car descending. As always, the cold air from above was falling through the shaft and the humming empty noise went on; but Brann saw no cars coming.

"It's empty," he told the others. "What could make that happen?"

Halsam crowded up next to Brann and stuck his head through the partly open doors. "I'll bet I know what's hap-pened," he said. "They're all down at the bottom. I'll bet none of the runners would bring his car through the up. They're probably all piled up down there with no one to bring them back." He moved away from the doors and ges-tured to the south. "It was like this at the next elevator sta-tion; the marketplat all empty and no cars running in the shafts."

"Maybe there's nothing moving in all of Tailend," Liza said. Did Brann sense awe in Liza's voice? She seemed not to believe what she had said: *nothing* moving in all of Tailend? "Maybe everybody, all of the folk are gone?"

She stopped and turned toward the verge. "Did you hear something?"

"No," said Brann. He listened and then he heard it also; a voice, tiny and distant-sounding, as of someone making a speech.

"Where is it coming from?" Halsam asked.

"It's across the parkplat somewhere," said Liza. "Someone is here after all."

The three ran out of the littered marketplat toward the path that crossed the park. If one were watching from an empty stall, he might have seen only three running, not any longer children, not quite yet adults. Their bare legs moved swiftly, and their loose, bright-colored shirts caught the illumination of the sunlights. Perhaps, if the empty stillness of the gallery were ignored, one might think them three young folk racing. Their footsteps sounded light on the dirt of the path and possibly one gave out with a lighthearted shriek.

They came to the dome of the Isocourt Hall. The structure, which towered to nearly the ceiling of the gallery, seemed different somehow, crushed partly as if the absent motion of a giant's hand had brushed it. Part of the dome halfway up had fallen away, and though the doors of the Hall were closed, it was from this aperture they could hear the voice. It spoke in a bass monotone continuously, waiting for no answer, offering no interruption for others to speak. From here, outside the dome, the voice was unstructured; speech without words.

"Are there Magistors still here?" Liza asked.

Halsam laughed, "Vardan still would be. Vardan goes on forever."

"That's not Vardan's voice," said Brann. "I never heard that one before."

Liza made a tentative move toward the nearest door. "Do we go inside?" They looked at one another. At last Brann nodded and the three went in. Inside, save for the open patch near the dome's zenith, the structure seemed intact. At the periphery of the pit, sections of the first two platforms had fallen in, and the ramps that ran to them were canted and sloped at impossible angles. The green floor of the pit itself had sunk partially at the opposite end of the dome. One small arc of it had collapsed entirely and from that open crescent of floor lights came and the suggestion of that network-like image of human veins seemed lit and brilliant as it never had been before.

"Who is talking?" Halsam cried out. He stepped cautiously out onto the sagging rubberoid floor of the pit.

The voice was intelligible now. But at first the words it spoke were not. Its speech was like that of other galleries, the words muted slightly, the vowels soft and broad. Was there someone here from another tier? Brann wondered; maybe someone crazy was here, ranting in the Isocourt Hall. He looked around the open chamber, but the source of the voice was not any of the chairs ranked around nor any of the closed chambers beyond. It seemed to come from the dome above, from some central point over their heads.

"There's nobody here," Liza said. Brann saw it was true.

Partially it was the acoustics of the dome that were to blame. Its ruined symmetry made the voice indistinct, and when Halsam asked again who was talking, Brann shushed him.

"Listen," he said, "it's not very different from how we talk. There's something wrong with his voice, is all."

They listened: "SOUTH CROSS ONE," it said, "WE ASK AN ASSESSMENT OF YOUR PLACE." It paused for an instant. "NORTH CROSS ONE AT HIGHROAD, WE ASK AN ASSESSMENT OF YOUR PLACE."

"It's talking to someone," Halsam said.

"It's talking to south cross one, at the south flank," said Brann.

"What does it mean, 'an assessment of your place'?" Halsam asked.

"Maybe," Liza said, "it's trying to find out what is happening at the south flank."

"How could it talk there?" Halsam asked. "Nobody could hear it *there*, from here. We couldn't even hear it outside in the park."

Brann shrugged. Then he recalled what Ebar had told him—perhaps it had been the truth. "My Grandmother Ebar said that there were ways once to speak from flank to flank of the gallery, and farther even than that. Maybe this voice is part of the way they could do that once. Maybe the shaking woke it up. What's below us seems alive now." The voice scared Brann, it scared Halsam and Liza half to death so that curiosity and fear were balanced but the strange boom of the voice won out and they stayed to listen. The voice went on asking, north and south by intersection and crossroad to give the "assessment of your place," imperturbably, though nothing ever answered it.

"Do you see?" said Brann as he went across to one of the desks at the pit's circumference. "The window in the desk has lights in it and words."

The lights pulsed in steady sequence, showing vague darkened shapes sometimes and sometimes nothing but unresolved blackness. Brann sat down as a Magistor might, feeling foolish and important. Liza and Halsam watched over his shoulders.

"It's saying the same thing," Halsam said. He read off the words as they appeared, *"South cross nine, north cross nine,"* just like the voice. "Hey!"

Once, the window did not stay dark; it lit for a moment with a picture. They saw a building with spires and arches as if they were looking down from directly above.

"It's like what we see from the grill in your secret room, Brann," Halsam said.

And Brann knew it, too, and wanted to go to that room and see how the Isocourt Hall and it could be connected, if someway he and Hals had been watched while they were in there and the picture of them seen here.

"It's the gallery school," said Liza. "Our school. It's on fire!"

Flames climbed on the stone spires, eating off paint and wooden decoration. The words of the picture said: *"School, south cross 28."*

Then again the window went dark with only words showing. Once more there came a picture, stark greens and browns of the parkplat and then the marketplat and the frozen elevator doors.

"It's showing us the gallery," Liza said.

"If there could be cameras," Brann told them, "which took pictures like those Ebar had and those Mama kept, couldn't there be cameras that can show us what the gallery looks like now? Ebar says that there are things we have forgotten and things we don't even know we have forgotten, things like this hidden all around us on the gallery." The sequence went on to its end.

"GENTLEFOLK," the voice said after a pause, "WE MEET AN URGENCY FOR THE GALLERY. I ASK FOR A POLLING OF THE MAGISTORS PRESENT AS TO AN ACTION COURSE. I AM AT AN END OF RESOURCES. I HAVE NO SPEECH FROM OTHER BRAINS ON TIERS UP OR DOWN. I HAVE NO SPEECH FROM STATIONS ALONG THE HIGHROAD HERE. IF ONE OF THE MAGISTORS HERE ASSEMBLED HAS A THOUGHT ON THIS, PLEASE RESPOND. I WILL POLL THOSE PRESENT NOW."

On the window now a chart of the Isocourt Hall appeared. Each of the hundred desks was pictured in the circumference of the pit. On this representation of the dome, one of the desks lit more brightly than the rest. "MAGISTOR ALM BARKALM, CAN YOU REPLY?"

Across the pit a chime came from one of the desks and the voice moved on:

"MAGISTOR VERNA DUNMADDEN, CAN YOU REPLY?"

Again the chime came and again, after an instant's wait, the voice resumed. The three listened as the voice inquired steadily at desk after empty desk whether any of the Magistors had a solution to the problem the brain had posed. It seemed to Brann as if somehow the voice were blind, asking empty desks in turn, oblivious to the emptiness, as if it might continue around and around the circle, asking.

"It's coming around to us," Halsam said. "It's going to ask us what we want to do."

"Are you going to say something?" Liza asked.

Brann shook his head. Two desks to the left a chime sounded and now the voice issuing both from the point somewhere above and from the desk next to theirs asked if that Magistor had a solution. Then the chime sounded and the voice moved on. The window in front of them glowed brightly and from somewhere in their desk the voice of the brain asked: "MAGISTOR LUDEN GOBI? CAN YOU REPLY?"

Brann shook his head again.

"Brann," Liza said, "talk to it. It's going to go past us."

The chime didn't sound; instead the voice asked a direct question only through the desk before them; its companion above remained mute. "MAGISTOR LUDEN GOBI, DO YOU WISH TO STATE SOMETHING?"

"It thinks we're Magistor Gobi," Liza said. "Brann, talk to it. I want to know what is happening. I want you to ask it where the shake comes from."

Brann looked at both of them. They leaned over his shoulders, the yellow light from the window painting their faces luridly. He, too, wanted to know what was happening. He knew that not even the Magistors of today had been aware of the voice of the brain—Mara had told him, the powers of that reticulate net of light below were mysterious to all—this had existed among them all this time, unknown, what more could it tell them, if he knew what to ask?

"DO YOU WISH TO POSE A QUESTION, MAGISTOR?"

Brann whispered to it, scarcely sure it could hear him, but frightened to speak out boldly, "Yes, tell me, what . . . what caused the shaking?"

Something worked below, some change came subtly to the light. Did they hear the question repeated, dissected into substrate meanings? Other voices seemed to whisper. "MY MESSAGE SOURCES ON THE FIRST TIER HAVE NOT REPLIED, DO NOT REPLY, CANNOT GIVE ME THE REQUISITE SEISMIC STUDIES, MAGISTOR. MY BEST ESTIMATE IS AN EARTHQUAKE. I WOULD KNOW MORE BUT THERE SEEMS TO BE A, SOME, DISCONTINUITY IN MY CONNECTIONS. I HAVE A TIME DISCONTINUITY. SOMEHOW SOME OF MY NETWORK IS MISSING . . . SOMEHOW I CANNOT ANSWER YOU. MY BEST ESTIMATE IS AN EARTHQUAKE."

Liza was perplexed. "It's not saying anything."

"WHAT IS THE DAY?" the voice asked plaintively.

Halsam looked to Liza. "It's crazy, isn't it? Why is it asking that?"

"WHAT IS THE DAY? CAN YOU TELL ME, PLEASE?" the voice took on a fearful quality, like that of a bewildered child.

"It wants to know what day it is," Halsam repeated. "What's wrong with the thing?"

"I don't know," Brann said. There was a stench coming now. It was of fire and he couldn't tell if it was from outside or below. Was the brain itself burning? For an instant there was a chuckling, roaring noise from below as if a horde of monklers were racing through the tier. The center of the pit sagged a little. Halsam grew wide-eyed.

"Brann," he said, "something's happening. Let's go!"

"PLEASE, MAGISTOR LUDEN GOBI, THE DAY!"

What day *was* it, Brann wondered. Had it been two days since the Sabbath? "It must be Twiday," he told the brain.

"NO, NO, THE DATE, THE YEAR. I HAVE A DISCONTINUITY, SOMEHOW THE TIME IS GONE."

"I don't know the date," said Brann. "It must be somewhere near summer-end, eighty-one, eighty-two, I'm not sure . . . gallery year 1211."

"THE GALLERY YEAR 1211?"

"It is," said Brann.

Was there a moaning from the voice? Did the window in the desk top dim? "CAN IT BE TRUE? I SEEM TO HAVE LOST FOUR HUNDRED YEARS." Then it paused again while the echoes below analyzed that and a question built in them rising to audibility: "ARE YOU MAGISTOR LUDEN GOBI? MY VISION SEEMS GONE HERE. HOW COULD YOU BE THAT MAGISTOR? THE FOLK DO NOT LIVE SO LONG."

"None of us is that Magistor," Liza told the brain. "I've never heard of him."

"JUST SOMEHOW IT HAPPENED. FOUR HUNDRED YEARS!"

Halsam was right, the brain was crazy. It made no sense. How could it lose 400 years? Brann couldn't conceive of something with a life that long. What was it made of? It was impossible, wasn't it? It was crazy, but maybe it could help them. The empty chamber was very warm. There was smoke now in the air and it meant that the fire approached. He saw that Halsam wanted to leave. Hals was held only because Brann still sat in the desk chair and Liza stood next to him, watching the light of the window. Halsam was Liza's age, but younger often in his actions, more a child . . . *But Hals had dared the empty elevator shaft when no one else would, and that had been years before* . . . Brann would have gone now, too; the brain was certainly crazy, but there were things he still wanted to know.

"Our folks have gone on Pilgrimage," said Brann. "Where have they gone?"

"THEY GO TO KEEP THE CITY IN MOTION."

"But the city doesn't move!"

"THEY GO TO FRONTEND TO COMPLETE THE CYCLE OF THE CITY'S MOTION."

"How *can* the city move?" Brann cried out.

"IT HAS ALWAYS MOVED," said the brain. The window's picture changed. "SEE THIS: THE CITY AS IT WAS!"

There were the mountains to the east in the picture, much closer now, on a day without fog or clouds. There were no Foundations to be seen. Even the Farmy Fields were absent. Instead, the land below was an open, mottled green, as if the Foundations and the Farmy Fields never were. They could not tell from what height they viewed this scene. It moved gently beneath them and the mountains came closer. The mountains were different somehow, a shape squared off their jagged aspect. The afternoon sun came from behind and its light cast the mountains in a yellow-orange pattern stretching across the horizon. A brilliant sun/sky reflection of mixed orange and blue blazed from the blocky thing on the mountain crest. They came closer still, and the three young folk could see that there were striations on the blocky shape, layerings like galleries, rising in tiers high above the mountains' highest crest.

"It's like Tailend," Halsam said. "Like someone put the city up there where it shouldn't be."

Now the view was closer still and they could see that the blocky shape cascaded down the mountain scarp. Buttresses rose from granite carved into naked stone facings. The scale was beyond their understanding. They had never been outside the city and even the immense reach of Tailend from the roof down to the Foundations they could only see in foreshortened perspective, dwindling to toy size in the distance. They were not prepared for, nor able to realize immediately, the scope of something so large. Only the scale of the mountains made the real size of this city apparent.

The city shape clung to the mountain face as if it had grown from it. It filled crevasses and openings in the mountain mass in a way almost organic. They flew now over the roof of the city. It was as the boy from the 113th tier had told Brann: black and white in a checkered pattern, snow and clearing. The city below them spilled out onto a plain to the east and ended. Their view came close again and now it was as if they were seeing Tailend.

"Brann," Liza said, "I see Structors there."

And Brann saw that Liza was right. There were Structors doing as he had seen the Structors doing on the Tailend of their own city. As he watched, the Structors worked with a slab of a tier in the way that the Structors on the Tailend of this city worked. He saw something else.

"Look there," Brann said to the others. "What is that going away from the Tailend?"

"It's Foundations!" Halsam said.

"Yeah, it is," Liza confirmed. "They're going on and on to the east."

"There is no city there now," Brann said. "Where did it go?"

"THIS IS THE ONLY CITY," the brain's voice told them. "IT IS THE SAME CITY YOU LIVE IN NOW. YOU SEE IT AS IT WAS THREE THOUSAND YEARS AGO."

"It didn't move from there," Halsam rejoined. "A whole city doesn't move like some power cart."

"IT DID."

"Is it still moving?"

"IT IS."

Brann studied the picture in the window, taking in the awesome concept of a city the size of the one he lived in (*so far it has no end,* the boy had said) moving somewhere, climbing down from the mountains like a worm from the parkplat, climbing down and crawling across the Farmy Fields for three thousand years, leaving a trail of Foundations. He saw the others gaped at it, too, and he asked the only logical question (he was not the first to ask it, but he was the first in a very long time).

"If the city is truly moving," Brann asked the voice of the brain, "where is it going?"

The brain did not answer. The picture went away from the window and no other picture replaced it. Halsam was scared; he made a small noise and pulled at Brann to come away. Liza, too, seemed quite ready to leave.

"I want to know," Brann told them. "It will tell us if we wait." He ran his fingers along the tarnished silver contacts on the desk top wondering at their functions. "Can you hear me?" he asked the brain.

It answered in a slow and tired voice. "YES, MAGISTOR, I

CAN HEAR YOU. I HAVE A DISRUPTION IN MY CIRCUITS. I HAVE
FIRE IN MY CIRCUITS. I HAVE NO ANSWERS FOR YOU NOW."

"Where is the city going?"

"WHERE? GOING WHERE? NO ONE EVER ASKED ME THAT
BEFORE. I HAVE FIRE IN MY CIRCUITS."

Smoke came from the chamber below. The floor of the pit
sagged at its center and the green rubberoid surface began to
bubble.

Halsam pulled at him again. "We have to go!"

"Where are we going?" Brann demanded. He beat at the
darkened window and his face grew red. Tears of frustration
came down his cheeks.

"IF IT IS FOUR HUNDRED YEARS," the voice said calmly,
"WE ARE MOVING NO LONGER. IF IT IS FOUR HUNDRED YEARS,
WE ARE THERE. IF IT IS FOUR HUNDRED YEARS FROM HERE,
THEN THE STRUCTORS HAVE DISBANDED AND WE HAVE AR-
RIVED."

"Where is it we have come?"

"I DON'T KNOW!"

"The Structors work as always; you are wrong."

"WE HAD ONLY FOUR HUNDRED YEARS LEFT UNTIL . . ."

"The Structors have not ceased; what are you saying?"

"THEY MUST!"

"They have not."

"IT IS WRONG . . . WRONG . . ."

Across the chamber flame appeared suddenly and the
bright light of fire spread up the ancient curve of the dome.
Halsam was pulling at Brann's shoulders, and Liza had
picked up their satchels. The chamber was hot so that the
tears on Brann's face became mixed with perspiration and the
flames rose in a sheet along the far curve of the chamber.

"I BURN!" the voice shouted. "SOMEONE STOP THE FIRE BE-
FORE I BURN!"

"Please, who would know the answers?" Brann asked.
"Who would know where the city is going?"

"ASK A POSTMAN! THE POST GUILD KEEPS THE HISTORY.
THE POST GUILD KNOWS THE WAY."

The voice cried more loudly, begging for Fire-fighters to
come and save it, crying for the Magistors to do something.
It cried and the voice became a garble until Halsam managed

to pull Brann from the chair, and seeing the flame now all around them, he joined Hals and Liza and they ran.

The Post Guild would know. Brann went to the Post House, to the plat where he had gone many times before for mail from other folk on the gallery and for messages from far away on the tier. He went up to the old open stone gate of the structure. With Halsam and Liza tagging behind, he stepped into the empty entry hall. The stones confused the sounds of their footsteps on the slate floor, sundering them and bringing them back from everywhere at once. The huge room was lit as it had always been with the high chandelier flickering as if from candles. It was empty, though. All they saw was dust and silence and disarray.

But on the stones of the hall to the left of the entry someone had written in a scarlet stain:

The prophecy proves true. Tailend is emptied. Post folk rejoin five frontward at the Post House on Tier 99.

Brann sat down on the cold slate floor. He stared at the message whose words seemed splashed on the stone in terrible haste. The paint bucket still lay beneath the message, and a red puddle spread from it out over the brush. The paint was still tacky as if the Post Folk had only just fled.

Halsam knelt next to Brann. "I'm frightened, Brann; what do you suppose is happening?"

Brann shook his head. "I don't know, Hals."

Liza paced the empty hall looking for signs of the Post Folk. She peered into the dark interior of the house where the folk never went. She saw something strange and called to Brann.

"Look at this;" she said. "All their devices are gone. They tore them out and took them away and there's nothing else here." Then Brann and Halsam heard her utter a clipped shriek and come scuttling out into the main hall.

"There's a dead man there, like the dwarf. Only he's not a dwarf at all. He's very big. I never saw anyone so tall. He has a knife in his back. . . ." She was shaking.

It was a man like the dwarfed giant, and what he held in a death grip so fierce that whoever of the Post Guild had killed him had been unable to wrest it away from his grasp was one of the Post House devices. He had apparently been trying to carry it away. An immense wound was in his back and a knife protruded there, one of the swords that the Post Guild always carried ceremonially.

Brann decided. "I'm going to where the message says, to the Post House five Frontward on the 99th tier," he told Hals and Liza. "Maybe you two should try to find the end of the Pilgrimage and join your parents."

Halsam looked at Liza. "Are you going to?" he asked her.

Liza shook her head. "I'm going with Brann," she said with finality.

Halsam stepped up to join them. "Well," he said, "then so am I."

Chapter Four

Driver

The dead giant had scared them. It was nothing like the unknown forces which the brain had called an *earthquake* and which, though destructive in immense proportion, were after all no different in quality from the actions of the Structors. Perhaps it even *was* a consequence of the Structors; Brann and Liza and Hals speculated on that. But the dead giant was a symbol of combat whose scope stretched beyond the confines of the gallery and whose duration was beyond knowing.

Brann resolved not to think about it, but his thoughts returned restlessly to the sharp blade of the ceremonial knife and to its placement at the base of the giant's wound. And the wound itself in the giant's back? Didn't it seem so sure and practiced, down the spine *so* and beneath the final rib? Had the knife been left itself as a sign? A warning to others like the giant? Brann was very quiet about it and his silence subdued Hals and Liza who walked beside him on the crossroad.

They had already passed through the gallery one-frontward of their own—a place nearly as familiar to them as their own gallery, where the shops and streets were often extensions of streets they walked all the time. It, too, had been deserted and the same signs of precipitous flight could be seen. The broken elevator gaped in that gallery's far wall. The market-plat there had been strewn with the same sort of refuse they had seen before. Here there had been no fire, though, and the reason for desertion was less apparent. Now they were through the one two-frontward also.

Here they found an anomaly.

This was a place just beyond their knowledge, where the known city ended. For some reason here the gallery wall was different. (How to explain it? It was as if a woman one had always known by sight from the waist up only had suddenly stood, exposed as a mermaid with fish fins and flukes from the hips on down, or a man one knew suddenly appeared with the hairy legs and cleft hooves of Pan.) Where there were archways in their own gallery, here there was a solid wall. The gaps in the arches had been filled with masonry and great grilled gates blocked the few openings. North and south along the verge of this gallery the gates were shut and locked.

"My cousin Vill told me that there were places like this on other tiers," Brann said. "He told me that sometimes the folk in one gallery hated the folk of another so much that they closed up the way through and made it very difficult to travel between. He told me that eight-up, on the forty-fifth, it's like that. They have something called a tariff gate you go through when you get off the elevator. Sometimes, he said, for no reason they wouldn't let a person off and that one had to go on to another level to get off."

They sat on the counter of an empty stall. It was one so like the stalls in their own plat that with little effort Brann could pretend they had never left home. *This is the closest I'll ever see to it,* he thought, and he felt the smooth stone almost with desperation. Halsam had gone wandering among the other stalls and returned with two loaves of stale, odd-shaped bread, yellow and twisted, and a bottle of water from the central siphon in the plat. Somehow it would not shut off when he tried, and water ran in a wide sluggish stream into the nearest of the open elevator doors. They could hear it splashing far below.

Halsam broke the bread and handed each a chunk. "Something's broken in the siphon," he said. "Do you see the water won't shut off?"

"Everything is like that here," said Liza. "I wonder if the whole city could be broken."

They watched the water running and looked on past it to the heavy crisscrossed bars of a gate.

"Why would some folk want to lock themselves away like that?" Halsam asked.

Brann made a face. "Grandma Ebar said that folk on some of the tiers have more than others; they know more things. Like how to make the little dancing dolls, one of those I gave you, Liza, that cousin Vill brought back for me—things that you can't get anywhere else. She says that they want to keep it for themselves and won't trade. Then sometimes there are fights between the galleries." He let them contemplate the concept of such huge collective fights—he expanded on it. "Ebar told me that there was one, called a war, one time where everybody in one gallery got killed because of it and it stayed all empty afterward."

Halsam looked incredulous. He was used to Brann's exaggerations. "I never heard of that," he said.

"Yeah," Liza agreed, "where did that happen?"

"Maybe here," Brann said. "Maybe that's why the gates are closed."

They were barely two miles from the center of their own gallery. But the way had been tortuous. Whatever the Structors had used to build the homes of this gallery, had withstood the shaking poorly. Houses were tumbled from their plats, creating mounds of impassable rubble in the narrow side roads of this gallery. They left the memory of the dead giant behind. As they became used to the singular stillness, they became playful. Brann chased Liza up the sloping wall of what had been a house, ducking into windows that lay sideways, chattering like children. Once, they boldly entered the shop of an expensive clothier. They made for the fine racks in the rear where the stuff of the wealthy hung, unattended now. Brann had often watched his mother make such things. They were cut from a fabric of distant manufacture. The Gads brought it mostly, as the Gads brought everything really strange—as they brought the circuses and the caravans coming from who knew what parts of the city, so distant they spoke only a little of Brann's folks' speech and spoke instead a tongue entirely divorced from anything known, calling it Tzingaro or the Rom and claiming it to be more ancient than anything spoken in the city. Gads, Brann remembered, had once camped in the parkplat for a week, and had set up a traders' market in the marketplat. Brann recalled their olive skin and black clipped hair in ringlets. There had been one called the Romking who had worn a bushy mustache in the way the Post Folk wore their swords. They had sold cloth like this with a patterned weave so fine that the separate threads of woof and warp could not be told and which would not wrinkle and which came clean with a single soapless rinse. Brann's mother had made his clothes, but he'd never had anything of the Gad's cloth, except once a scarf made from a bolt end.

"Two hundred Paad," Liza said. "Can you believe this?" She held up a dress of creamy white that clung to her as if it were a skin. She shucked her own travel-stained shorts and shirt right there to put it on. This embarrassed Halsam a bit, for privacy in the confines of the city was prized and nudity was not quite so common as might be supposed. Since the previous morning when Halsam had discovered Brann and Liza together beneath their blanket, he had felt—without really being certain just what he felt—a certain closeness in them that excluded him at times. Now Brann had also undressed and chosen from the rack knee-length pants of a soft green weave and a puffy-sleeved shirt in whose pattern of brown and white Halsam could perhaps discern flowers woven.

"Take something, Hals," Liza said, and she found him a suit whose azure blue tunic and cobalt blue pants made him look, she said, like the sky at sunrise.

Hals smiled tentatively and held the garments. Then he saw the mischievous looks which had come to Brann's and Liza's faces. They circled about each end of the aisle and chased him down to a curtained cul-de-sac where all three went down in a tangle on the carpeted floor. They undressed him in spite of his struggles, and in spite of the closeness of Liza's red, sweet-smelling hair and soft laugh which scared him immensely. Then, grinning, they paraded him in front of a mirror in clothes which his father's gardener's wage could never have purchased. It felt to him that the clothes were not really separate from him, and in the azure cloth he saw scenes possibly woven which he could not quite determine, but which if explicated would have been, he was sure, landscapes never viewed from the galleries of Tailend. Neither Brann's nor Liza's garments were quite like it. It did not surprise Halsam to read the tag that priced it at 1299 Paad.

There was silence in the gallery that night. Of all the changes, Brann found this one hardest to bear. In all his memory there had never been a time when the gallery was totally silent. Always from somewhere came the sound of an elevator car rising or the low grating noise of the car doors opening. On the highroad there was perpetually the distant motion of a power cart whose hum swelled and faded in travel. There were voices even in the rarest moments before dawn. And always at the verge the remote and brittle noises of the Structors came, metal upon metal, and metal upon masonry and winches moving and engines' thrum. Ceaselessly there had been the sough of wind moving outward from the city's interior, a noise so constant that its absence now was fearsome, an augur of great events somewhere inside.

"The monklers are gone," Liza noted. "I haven't heard them since the shaking."

It was true. The little Lemuroidea were no longer in the trees of parkplats they had passed. They had nested everywhere, climbing from tier to tier and skipping along through galleries without hinderance. But Liza said she had not seen the short soft muzzle or wide staring eyes of a monkler since the shaking. Now and again there were birds—the great ones which seemed denizens of the world outside the city and visited Tailend irregularly; and the small ones, descendants of wrens and of captive birds set free into the city's larger cage long ago—and the birds still sang. They were nervous since the shaking and stayed more constantly in the air. But the soft chitter of the monklers was absent.

"I hear them," Halsam said.

The three were in their blankets, Brann and Liza together, Halsam separate just a bit, all settled onto a litter of old excelsior that had once been the protective packing for fruit from the Farmy Fields. Now, two galleries inward from their own, it was very dark in the night. Nothing of moonlight from Tailend penetrated and the few moon lamps in the ceiling were distant and dim.

"I hear it, too," Brann said. "It's not monklers, though."

"It sounds like monklers to me," Hals said.

Brann shook his head. "No, listen, it's more like singing, all together, only I can't make out any words."

Liza sat up. "The noise is coming from the other side of the gate," she said. "Do you suppose there are folk in the next gallery?"

"I never heard any folk sound like that," Hals whispered. "It's like noises of animals, like the animals the Gads bring when the circus comes. Only sometimes I think I can make out words in it."

There came a long wild calling like the yapping of a wild dog, were there any dogs in the city save for those in the Gad's menagerie, and a single cracking report. Something white and luminous in the dark came fluttering down onto Liza. She shrieked and flailed.

"What is it, Brann? Help!" And Brann started laughing.

"It's your dress, Liza." The thing had slipped, perhaps moved by the sudden noise (or coincidentally) from where Liza had draped it on the overhanging counter of the stall. The white cloth, ghostlike in the night, had fallen onto Liza. She struggled free of the blanket and stood grimacing at Brann. Halsam saw her in the stripe of moonlight that stroked down her spine from the nape of her neck to her buttocks and slipped across arm and breast as she moved. She flung the dress at Brann and would not look when he held out his arm.

Brann stifled his laughter. "Please, Liza. I'm sorry. Come here."

She turned her face away, but slowly she looked back at him and soon she took his hand and settled back to the blankets. They would not have understood why Halsam picked up his blanket then and moved it outside the door to the stall, lying there with his hands pressed over his ears. Brann and Liza were not especially attentive to the resumed noise from beyond the sealed arches of the gallery, the low, speechless, incessant chant.

"Halsam!" Liza was calling. Brann woke with the dusty odor of wood shavings in his nostrils. He found his way out from beneath the blankets. He ruffled his hair, feeling excelsior there, and sneezed.

He heard Liza call "Halsam!" again.

"He went outside last night," Brann said. He shook wood shaving from his pants and pulled them on. Taking his shirt like a towel around his neck, Brann stepped out into the entrance of the stall where the full beam of the sunlights made him squint.

Liza squatted amid the disarray of Halsam's belongings.

"He's gone somewhere," Liza told him.

"Maybe he went off to find something for breakfast," Brann answered. "He's good at that." Brann moved over to where the stream of water still issued from the siphon in the center of the marketplat. He put his head under the stream and washed away the dust and the excelsior. He toweled the water from his arms and chest with his shirt.

"Brann!" Liza called sharply.

"What?"

"This isn't funny. I think something has happened to Hals." She pointed to the contents of his satchel, utensils, matches, a flashlight, odd torn bits of clothing strewn over the flagstones. A packet of dried apples had been torn open and the contents were gone. Crumbs of the fruit, as if hurriedly eaten, lay among the belongings.

Brann felt ashamed that he had laughed before. Something had happened that had taken Halsam from his bed in a hurry. He joined with Liza and they called for him. "Hals, where are you? Halsam! Halsam!" Their voices went on, repeating into the silence of the gallery. Then Brann took his knife and moved among the stalls looking for some sign of Halsam. His fear now—he didn't tell it to Liza—was that some straggler from the exodus had murdered Hals, perhaps for his food and dragged Hals's body to some deserted stall. All the stalls were empty. Halsam was gone.

Liza and Brann stood together, abject, in the center of the marketplat, near where the siphon bubbled and ran. They wondered to each other why Halsam had gone outside the night before and where he might have gone.

"What made him leave?" Liza asked.

"Maybe we kept him awake," Brann said. But it wasn't funny.

In their frustration they began to argue as to whose fault it had been that Halsam had gone. Not looking much at each other, they gathered up their belongings and packed their satchels. Outside, Liza repacked Halsam's satchel and refused to allow Brann to help. Brann, angry, moved away. He walked toward the wall of the gallery where the gate blocked further passage and he looked through the grillwork into the gallery beyond. From where he stood he could see only ruins. They were the tumbled walls of houses, the stone and masonry worn and dirty. It seemed to predate the shaking surely, as if some disaster had occurred there long before. Dirt had covered the flags on the other side of the gate and only in one place was there a path leading over it where the dirt was swept from the floor. It led back amid the rubble and disappeared. Misshapen walls blocked further view into the next gallery. Brann took hold of the gate thinking to climb a bit and perhaps see where the path led. The gate swung with his weight. It swung silently as if it opened often for some purpose and Brann saw that there were footprints in the dust going both ways. He leaped clear and crouched, breathless.

"Liza, I want to show you this," he called. "I think I've found where Hals went."

She came at a run, dropping any pretense of anger. Brann showed her the footprints beyond the open gate.

"Look," she said, "the lock has been cut open. Was it like this before?"

Brann shrugged; he couldn't recall.

Liza bent to examine the massive dead-bolt which should have held the gate shut against almost any force. The bolt was on their side of the gate. "Someone has cut right through the grill from the other side," Liza said. "It's still all fresh, bright metal. Maybe it's only been a little while since it happened."

"We would have heard," Brann protested.

"No, we wouldn't."

They heard the noise again, the low, eerie chanting which was not quite speech. Its source was beyond the tumbled walls of the next gallery. The cracking came and the loud yapping that they could now hear as words.

Liza called, "Halsam!" cupping her hands and shouting through the ruined gate. There was no reply. The chanting continued. It rose into a grumbling cacophony after the cracking noise and settled into its eerie rhythm after a moment. She shouted, "Halsam!" again and would have shouted a third time—she had her hands cupped and the word on her tongue—when a woman appeared. She came from behind the farthest wall visible on the path.

The woman's jaw had a dead slackness. Her open mouth showed stumps of teeth. Seeing Brann and Liza there, she peeled her lips back further in a loose-lipped grimace and her pink tongue came uncertainly to her lips. She wore nothing except a harness, and her hair ended raggedly at her waist. The leather of the harness crossed above her flat breasts and between them, coming down over the doughy flesh of her belly. Her color was dark but it was the darkness of dirt, not pigment, and neither Brann nor Liza could tell harness from flesh. Even without the motion of air, her odor came rank and sour so that Liza gagged at it. For the briefest instant the woman remained. Then her arm came up and she flung something which splattered on the gate and through it, and would have splashed on Brann and Liza had they not seen it coming and dodged back from the gate in time.

Liza wrinkled her nose at it. "It's shit," she said, "or something else just as rotten."

They looked back through the grillwork but the woman was gone.

"I never saw anyone as filthy as that," Brann said. He did not even have time to imagine what else might be in the next gallery nor to do more than lick his lips, which seemed somehow to have become very dry. The chanting picked up in cadence and also the yapping shout. The cracking sound rang out several times swiftly. The rumbling of something immense, moving, began and they could feel the vibration of it through the concrete of the gallery floor.

"Hals is there, I bet," Brann said.

"Do you want to go in there?" Liza asked him.

"No."

"But we have to if Hals is on the other side of the gate, don't we?"

"Yes, I suppose."

He saw that she wasn't angry anymore. Though she tried to hide it, he made out the faintest smile when she turned to pick up her satchel. Somehow Brann had found he wasn't as afraid as he had been, because whatever had happened to Hals had to do with folk of some sort and he *could* deal with folk, as opposed to giants or things entirely unknown.

Brann picked up his own satchel and Halsam's. Avoiding the foul stuff which still dripped from the gate, he pulled the grill open and they stepped through.

The rumble came louder now as something rolled with gathering momentum. The chant picked up in cadence to what might once have been a song. The meaning of it had gone and even the volition until it sounded as if it were imperative, a noise inseparable from action. The hair on Brann's arms rose and he felt goose bumps. Liza walked on her toes like one afraid to touch the ground. The ground was gritty like sand under their bare feet. Wherever they stepped, little puffs of dust came up. The smell of it was dry and unpleasant.

"I wonder how long things have been like this on this gallery?" Liza whispered. "These were houses once, I think. Maybe like ours, but you can't even really tell except by the shape."

The path wound through the haphazard mounds. They were not really used to the dirt. Their own gallery had always been swept daily so that the paths and crossroads were spotless and they could go barefoot without a thought. Here, a masonry wall leaned over a hill of rubble so that a cave was formed. They couldn't see inside, but in a cleared space at the entrance there was a fire circle. The stones were sooty as if many fires had burned here. In a midden nearby were dry and splintered bones. Had it not been for the thought of Halsam, one could hardly imagine which of them would have said, "Let's go back!" first.

The only colors in this ruined gallery were the grays of fallen stone and the black of soot. A fine dust soon layered their clothes. Everywhere in the dust there were directionless footprints, and once they came across a rubble-strewn highroad where the dust was rutted with the mark of great wheels. The air was filled with dust like a dry floating mist.

The noise was very close now, just beyond a broken ridge of stone which seemed to have been moved aside by some engine—perhaps a bulldozer of the Structors, though Brann could hardly imagine the Structors coming so far into the city in any past time. The path intersected another one there and turned to parallel the ridge. On the other side they could clearly hear the sounds they had heard before, moving steadily toward them.

Brann found a place where the ridge seemed to have been climbed often before, where dirt was packed into the space between the rocks and the way was easier. He motioned to Liza that they should be quiet, and together they made their way up the ridge. At its crest it reached perhaps a third of the way to the ceiling.

The cracking noise came again very suddenly as they reached the ridge crest. Brann cried out, "Wha . . . !" involuntarily. A rock rolled from beneath his foot and he went down onto the rock.

"Are you all right, Brann?" Liza asked. She scrambled up next to him. "You're bleeding!"

"I scraped my knee; it's not bad. The noise startled me."

"I'll clean it," she said, and she began to open her water bottle, but Brann motioned her to silence. Dust was floating thickly below, and from their left the rumbling noise grew loud.

"Oh! for the Lord above!" Liza exclaimed.

Brann hissed at her, "Shush . . ." He lost sense of the hurt knee, and he and Liza both stared at a most remarkable scene.

First in view were the folk, pulling. They were like the woman briefly seen before, naked but so filthy that the dirt almost clothed them. Lines of them spread out, harnesses linked to a fan of ropes which converged behind them and disappeared into the dust. The folk, men and women, moved, pulling against their harnesses and ropes like draft animals, heaving step by slow step into their traces, while their slow mouths moved in the mumbled incomprehensible chant. Their eyes had no intelligence at all, no independence, no curiosity. They just stepped and moved, leaning, pulling their weight against the ropes. Then what they pulled came into view, and Brann knew it at once from what Grandmother Ebar had described. It rolled on wheels twice man height, iron like the spoked pulleys of an engine. Over the axle was a platform of meshed boards and metal lashed together and glued together. The two watching could not imagine *what* the glue was. As Ebar had said, it was more like a nest than the construction of something sentient.

"Is that Halsam there?" Liza asked.

"It can't be him," said Brann.

"Those are his clothes."

"It's not Hals," Brann said.

"Where is he then?"

It did seem to be Halsam standing in the nest. It was Halsam's size, a man as filthy as the rest, but seemingly awake and aware. He guided the team of folk with a long whip which he cracked over their heads. The lash licked out, touching one naked back or another. The whip elicited no reaction from any of the pulling folk who seemed not even to feel it. The Driver cried out with each crack of the whip in that yipping howl, which might in some precursor of the Driver have been distinguishable as words, but which had become over generations a stylized, empty cry. He wore Halsam's clothes, the blue and azure of them the only bright color apparent in the gallery. Fixed in the center of the Driver's chest was some sort of jewel, crimson and large as a fist.

"There's Hals," Liza said, pointing. "See, they've got him tied to one of the ropes, pulling."

"Could that be Hals?" Brann wondered. "How did he get here?"

"They must have heard us last night and seen Hals sleeping outside," Liza whispered. "That must be how they get folk to pull."

"I wonder if it's the same ones Grandmother Ebar saw," Brann said. "It was when she was just a girl, maybe seventy years ago." He told Liza what Ebar had described.

"We have to help Hals," Liza said. "We can't leave him there."

"How?"

"I don't know, but look at him, his back is all cut from the whip. They'll kill him if we don't get him out."

Like the others, the boy wore nothing but a harness and his back was bloody where the whip had touched it. From time to time Halsam looked around hopefully at the ridge line. *He's looking for us,* Brann thought. *He's waiting for us to help him.* They could see that he had been crying; the dirt on his face was streaked where tears had run and dried. He seemed beyond crying now and it was clear that such treatment for days and longer would reduce him to the state of the other folk, mindless, a draft animal. The stench from below was awful, like the woman's redoubled, and Halsam seemed to reel along in it hardly aware anymore of his condition.

To the right a portion of the ridge line had slid down, perhaps from the force of the shaking. It covered the road that the wagon would travel, and the folk pulling it came there and stood dumbly. Those behind piled onto those in front and they milled about tangling the ropes. The Driver cried out something else in that yipping voice and the wagon came to a halt. At that, all the folk simply settled to the ground where they stood.

The Driver clambered down from the wagon, and something else climbed down with him, mimicking his moves precisely. It seemed like a monkler grown large, and as the Driver walked up to the slide it paced him step for step.

"That's a little boy," Liza said, "a child Driver. Can you imagine them, father after son for generations of the city, riding on that wagon?"

"I wonder how far they've been," Brann said.

"Or where they were ever going in the first place," Liza added.

The Driver stared at the masonry and kicked it, morosely. He heaved at one immense boulder and when it wouldn't move, he kicked it savagely, barefooted, and hurt himself. He let off with a string of yipping sounds in which there were almost words buried like tangled obscenities. The miniature copied him precisely.

The scene might have been comic, except that as the Driver cursed he struck one of the nearby folk with the butt of his whip, battering her to the ground. He shouted something else, and with the whip laid about beating at the folk. Slowly some of them got back to their feet and began undoing the links to the ropes. Then one by one they formed into a ragged line. A big man at the front began lifting the rocks one at a time and passing them to the next in line, who passed it to the next, oblivious to the shouts of the Driver. The Driver and his shadow ranted, dancing up and down the line. The first rock reached the far end of the hundred-some folk and only then did the man at the front pick up the next one.

"It will take them forever to do it that way, from there," Liza said. "Don't they see what they're doing?"

Brann shook his head. "I don't think they know any other way to do it. Maybe one time there was a reason for it. But I think they've forgotten the reason and don't know anything else to do but this."

Some few of the folk had not been unlinked from the ropes, perhaps half a dozen. They all seemed younger than Halsam, who also had been left tied. They looked a bit less subhuman than the other folk. Two even appeared to be talking together, a boy and a girl, possibly in their early teens.

"Why doesn't he let them up to move rocks?" Liza wondered.

"Maybe they're new ones like Hals and he doesn't trust them yet," Brann answered.

"Pretty soon they'll be just like the others," said Liza. "I wish we could help them."

To Brann they looked far gone, already beyond help, even the two talking seemed so; he pointed out to her how dead their eyes seemed, how listless they were, how their conversation when it drifted up was a gabble, a play at remembered speech. "We can't help them, Liza," he said. "We'll do well to get Halsam out."

They watched the slow, excruciating movement of the rocks.

"They are going to be at that all day," Brann decided. "I'll bet they stay here tonight and move on again in the morning."

They watched Halsam, who sat dazedly where he had stopped. Liza watched Halsam, who from time to time, picked at his knots which held his harness to his ropes, but they seemed beyond the ability of his fingers to loosen. Brann watched Liza and as a tear began down through the dust on her cheek, he put his hand onto her neck and moved it gently, almost crying himself. He knew that Liza felt helpless. He felt the same.

Throughout the day they lay in the rocks at the ridge crest and watched the steady procession of stones moving down the

line of folk. Slowly the slide dwindled. The big and little
Drivers ranged up and down the line shouting their curses at
the uncaring folk. Now and again one would drop out and
relieve himself. At that, the whole process came to a halt and
didn't resume until the man or woman rejoined the line.
Brann and Liza only watched. They ate some of the fruit and
bread they had scavanged from the marketplat where they
had spent the previous night. They discussed in a low whisper
plans that might free Halsam and they discarded them. No
form of attack, neither stealth nor a frontal assault, would
succeed during daylight. The rocks down the ridge offered no
cover. It would have to be after dark. Even then it would be
hard.

"What if they have a fire?" Liza asked. "What if there's a
moon lamp overhead? From here they'll see us. We'll never
get down that way."

"Do you want to just leave Hals?"

"No! But I'm telling you I'm afraid of *them*."

"Probably, they're just as much afraid of us," Brann answered.

And it occurred to him that it was true. The woman that
had seen them first had been terrified of them and had run.
He began to see possibilities, and in those possibilities it
seemed there might be a way to rescue Halsam. He told Liza.

"Maybe it will work," she said.

It was sundown. The sunlights in the ceiling began fading
spectrally from their daylight yellows into soft orange-red
tones that the sky seen from the verge of Tailend seemed to
imitate. Brann sometimes wondered if it was not in fact the
other way around, if the lights did not imitate the sky and
sun. What would Hegman Branlee say to *that*? There were no
moon lamps above where they lay on the peak of the ridge,
though a hundred yards to either side the cold hazy-blue of
moon lamps shone, creating doubled shadows below on the
road. As the sunlights faded, the folk below became listless.
A chunk of stone halfway down the line came to a man who
dropped it suddenly. He moved away from the chain of folk
as if the task he had been performing had been suddenly forgotten. Others began drifting off also and the chant—different
in some vague way from that used when they pulled the

wagon—broke down into dissonance and became an abusive
gabble directed at the Driver.

"Lord above," said Liza as she shook Brann's arm urgently
to bring him back from where he had been lost among sun-
sets and the mystery of the moving sun. "They're building a
fire, Brann. They'll see us when we go down and it'll be the
end."

"I don't think so," said Brann. "All that flickering and
shadow should be good for us."

"Look, they're eating," Liza whispered. "What is it?"

The Driver had taken a bag from the wagon. It was
stained and greasy and contained what seemed to be meat.
Brann didn't want to speculate on the form of it because he'd
never seen meat in just that shape, long and lean, *and were
there fingers on it?* He couldn't look again to see until the terrible piece had been taken. The Driver cried an almost familiar phrase and flung out things from the meat sack. For the
first time the folk moved swiftly, snatching up the flesh and
fighting among themselves for it, ripping skin from bone and
gulping it unchewed. The fire had some other purpose (vesti-
gial, perhaps) having nothing to do with food. And in that
feeding frenzy, the gabble from those folk was full of fierce
growls and a harsh jabbering that brought the goose bumps
back to Brann's arms.

"Will they eat him, Brann?" Liza asked. Was she crying?
Brann wanted to but he couldn't seem to breathe and pain
came as he felt his teeth bite into his lip. The Driver flung
out more meat. The little Driver mimicked him, tossing tiny
gobbets, and it disappeared *that* fast, torn away as it fell.
"They're cannibals. That's why they wanted Halsam."

"We have to wait, Liza. We can't go down there now.
Probably they have enough for tonight so that they'll leave
Halsam alone."

It seemed so cold there on the ridge. The moon lamps occasionally lit mounds of rubble, making bright spots in the
darkness that went on, on all sides, silhouetting the hills and
casting strange elongated shadows. Only the fire gave any
color to this scene and it was an orange flickering in which
the mindless folk moved restlessly. They settled down into a
loose mass, sleeping on their haunches, curved and curled as

the monklers slept. A low chuckling jabber came ceaselessly from their camp and always there were some awake.

Halsam and the other new captives were still chained to the ropes. He huddled with his knees drawn up and his arms around them and he looked about. He seemed to be crying again. The fire had burned down so that it was an orange mound that gave little light.

"We have to do it now," Brann said.

"You start," Liza whispered.

Brann felt for the pile of stones he had gathered during the day. He found one pebble curved to fit neatly in his hand and he cocked his arm. He whistled. It was a low chirping note that imitated the birds. Vill had taught him that.

There was a gabble; one of the folk called to another.

Brann whistled again and Liza moaned with her hands cupped to her mouth. Brann tossed the stone. It went out in a high arc and landed on the shoulder of a sleeper. The woman started awake.

"Wooooooooooooooo!" Liza called. Brann whistled again.

Below, the folk stirred. Brann tossed another stone which fell into the fire sending up a brief yellow dazzle. Another of the folk woofed uneasily.

"Halsam," Liza called, "we're coming!" And Brann tossed a handful of tiny pebbles. They rained down on the folk, who turned and twisted savagely, searching for the source of torment. They began to press back into a tighter group around the fire.

"I'm starting down," said Brann. "Give me the doll."

She took the little silver object carefully from her satchel and handed it to Brann. He held it in his left hand; in his right he had the knife. "I'll call you to come down," he told her. "Keep calling and tossing stones until then."

Brann slithered down the steep bank of the ridge. From above he heard Liza give out an eerie moan that scared even him. It seemed to terrify the folk who were gathered in a tight group about the dying fire. They woofed and jabbered and appeared thoroughly confused. Each time a pebble fell among them, they would scramble away from it, bleating. Several times different ones of them stepped into the fire, and seemed not to notice it as if they didn't understand pain.

Brann edged down into the camp toward where Halsam sat.

"Hals," he called. The boy looked up. He seemed dazed, as if he didn't comprehend what was happening.

"Hals, it's me, Brann. I'll get to you in a second."

"Brann?" Halsam replied slowly.

"Yes," said Brann, "just a second." He darted out into the open space of the camp. The stench there seemed palpable and he felt things beneath his feet, damp and squashy. He was reminded of the strange thin strips of flesh and he gagged. One of the folk, a heavy woman who might have been very old except that her hair was dark and did not appear gray even in the dim light of the camp, saw Brann and began calling urgently in an ugly bawling voice. If the sounds she made were words, Brann didn't recognize them. She moved toward him, still bawling, her eyes showing some primitive sort of fear. Slobber ran from the corner of her mouth. She came on, menacingly. Behind, perhaps gathering courage from her, others of the folk began to move. Brann brandished his knife. He couldn't seem to breathe deeply enough in the foul air. His limbs felt weak and he found a noise coming from his own throat. He wanted to run. The woman ignored the knife; seemed not even to realize its significance.

"Liza," Brann cried, "now! Do it now!"

There came from the ridge the loud, unearthly cry as of someone being dismembered. The sound froze them all, even Brann who knew that it was Liza calling. A steady rain of pebbles began to come down. In this interval, Brann set down the doll nearly at the feet of the woman. Liza howled again and the doll began its dance. It was a miniature human, perfect in form. Its polished silver skin picked up the highlights from the moon lamps and from the scattered coals of the fire. It turned and it moved, drawn toward the fire's heat energy and drawn also toward the compacted animal heat of the folk. It turned toward the woman, whose attention left Brann as though he had vanished. It approached. She shifted her foot away and sucked a hissing breath. The doll touched her foot then and she fled, wailing, charging through the fire blindly. There came a collective moan of terror. They ignored Brann now and the noises from above; they ignored everything but the little silver man that stalked them lithely through the stones and scattered coals of the camp. It touched the foot of another woman not quick enough to flee, fell over and righted itself. The folk watched as if they were being stalked by a monster.

"Liza, come down!" Brann called. He turned back to where Halsam squatted among the ropes.

Hals at last seemed aware of what was happening. He begged Brann to hurry, his voice hoarse from crying. "Cut me loose, please! From here, cut me loose!"

Brann sawed at the harness, which was made of stuff tough as wire. "It's hard, Hals."

"Hurry," Halsam said. He pulled at the knots and got in Brann's way. Liza was with them now and she sawed at the harness with her own knife. The leather began to give.

There came an angry two-voiced yipping from behind them and the whistle and crack of a lash. There the Driver stood on the platform of his wagon, the little Driver in the same menacing pose between his feet. The Driver seemed all blue in that smoky haze in the camp; moonlights behind made his hair a halo. The blue of Halsam's clothes and the gray of his skin made him seem transparent, a thing of the light. On his chest the red jewel gave a light of its own.

He shouted gutturally. The lash cracked against Brann's cheek, burning. The Driver turned and began sending the long whip out into the crowd of folk, but they paid no attention though he cursed at them and danced in a horrible rage on top of the wagon. The miniature danced and cursed, also, dodging the Driver's feet and shaking his small fist. But the folk were still transfixed by the terror of the unknown little dancer. They shied away from the whip or ignored it altogether. The Driver turned his attention back to Brann, Halsam and Liza, his anger heightened with frustration. The whip cracked among them and Brann felt it cut him this time, biting into the skin on the back of his left hand. A sudden turn of the whip took Liza about the legs, pulling her off her feet. Brann caught a turn of the leather whip. He held it against the Driver's pull and heard Liza shriek, grasping at the smooth gallery floor. The strength of the Driver dragged her even with Brann pulling back.

"Let her go!" Brann yelled.

"Nnnnnnggggmmm!" the Driver shouted back. He heaved on the lash and it tore free of Brann's hands, spinning Liza like a top. Brann lost his knife. He saw it tumble among the rocks at the base of the wagon. The lash came down repeatedly, slashing at Liza's legs. She shrieked again, scrambling away from it.

Brann found a rock that filled his fist and he ran, bellowing, toward the wagon. He found that he felt nothing, not the pain of the lash cuts, not fear, not even anger. He felt hate and he leaped clear of the slippery ground, finding purchase on the ragged lip of the wagon. He shouted "No!" in a wild scream that surprised him and he felt his heart beating hard and his breath wailing out the sound. Somehow the rock was in his fist and somehow he swung it toward the driver, who cried "Nnnnnnggggggmmmmm," as if it were the remnant of some long-remembered powerful curse, and who stopped crying all at once. He fell, voiceless and still, onto the wagon.

Brann stood. He looked at his hand. He felt the throb of blood in his fingers where they had been crushed between rock and the skull of the Driver. The rock slipped away and he dropped his arm. Brann found himself wondering what had happened, as if it had all occurred in a fugue. The Driver was between his feet still breathing but unconscious and limp. Brann moved his fingers and decided that they were unbroken. He saw that Liza was standing next to Halsam, cutting him free of the last harness straps. Halsam was saying "thank you" over and over and embracing Liza, and Liza was crying and Brann saw bloody welts on her legs.

"Is he free?" Brann asked. "We have to go before something happens."

Halsam stepped away. "I want my clothes back," he said.

Brann looked down at the Driver. "They smell," he told Halsam.

"I don't care. I want them back."

Brann helped Halsam up onto the wagon and together they stripped Halsam's clothes from the unconscious Driver. Seeming not to notice the stench, Halsam put them on.

"They were going to eat me, I think," he told Brann. "It was people they were eating; they had parts of them in the bag."

"I want to get out of here," Liza said.

Brann nodded. "Me, too."

Brann went to retrieve the doll. By this time it had begun to wind down in the darkness. But the folk were not hostile now. They backed away from Brann and watched, as a band of monklers might, when he picked up the doll and touched a contact to shut it off. Liza had brought their satchels. They moved toward a path Frontward through the mounds of rubble and were soon lost to sight.

Beneath the wagon a shape whimpered and moved. It was the little Driver. He climbed back into the haphazard nest and crouched over the form of the Driver. A small hand came down and grubby fingers moved the Driver's head from side to side. The whimper grew and the creature's savage little eyes narrowed. Then the whimper became a raucous yipping, and the little Driver climbed to the Driver's chest. There he wailed his terror and despair. Beneath, unnoticed, the Driver's hand twitched and began to move.

"Do you think you killed him, Brann?" Halsam asked.

"He was breathing, Hals. You saw."

"Yeah, I saw. I wish you'd killed him. I would have."

Beyond the camp the path became tortuous. Rubble, past all relationship to dwellings, was mounded into crazy mis-shapen hills. The paths through it were a labyrinth. The odor of the dust was stale, as of stagnation since long before the shaking. They navigated by the familiar alignment of the moon lamps, spaced wider north and south. Once they came to the stub of a staircase which rose out of the rubble half-way to the gallery ceiling. And in that ceiling, plugging the stairwell, was a conglomerate of concrete and stone. But here, too, Brann marveled at the persistence of the Driver and his folk. A mass of old metal beams climbed on, in a rat-pack snarl, up to the plug. And here the softer stone was half eroded as if by the steady, timeless labor of the folk. Perhaps in time, Brann thought, they would get through.

"What's that jewel the Driver was wearing?" Liza asked. She reached out to Halsam's chest and stroked the jewel lightly. "It's warm," she said, "as if something were heating it from inside."

Halsam felt it himself, his fingers atop Liza's. "I know. I can feel it on my skin."

"Take it off," Brann said. "Throw it away."

"Why?" Halsam demanded. "You think it's dangerous?"

"I couldn't know," said Brann. "I'm not sure it's a good idea to keep it."

"I'll keep it," Halsam said.

"Why do you think the Driver wore it?" Brann asked. "Possibly it gave him some sort of strength. He was strong."

"Maybe," said Liza, "it made them all stupid as they were."

"No," said Halsam, "I think it was special and important, something that made the Driver not like the others. I'm going to keep it. It's fixed somehow on my shirt anyway."

Liza wrinkled her nose. "And you better wash that shirt soon, too," she said.

They walked on through the landscape of rubble mounds, made dark and menacing somehow by the moon lamps. It was very quiet and Brann listened for the chanting to resume. So far he had heard nothing. Had he truly killed the Driver?

"Can't we stop now?" Liza asked. "My legs hurt from where the Driver's whip cut me. We didn't either of us sleep, Hals, while we were waiting to rescue you."

"I don't want to stop here," Halsam said. "I want to get out of this gallery entirely."

"Maybe there is no way out," Liza said. "Maybe all the doors and things are blocked up to keep those people in."

"We'll get out," Halsam said.

Brann stopped walking and turned to look backward over the path they were taking. "Do you hear that?" he asked.

"It's something," said Liza.

"It's them," Halsam said. "They're coming."

Liza's eyes searched the rubble around them. "We can hide."

"No we can't," Brann answered. "We can't hide from them. They can smell us out. There are so many of them."

"It is," Liza whispered. "It's coming closer, like screaming. Like they're so mad at us."

Brann picked out a path that seemed to lead Frontward. He pushed at Halsam and Liza. "We can't let them catch us. We can't!"

Then they were running. The path led through the rubble, twisting, joining others. Side paths led off into darkened gullies among the piled stone. They came to a forking. Neither of the divergent paths seemed to lead Frontward.

"Which way?" Halsam asked.

Brann leaned over, hands on his knees; his breath came harshly.

"They're closer, Brann," Liza said. "Which way do you think?"

Brann couldn't think. The cry of the folk was full now and clear, full of menace. It drew nearer even as they stood. The moon lamps were wide-spaced here and both paths led off into unlit night. One was wider, seemed more traveled. "This one," Brann said, pointing.

"But that path looks like it circles back, maybe toward the north flank," Liza objected.

"Lord above," said Brann, "then *that* one."

The sounds of pursuit grew behind them and without even time to catch their breath they ran again. The path they had chosen turned gradually Frontward. It was straight and easy. Brann thought perhaps the cry of the folk was diminishing. Had they given up?

Halsam, who was a few paces in front, called back breathlessly, "It's getting narrower, I think. The walls are coming together."

They were in a sort of canyon between near vertical walls of stone, as if somehow the rubble near the verge of this gallery had been compacted into a stone barrier. This was the only path now, the only breach. They were not really running anymore, stumbling instead on the uneven floor. Brann could hardly hear the cry of the folk behind; the sound of his own blood moving, the sounds of his breath, drowned it. A single moon lamp was lit in the ceiling, which was dark otherwise, so that only a faint light from far behind and to the flanks came.

"I see the verge," Halsam called. "It's not far now." Somehow he still had the strength to sprint and he moved out ahead of the others around a curve of the wall. Brann lost sight of him in the darkness. Then Liza fell. Her legs, sore from the beating she had taken, gave out and she tripped over loose rock. Brann ran full into her from behind. Their legs tangled and they went down together. The baying of their pursuers became terrific. Liza was spent. Brann got back to his knees and pulled at her, saying, "Get up, they're close. We have to get up," and Liza just clung to him and shook her head.

The baying stopped.

A stench rolled over them as of things dead a thousand years. Brann pulled away from Liza and turned. There stood the Driver. His face was a rictus, past speech. The Driver's tongue worked in his mouth. Blood, a black line in the moon lamp's small light, ran down from his left temple. His left eye was swollen and half closed. There was a brightness in his right hand. He extended the arm and Brann saw that the brightness was a knife—Brann's had dropped during the struggle in the camp.

The Driver's mouth worked and out of it came a single, half-coherent "Nnnnnnnggggggg!" Liza hitched backward, dragging herself through the dust. Brann slid backward also, his eyes never leaving the sharp edge of that knife. In the blue darkness behind the Driver, Brann saw eyes, the only evidence that the Driver's folk waited beyond. The little Driver paced at his teacher's feet.

Slowly, in hideous ballet, Brann and Liza crabbed backward around the bend in the wall. And just as implacably the Driver followed them, his knife-point weaving before Brann's face. Space opened in the pathway behind them and Brann heard Liza say, "Halsam! Where . . . ?"

"It's sealed," Halsam said. "The gate is shut."

Brann heard motion behind, Liza standing. He couldn't take his eyes off the blade that moved inches from his face. He stared at the Driver. And a change came over the Driver's face. His eyes widened. The motion of the knife stopped. He seemed to stop breathing and tendons stood out in his neck. The mouth worked, beyond any noise now, and the knife dropped, forgotten, at Brann's feet.

The Driver was looking past Brann now as if Brann had vanished. Brann craned his head around to see Halsam standing, half turned, next to the walled-over gateway to the gallery. On Halsam's chest the jewel burned with a bright scarlet light that grew steadily more intense.

Firmly, the Driver's eyes were fixed on the burning jewel, and in his throat a terrible, piteous moaning began.

Chapter Five

The Stairs

It was the jewel the Driver wanted as if it were his soul. Somehow in the generations that the jewel and the Driver were one, the jewel had lost the separate identities of function and device. It had lost even the clear delineation between Driver and ornament. In this generation, Driver and jewel were inseparable. Yet now they had separated and Brann saw the consequence of it in the faces of the dumb folk. They came into the glow cast by the jewel. Women and men of the folk pressed into the space at the end of the pathway until they were a solid mass. The air seemed a tangible thing, their stink a physical force that battered Brann until he felt disoriented.

The jewel's light was great now. In it the Driver's skin shone with the slickness of sweat and he shook as if spastic. His naked skin twitched. His eyes rolled. His voice rose to a warble and his arm, as if controlled by a poor puppeteer, jerked out over Brann's head to reach for the jewel on Halsam's chest. Brann found his knife.

"Stick him, Brann," Liza said.

"Stick him," Halsam echoed.

Brann brought up the knife. He was dizzy in the hot air and he found he couldn't focus on the gyrating body of the Driver. The little Driver mimicked his father's moves. His tongue lolled carefully. He mewed and spat and pawed at dirt, trying to share some of his father's rage over the loss of the jewel, matching the larger creature's frenzy. The Driver stepped on the little Driver's foot. The little Driver howled, turned and stepped on the foot of one of the dumb folk. And the dumb folk began stepping on each other's feet, woofing, snorting, thoroughly distracted.

"Stick him now, Brann!" Halsam said.

Brann tried to answer. Halsam moved and the Driver's voice caught as though he were choking. Halsam reached down for Brann's arm, pulling it to get at the knife. In that movement something shifted inside the jewel and a crystalline ringing began inside it. The Driver screamed and leapt simultaneously. Brann felt the rough horn of the Driver's feet trample him. He saw Halsam and the Driver grapple. He felt Liza pulling at him, and perhaps she said, "Help him, Brann," and the light was doused as Halsam and the Driver came together.

"You!" Halsam was screaming. "You!" And Brann, finding his feet, stood in the darkness.

"He's killing Halsam," Liza said. The dumb folk noticed the fight and left off their foot-stepping game. They pressed and shifted closer so that no open space remained. Hands touched Brann. Liza flailed at the hands which felt her. In the red light issuing from between them, Halsam and the Driver were shown locked together, grappling. In that light Brann saw the Driver's strength, and he wondered at Halsam's and how his friend could hold his own in the struggle. Brann reached out to help and felt hands of the dumb folk come between so that he could only watch. The Driver's strength was telling. His fingers found new purchases, working closer to Halsam's throat. The little Driver strangled Liza's knee. She kicked him. Brann flailed with his knife. He felt it bite into flesh and he knew he was hurting some of the folk but they made no cry of pain. Steadily he was pulled farther from Halsam's fight. Liza was next to him.

"The Driver's killing him," she said.

"I know," Brann answered, and he shoved helplessly against the mass of flesh and groping hands.

Then a different note came from the jewel, a sudden high trilling as if a bird were captive inside. A distant muffled rumble came, the grinding of ancient machinery. Brann felt the vibration through the concrete of the floor. The grinding grew. The hands of the folk stopped and woofs of uncertainty sounded. Brann saw Halsam and the Driver pressed hard against the stone of the passage's end, pinned there by the pressure of the folk. The driver's hands had found Halsam's throat. Halsam pulled at them. The grinding went on and the mass of the stone wall began to break with a cracking report.

Liza pointed at it and cried, "There's a light; the wall is coming open."

Through the new-riven opening in the stone mass a swath of yellow light spilled out. With the shriek of an engine long unoiled, a metal door pulled away from the imprisoning masonry and slid sideways. Beyond was the lighted landing of a stairwell, and into that opening the pressure carried Brann and Liza and the front rank of the folk. Broken masonry collapsed in dust. In it Halsam was buried, and the Driver, too, senseless from the blow of a falling brick.

Lights sprang on above and the folk shrank from them, pulling back into the blue darkness of the passageway. Brann found they were on an open metal grating that served as one landing in a spiral staircase that went up as far as he could see. Cold air blew down, and the irregular brick walls dripped.

"Get Halsam," Liza said to Brann. "Help me."

The folk still watched, keeping well back from the landing. Brann moved over next to Lisa and together they pulled Halsam out of the loose dirt and rubble that had fallen from the opened door. Once again Brann thought that he might kill the Driver, and looked about for his knife.

"You have to kill him this time," Halsam said, and he kicked at the Driver who lay unconscious in the dirt.

"My knife is lost," Brann said. Remarkably he was relieved that the knife was missing. He remembered the dead giant in the Post House and tried to imagine himself stabbing the Driver that way. There had been a time a few moments ago when it would have been possible. Not now.

The chimney of the stairway dropped away into extreme darkness. The walls of it were like the irregular brick interior of an oven. Brann had never seen a chimney or any such thing for comparison.

"I'll kill him," Halsam blurted. He cast about for a stone large enough to bash the Driver. The Driver was coming to.

The glow of the jewel had entirely faded. The magic of the scene was gone.

"We have to go up," Liza said. She pointed along the helix of the stairway. Its open risers were rusty and it wound up through a stairwell that seemed bored into the substance of the city. "We have to go up, don't we, Brann? That was the message on the wall of the Post House."

The masonry was rotten; it broke in Halsam's hands. Tears of fury ran down his cheeks as he beat with the stone at the Driver. Brann took Halsam by the arm.

"Hals," he said, "if you don't come away soon, they'll all be after us again. You can't kill him; there's no way and no time."

"I hate him," Halsam said. "You saw what he was going to do to me."

"Leave him, Hals," Liza told him.

Together she and Brann pulled Halsam away and they began to climb the clockwise spiral of the stairs.

"Where did all this come from?" Liza wondered. "I never heard of any secret stairways in the city."

"You never heard of giants before," said Halsam, "or of ugly stupid folk, either, that stink so awful." He squinted into the light that came from lamps set into the walls of the stairwell, looking down several turns toward where they had left the Driver and his folk. "Did you see the little one, making believe he was his papa, throwing stones at me and squeaking? Maybe if the Driver really is dead, the little one will just keep following. I bet the runty little thing would just keep coming."

"I wonder how far up this goes," Liza said.

"I can't know," Brann answered, "except that the air is cold like from the closed elevator shafts coming from way up on the city roof."

"That's far," Liza said. "I hope there's a way out before then."

Brann looked into the tightening spiral of stairs that twisted away above as far as they could see. Stone much harder than that which had broken below plugged what was probably an opening into the next tier. They stopped to probe at it and Halsam touched and worried the jewel, but whatever had worked to open the door below didn't function here. They climbed on.

"I bet the bastard Driver keeps following us," Halsam said. "I bet he keeps following us forever. He wants this back." He pressed his hand over the jewel which was dark and sparkled only in the irregular lamps of the stairwell.

"We have to get high up away from him," Liza answered, "clear away from all of them."

Halsam shook his head. "No, one time soon we're going to have to take him on. He'll keep trying until we do."

They looked back down the stairs again. Perhaps something clanked down there, and they speeded their pace.

Who had made the stairway? Brann couldn't shake the wonder of that. He had no doubt that it went on down to the Foundations, into the darkness below where they climbed. The brick of the walls was yellow and slick. In places where the brick had peeled away, Brann could see the gouge marks of some machine (of the Structors? he wondered) in the concrete of the city. The well went up like a corkscrew so that he could see no more than a few turns upward. If Liza was right, then there was no way out before the roof. They passed the plug filling the entrance to yet another tier. The shadows from the openwork risers cut the space into a network that shifted on their skins like a floating spider's web. The risers themselves were of iron, treated somehow so that there was little rust. Dirt encrusted them, mixed from dust and condensation.

The three moved up the leftward spiral, Halsam first, then Liza and Brann. They had climbed perhaps three tiers and Brann's legs pained him already. "The steps are so high," he said. "It hurts to keep stepping up them."

"Yeah," Liza agreed. "It's as if they were made for bigger people."

"They were made for the giants," Halsam said.

"Do you suppose giants like the one we saw made them?" Liza asked.

Halsam shrugged. "Who would want a secret stairway?"

"Huten would," Brann said.

"A story for babies," Halsam scoffed.

"Well," said Liza, "Huten is supposed to have tunnels like these."

There is a tale of Huten and his keys. It is told to frighten truculent children.

"Do you hear the keys ringing in the tier, jangling in the night? Huten comes for a child. Huten has his own ways about the city, paths he only walks, passages he knows. He has hair down over his face on his chin and cheeks, and teeth so big they are like yellow blocks of stone."

Children would vanish. It happened to Larsa, a schoolmate of Brann's. She, brown hair, brown eyes, a pudgy ten-year-old, vanished. She had walked past the derelict plats of the inner wall north of the marketplat.

Elders whispered, "Huten!"

A troop of Gads was arrested by the officers, interrogated. The Romking grinned, gaptoothed, yellow, as was said of Huten.

"N'I," he said in his funny Frontward speech, "n'any Gad would steal a child o'folk. How d'you take us? T'be thieves. N'I!"

An old Gad woman, face as dark as a monkler's, eyes like one, too, small and never still, had whispered to him in Tzingaro.

"Tsa!" he whispered back.

She made motions about her face, pointed to the Romking's mustache, which was only black hair cut from his head and fixed on his lip, waxed and drooping, a strange, fierce ornament.

"Potko!" he grunted. He shook his head violently.

"W'the keys took her," the Romking explained. "The goodwoman says, w'the keys come ringing, took'er."

"Stupidity," the Schoolmaster said. "Huten is an old tale. She's taken it herself to wander from here. She'll turn up or not. It was foul play or not, but not Huten."

In Brann and Halsam's hiding hole above the conduits, they had listened for the keening in the pipe and fancied footsteps going away.

"Is Huten real?" Brann asked Ebar.

"Perhaps," she said. "We have evidences. A noise does

come sometimes at night, the ringing. Have you heard it?"

"You said it was air moving in the old pipes and water maybe." In Ebar's green room sunlights fought with the light outside fading; shadows moved two ways.

"Huten," she said, "not the fabled monster, do you understand, boy? Not some inhuman thing. But you know there are things we have lost. We have lost this. There are ways through the city we do not know and folk who use them and these folk are hairy of face and chin and they are tall. I've heard some of the Post Folk speak so. Other tales, too." She would say no more.

"Post Folk speak to you?" Ten-year-old Brann was awed. Ebar talked with Post Folk!

"Much is missing," Ebar said. "Perhaps this was once known."

"But Hutens?" protested Brann. "Do you mean there are lots of them?"

"Where is Larsa, your friend?"

In later years Brann would say *Huten* to Grandmother Ebar.

"Trash and fool stuff," she would say. But dim bells sometimes rang at night and perhaps there were footsteps through solid walls.

It was Halsam who heard it first. Far below was a humming sound like voices blended into the motion of feet. He rose on his elbow and looked over the sleeping forms of Brann and Liza. The light in the stairwell was exactly the same as before. It was entirely independent of the sunlamps on the tiers. He sat up, feeling the ache in his muscles from his exertion and from the continual damp.

He shook Liza. "Do you feel it?" he asked. "I think the Driver is coming again."

She squirmed out of the blankets. "No, do you mean it? They couldn't be coming."

Brann woke. "I hear something, too," he said. He massaged his legs.

"They're coming," Halsam said. "I knew they would."

The three scrambled to pack their belongings.

"How far are they?" Brann asked. "What do you think?"

"Maybe they're just starting," Halsam answered.

"No," said Brann, "they could be close. The air is blowing down from above and it might be carrying the sound away."

"Won't this stop?" Liza asked. "Will they just keep following us? We've climbed seven tiers. Will they just keep following us until we get to the city roof?"

"I can hear them singing now," Halsam said. "Let's go."

"I'm hungry," Liza protested. "We have no water left." She probed at the mortar which plugged the gateway. "We surely can get out here."

The plug was scored with the marks of others who had tried. Brann pointed to this. "We don't have time for it, Liza. Come along."

He handed her her satchel and they turned to the stairs again. The steps passed beneath them, each one pulling at hamstrings and calves over the wide risers. Breath came harder until the words of encouragement they called to each other dissolved into a steady panting without voice. They passed two more landings and finally stopped, exhausted, at the third. Here even the signs of a doorway into the tier were obliterated and the stairwell rose smoothly.

Vibration came through the metal of the steps and they resumed their upward flight.

It was on the morning of what Halsam reckoned to be the eighth day, at possibly the 72nd tier, that they came to the end. Halsam came upon it first and he cried out, "Hey."

Brann and Liza came up to that landing. Here the stairway stopped.

"What happened?" Brann asked.

"It's all tumbled down," Liza whispered.

Halsam pried at the wreckage and shook his head.

Somehow, long ago, the stairway here had broken free of its wall bolts and fallen back into a tangle on the landing. It had happened so long before that the broken ends of metal were as rusted as the rest. Water ran freely on the walls.

"Maybe some main burst here," Liza speculated, "and rusted it all away."

A crude brick dam at the landing kept the water from falling farther. The stream entered a hole in the masonry plug and disappeared. Forgetting their danger for the moment in the presence of so much water, the three squatted on the landing amid the iron and drank from the trough.

"I was so thirsty," Liza said. She gulped the water and splashed it over her face and arms. Dust ran there in muddy streaks.

Brann filled bottles from their satchels.

"How are we going to get up?" Halsam asked. He began to climb carefully through the tangle. "Someone made a way here. It's been pushed back."

"The metal is sharp and rusty," Liza called. "Don't get cut."

Halsam answered derisively, "Come on. The Driver would really cut us to pieces."

Below, the chanting of the dumb folk came steadily closer, climbing the open stairs faster than they could proceed through the wreckage. Halsam watched them as they emerged. Everything here stopped. The stairwell from here on was a chimney. In places, bolts still stuck out from the bricks where the stairs had been anchored. Water ran on the brick and metal. The damp air smelled of corrosion and rust.

Halsam pointed up. "Do you see it?" he asked.

Brann and Liza looked upward also.

"I see ropes," Hals said. "Pieces of them fell. Maybe they rotted in the damp down here."

The rope ends hung free, ending three times Halsam's height above the spot where he stood on the highest protrusion of broken stair. Dust streaked his hair and rust smeared blotches of orange on his face and arms. He did not look all that different from the Driver now in his dirty Gad's cloth shirt and shorts. A meanness had come over Hals since his encounter with the Driver, as if he were angry at himself for what the Driver had done to him. Hals was Brann's best friend and now he scared Brann a bit, with the intensity of his anger especially.

"We can get up, I think," Hals said, and he stepped straight across the broken stairs though metal teetered under him and threatened to collapse the whole unstable pile. Halsam set one foot to the stub of a bolt and began to climb.

The fact of the chase had told on Brann. He stood with his arm around Liza's waist, watching Halsam move from one to another of the projections. Hals was silent, determined; only his breathing gave any sign of the strain. Partly it was that the chase seemed interminable to Brann; no matter their own pace or endurance, the dumb folk just came on. Were this not the finish of it, if they moved past this spot, wouldn't the Driver continue behind them? Partly also it seemd to Brann that momentarily he would step out of this dream unscathed as the heroes always did in the comic pictures which the Gads showed in one special tent. Those heroes were manifestations of the light from lamp to luminous screen and vanished in the brighter outside light of the tier. Still, Brann sometimes waited for this to vanish in a brighter light which would be Mama Adelbran awakening him. He watched Halsam perch on the uppermost of the bolts, one long enough for the boy to get both bare feet onto.

"Hals!" Liza warned, as he edged upward along rough brick, pressing upright and then extending his reach until he caught the end of one of the ropes.

"I've got it!" he said to them. Brann didn't even ask if the rope was too rotten to hold. It would, or not, and everything came to that single truth. Halsam edged farther, leaning out, his hands taking more rope. On his toes now, he groped upward until he reached a knot. Frayed shreds of it came free and drifted downward on the cold air. Halsam went hand over hand until his legs wrapped the rope and his feet found the knot. His shadow swung over the broken stairs; one single high lamp cast this shadow and a few more still higher threw bits of the ropes into light so that they seemed like so many dotted lines hanging.

"I have a longer one here," Hals called. "It's against the other side of the stairwell. I'll swing it over and you can get up easier."

"You next," Brann said to Liza. He boosted her onto the first bolt. Brann feared for her. It was not that she was less tough than the others. She had proved she was tough enough long before this—nor was their society one in which any such differences between men and women had meaning, so that Brann would not have even harbored such a thought. But she was smaller than the others, half a head shorter than Brann, a couple of inches less even than Halsam. So Brann boosted her up with the rising chant of the dumb folk as a goad and held his breath while she reached for the next bolt end just fingers' reach away. Liza stretched out along the rough brick, her hands slightly below the free end of the rope which Halsam dangled toward her. She looked down at the sharp rusted edges of the fallen stairs. The rope dangled and Brann cried, "They're right under us now."

Halsam did a wonderful thing. He twisted his legs about the rope he hung on and turned himself upside down so that his arms reached to where Liza stretched toward him. Halsam's face was purple with the effort. He caught Liza's hands and with a cry she swung free from the bolt end and they both dangled, moving over Brann and the broken stairs. Liza clambered up over Hals's body and onto the rope. Hals righted himself. "Come up," he told Brann.

A head appeared in an opening of the stairs. The dead eyes were not the Driver's. Brann kicked at the man's face and a woof came from the slack mouth. So fast, the man's hand lashed out and caught Brann by the ankle.

"Climb!" Brann told the others. He pulled a scrap of railing from the junk and pounded at the arm which held him.

Halsam made a move to come back down, and Brann shouted back in a fury that they could not help, that they had to go on now. The hand hurt his ankle and Brann felt terribly stupid that no heroic action came to him. He only beat at the arm stupidly and listened to others of the dumb folk making excited noises beneath. Perhaps the broken stairs would erupt with dumb folk. He beat at the arm, and the man's grip relaxed. For the first time, one of them reacted to pain, crying out in a high bewildered voice and pulling back his injured arm. Brann kicked free, and the man slid back into the stairs, blocking pursuit for a time.

Brann caught at a bolt and went up the wall, bits of brick falling away beneath. The jungle of metal stairs shook as if some engine of strength gripped it and the notes of the dumb folk's chant built toward a frenzy. Brann stretched far toward the rope and caught it. He motioned for Hals and Liza, who had been transfixed, watching the struggle below.

"Get out of my way; climb now," he said.

They went up, pulling themselves from knot to knot. Liza and Hals climbed together steadily with Brann's weight to hold the rope down. But under them the rope whipped about so that Brann was nearly thrown free. Time after time his hands came to the same knot on which Hals's feet rested, and once he even thought to swing over to another rope but it was rotten and the weight of Brann's arm on it tore it free to go snaking down into the open stairwell. The rope stretched upward, perhaps two full tiers. The skein of shadows thickened so that the stairwell was darkened and indistinct.

The loose rope below Brann came taut. He knew someone had taken hold. "The dumb folk are on the rope," he told the others. "They're climbing up after us."

"Lord above," Hals replied.

They moved up along the knots through the darkening shadow of the stairwell. The dumb folk climbed up several ropes now. At last Liza announced, "I'm at a landing." And she pulled herself over the edge where the jagged ends of risers told of fallen stairs. The lights were dim yellow and the shadows deep. Somehow Brann imagined shapes above, globular and still in the stairwell. He pulled onto the landing and lay while his raw hands burned and the blood pounded in his head.

"Cut the ropes," Liza said. She pulled off her satchel and felt for a knife.

"That's the only knife we have," Hals said. "Don't drop it. I want to use it on the Driver."

She reached over and sawed at the ropes' tough fibers. Six rope ends were tied there but now only two were intact. A third had broken free carrying dumb folk down. Liza showed them that the rope they had climbed was cut half through by wear. It hung very straight under the weight of a number of dumb folk. They had breath to chant as they climbed. Their voices continued smoothly. Brann wondered how they could breathe. He could see them down there, gray shapes like slugs moving up the ropes, and it didn't matter to him as Liza slashed the rope end free. It hissed downward carrying perhaps ten of them. She moved to the other rope.

"This one is tough," she said.

"They're very close now," Brann told her. He began to hunt along with Hals for something to throw down at the dumb folk, but the landing was clear.

"I'm getting it," Liza said.

But then a face came into view, a woman this time, but

not different otherwise from the man he had beaten below. The woman's arm came onto the edge of the landing. Her other hand reached, fingers feeling for purchase. Liza cut through this rope, too, and it dropped under her. Like the first rope, it fell with a hissing noise into the throat of the stairwell. Brann heard faint cries and the rattle of broken metal. The woman reached for the stairs, her face contorted. Brann saw sweat on her breasts and her paunchy stomach. Then her fingers began to slip. Her mouth opened, pink tongue pressed forward through rotten teeth. Her grip came loose. She was still staring as she fell. In all this she didn't make a sound.

Once more they climbed, this time in light so dim that shadow and form were melded. Something obscured their vision overhead and rattled softly (not metal, something else) in the motion of the air. The lights grew rarer and this seemed the last light entirely in the climb toward the city roof. A brightness began at Halsam's breast, a slow, steady accession of red. The jewel glowed again, and again it held a minute singing of power.

"It's warmer," Halsam announced. They were surrounded by shadow and bobbing, rattling shapes.

A trap snapped shut.

Halsam was ripped from the steps, caught in a tight-meshed net. He shrieked. Brann and Liza looked up and had no time to make noise themselves before a web, with the sudden hiss of torn air, snared them and they hung together in a tight-wrapped bundle that bumped against Halsam's and swung away in some wider open space.

"A trap," Hals said. "Someone set it to guard the stairs."

"Get your knife, Liza, and cut us out."

The jewel became brighter and the space about them was lit with its singular red light. Shadows melted in it.

Liza slashed at the netting but it was made of something metallic against which the blade slipped and became dull.

"It won't cut," she said.

"Lord above," Brann said.

The dark melted still further and in the red light they saw other swinging nets now and in them, skeletons. It was those which rattled. Now the brilliance of the jewel revealed a myriad of these snares, each with its own packet of bones, some crumbled and some newer so that dried remnants of flesh still clung. All swung softly and rattled in the cold falling air.

"Lord above," Liza echoed.

In the well below they could hear the noise of metal on metal pounding and the mixed noise and chant of the dumb folk working. They came as if deathless.

BOOK TWO

Chapter One

Huten

They heard a bell in the stairwell. It sounded distant as though it came through many inches of masonry. In the jewel there was an echo of it, and above them the net that contained Halsam started to rise. The scarlet light moved far above them so that it was only a feeble gleam in the wide space around the stairs. There came a grinding of broken stone like the noise which had opened the passage far below. They heard a guttural voice, deep bass. Halsam answered something indistinct, and all at once the net that contained Brann and Liza also began to rise. It bumped aside other nets in which only human bones hung. In one a skull bounced alongside them, chinless, long hair streaming over empty eye sockets. They stopped next to the net which had held Halsam.

Abruptly a face was staring at them through a place where the stairwell plug had newly opened.

"Huten!" Liza shrieked.

It was a giant's face, heavily ridged. His brows were thick and eyes dark. His nose was flat and slightly bent as if once broken and ill-repaired. But the hair!

"Look!" said Brann. "He had hair on his face all over, like the giant in the Post House."

"Like Huten would," Liza said. "Does he have a mouth?"

He did. He spoke a slow, deep-voiced sentence in which gutturals rasped. He poked out a finger at them as they swung in the net. He laughed. The hand was massive, hairy

113

on the back also. When he laughed the teeth were exposed, and as Huten's had been said to be, yellow and like stone blocks.

"Blig fie Ig endech!" The finger poked again.

Brann batted at it with the side of his hand. The man laughed.

"Huten," Liza repeated.

"Ech? Hugen?" He placed that hand on his chest, nodded terrifically. *"Hugen, hugen!"* he repeated.

"Lord," said Liza, "it's true."

"Couldn't be worse than that," Brann said. He pointed down to where the distant noise of metal told of the Driver still coming.

They saw that the man was a giant, of a size of the dead giant they had seen in the Post House. He wore a kilt of heavy weave, banded in blue and black. He wore a leather vest. His arms and legs were powerful, and the hair on them was thick, very black and dense as the hair on his bare chest. The language of the Tailend folk had no word for beard. Brann and Liza thought of it as hair, like an extension of what grew so thickly on his head, though coarser and intertwined. He wore sandals and his belt held a heavy sword with a hilt that looked to be bone. On the belt were other implements, some as strange and complex as those in the Post House.

One of these implements he took from his belt and reached out to a ring at the top of the net. He fitted it there and the net sprang open into single strands, dumping them onto the landing. For an instant, Brann thought to run, and he assayed their chances up the dark stairwell.

"Nag dunen," the giant said, and one of his massive hands came to the back of each neck. They found themselves pulled firmly out of the stairwell and into a low-ceilinged passage. Rubble from the plug had spilled out onto the floor of it. A woman of the giants sat there, dressed as the man was. Halsam sat there, too, caught between her knees. He squirmed but her strength was sufficient to hold him and she grinned at his efforts.

Her face was hairless. The two giants conferred, their voices big and resounding in the passage. The man pointed to the left where a series of doors stood open. Each led into a different branch passage.

"*Undle feg?*" he asked at last.

"*Chet,*" the woman answered. With that, the man began walking in the direction he had pointed, shepherding Brann and Liza along. The woman pulled Halsam to his feet and went after.

"They're so big," Liza said to Brann, "you don't even come up to his shoulders."

"They're so tall they have to bend for the doors," Hals said. "They can't even really straighten up anytime."

"Where do you suppose we are?" Brann asked.

"I think we're in the space between the tiers," Liza answered. "Who would believe there were people living here?"

They walked through hallways that turned into other halls. The ceilings became higher, arched a bit. Doors were along the passage, some closed with darkened glass panels in them. Some stood open showing empty cubicles with identical desks and chairs. Nothing else was in them but dust, lying untouched on every surface.

They wove and turned through the interconnections of the passages until Brann felt thoroughly turned around.

"I'm lost," he said. "Hallways go everywhere. I have no idea how far we've come."

He was lost. It was a remarkable sensation. The side roads and highroads of Tailend were generations known and were marked everywhere with this sign or that sign of all the ancestral folk so that the Adelbran name might be seen at a turning of a path or on a store front, so that the paths in parkplat and alleyway were all familiar, and from flank to flank of tier 37 Tailend there was not one place in which one might be lost. The fact that here they could turn a corner and not know what was around it, and worse, in the twistings of the path that they did not even know precisely from where they had come was something that made Brann feel like a child. Among the giants he felt so, and he saw that Liza and Hals felt that also, starting and grinning tensely.

Noise increased around them. Now there were lights in some of the cubicles. Other giants were in the halls, heavily built men and women in the same attire.

"Do you see," Liza pointed, "they're all strong and hard. None of them is fat or soft looking."

Like Liza, Brann knew nothing of soldiers; to him, they were like the officers of the Isocourt. "They all have those swords," he said.

They stood aside in the passage for a party of giants which exited from an elevator car. They were a grim bunch, their dress stained. Blood showed here and there. Some wounds were bandaged. But they could laugh, and they called good-natured greetings to the two who had charge of Brann, Liza and Halsam. One woman, blood in her hair and a bandage over her forehead, pointed at Brann and made a gesture which was pointedly obscene. *"Shmund!"* she said. And Brann seemed to know exactly what the strange word meant from the way she held her hands and moved them, and he blushed. Their captors laughed with the rest. The woman who held Halsam reached out to pinch Brann's cheek.

What it was, was that the giants hardly seemed monsters; Huten who came as the legends said to steal children in the night. Yes, they were large and very strong. Yes, they carried swords and other weapons. Yes, they obviously fought some enemy capable of holding its own with the giants in battle. But they were not grim monsters.

Liza saw this also. "They are more like us that the Driver's folk, for all they seem another race," she said.

But they *were* the Huten of old legend. What they would do now was an open—and frightening—question to the three.

He was the largest man they had ever seen. Not any of the giants, not their captors nor the warriors they had met in the passages, were like him. He was immense, built as if carved from a chunk of the city's stone. The beard down his chest was red, not the delicious auburn of Liza's hair, but a bright carrot red and thick like snarled vines in the wildest of park-plats. "Oten," they called him, perhaps his name, perhaps a title. He had some special place among the giants.

"Wag kommiga vah?" he asked them.

"Oten wishes to know you have entered here from where?"

"Tailend," said Brann. He tried another mouthful. It faintly resembled Tailend beer but with a bitterness and stench of some foreign herb.

"Haartsood kommad," the dwarf said back to Oten.

"Hartsood! Ha ha ha!" He drained the stone bowl of his own drink in a single swallow.

Liza squirmed upright in the pillows. "Why is Oten laughing?" she asked the dwarf.

The man, as did the other dwarf whose memory brought back to the three thoughts of Tailend before the shaking, stood as high as Brann, bandy-legged and bowed, with a huge head and prognathous jaw. He paraded across the hall between where Oten held a sort of court in a heap of huge pillows and where Brann, Liza and Halsam lay on similar pillows. A fire burned without smoke and torches on the walls of the hall burned strangely without heat. Between them stood other giants, watching. Oten's voice was cracked, an old man's, and only that gave his age away.

"How big was he when he was young?" Halsam whispered.

Liza shushed him. "Will you tell us why he is laughing?"

The dwarf pranced closer. "It is funny so; *Haartsood* is how I must describe from where you come. It is the single word for it. You know what is *horse?*" Liza nodded. "Well, *Haartsood* means to us, horse's tail or horse's ass." He bowed. "It is a joke, you see."

They were comfortable. Their clothes, the indestructible Gad's cloth, smelled faintly of a soaping they had not needed to come clean, and the three smelled of it also, a musky scent when a woman of the giants—fresh back from battle somewhere and reeking of blood and battle sweat—had stopped the party in the halls and demanded that they be bathed before Oten received them.

This woman, Riija, she was called, unceremoniously took charge and propelled the three young city folk into a side passage that led to a bathhouse. There she ordered other giants to strip them and they were plunged into an immense circular tub full of very hot water. Liza screamed that she was being boiled. Halsam protested that he wasn't a child to be bathed so. And Brann submitted, Liza watching him narrowly as though she could cast the evil eye. A woman of the giants, two heads taller than Brann, disrobed and plunged in next to Brann to scrub him thoroughly. But she dealt with Liza and with Halsam, also, sending them on to a man who pummeled them atop a padded table. Brann, who thought his modesty fled after his times with Liza, grew redder even than the flush brought by the hot water and fought futilely to keep the woman from washing him all over.

They attracted an audience everywhere. Warriors waiting their turns in the tub laughed. And laughed still more when once the woman had held Brann up by the ankle so that he hung upside down and dripping. Giants gathered in the halls about them, feeling the Gad's cloth, touching their bare faces, especially Halsam's and Brann's. Once, a sword came half unsheathed and a squat, powerful giant spat and growled something sharp. Once, a woman pinched Brann's arm harder that she ought and once, a young giant warrior gestured at Liza and smiled with an expression distinctly ungentle. But that was all; otherwise they were curiosities.

Here at the table, a low board for the giants, chest high to the three, they gorged on things they couldn't name and they answered Oten's questions.

From where had they come?

Tailend.

Why had they left?

The shaking.

Had strange happenings been encountered?

The Driver, the first dwarf.

Especially, Oten was interested in the Driver and in the properties of the jewel, to which his eyes returned repeatedly though his glance was surreptitious and swift. How had Hals come by the jewel, he inquired. What had caused it to open the gateways? When had it failed; when had it succeeded? He questioned them, through the dwarf, most carefully and seemed both pleased and satisfied that they knew little about it. But though he obviously desired it, he did not take the jewel from Halsam. One time he motioned for Hals to approach and his hand, great enough to enclose Halsam's head entirely, reached out to touch the jewel. It became very hot at Oten's touch and Halsam leaped back. Oten held a conference with the dwarf and a tall warrior over whose chest a ragged scar slashed. They pointed toward Halsam and it was plain that they discussed the jewel. For an instant it seemed that Oten's anger would engulf everyone and then he grinned, and as if the subject had never been raised, he did not deign to look at the jewel again. Something important had happened here and Brann didn't doubt that the red, flat-sized piece of stone would come to be contended for again.

Brann mentioned the Post Guild, saying that he had also held a desire to join them and that part of their journey was come of this wish to find the place where the guild recruited new members.

Oten climbed to his feet at this, bellowing, pillows scattered in his motion. The laughter of the other giants stilled. Oten stepped over the table, towered above the three so that he seemed to stretch to the ceiling of the big room.

"Brefmande?" he demanded. *"Di brefmande tech?"*

Perilously the dwarf stepped between Oten and the three young folk. "What could you want of the Post Guild, Oten inquires."

Behind the pillows was concrete, the section of a wall separating galleries. In terror, Brann wished he could tear through it and escape. It became very quiet in the hall.

"Why is he angry?" Brann asked the dwarf.

The dwarf answered directly. "It is the Post Guild we battle. They are our enemies, from a very long time. Hereditary, you would say. Hugen fight, Post Folk fight back. It has always been." He translated their question for Oten, who spat ceremoniously.

"The Post Folk are like the three of us," Liza said. "Why do you hate them and not us?"

Oten listened to the question and snorted through his mustache. *"Kigge,"* he said.

"You are children," the dwarf repeated. "We make no fight with babies."

"Babies!" Halsam shouted. "Who says that?" He climbed up in the pillows and glared about. He was not as tall even as the dwarf, and the giants laughed. Some tension abated.

Oten waved to the dwarf. *"Sa appad Ergluk di."* He sat again and crossed massive red-haired arms over his bare belly.

"Oten says for you to hear the truth of the Post Guild. It is something to make you understand. The story comes down many generations. Those with serving duty will bring more to drink. In a moment I will tell it."

"I have a question before you start," Halsam said.

The dwarf turned to him, head cocked.

"Do you have Structors among you to make places such as this?" He indicated the hall, which seemed so immense that Brann and he had wondered together earlier as they ate whether or not the city structures were different here, the architecture something entirely apart from what they knew. It was a tier high and dark in its upper reach. All light came from the orange firelight and the torches which they saw to be artificial lights burning without flame, gases uncased and incandescent, but cold. One could pass a hand through such a flame, Hals whispered, and he did. He said it tingled but he felt no heat.

"You are crazy," Liza told him, and Brann refused the trick.

"We have no Structors," the dwarf told them. "This is part of your city all here for us. Hugen found it this way when they come."

"Then the Structors built this for you?" Liza was incredulous. "And you say we have been fighting you always?"

Oten uttered a curt command. The hall quieted.

"You will hear," the dwarf said. He drew himself erect; it might have been a comic gesture, but none laughed. The giants were silent, intent upon him, and there came only the sound of swallowing and the dull noise of bowls on wood. It was an important tale and the giants seemed ready to sit through it even in an alien tongue.

"I am sorry," the dwarf said. "I speak this better in our speech. Perhaps I confuse you, but you listen the same, please."

His voice became slightly singsong. He stumbled as he started to translate and then quite remarkably, Brann, Halsam and Liza forgot him and his looks. (Possibly the ale did it but the lights were not so bright, the dwarf *was* taller.)

"The time of which I speak, it is tausenya, a millennium ago. The ocean is not so cold and I come ashore. The trees here are different from those of the island. We have come back, walking to sunrise twenty miles a day. Five walks. Gefa, the city, is closer. One hundred of us come this time, three ships. The city is far down the mountain now. Last time it was another ten days' walk. We look for our doors into the city. It is the rule that the city have doors for us no matter how it changes. But the doors are shut to us for the first time and we sleep outside about fires in the Farmy Fields.

"Of the Hugen none is so tall as Obavall, our Captain. In Obavall's camp in the morning there are three dead. Killed from swords. Their blood is in a trail of footsteps back to the Gefa doors.

" 'Are some folk lurking in there?' Obavall asks. 'Are some of the little ones in Gefa who are not really human and would want to kill Hugen? One tausenya before when we came it was not so. We were welcomed as was the law.'

"Obavall was the hero of Insel the seafight when Deton died. It was Obavall whose sword won the day from the Abusk raiders and brought Prince Spattan low.

"Obavall asks if it was not the law that once in a tausenya we come and receive the city's bounty, receive what Gefa offers. It was agreed so when we left Gefa for good five tausenya ago. Was it not so in the original pact thirty tausenya ago when all humans left the city except for those who feared and would not leave? When the city was called, only Gefa and we Hugen were left to oversee the rest.

"This time there is no bounty and the doors for us are closed. There are as many of us Hugen here as may be counted on ten hands of men. In Gefa are many millions and more too much to count. In the morning out steps one of the Post Folk who says tribute to the Hugen has ended and out rush more guildsmen in a tide. The Post Folk are small as all folk have come to be in the city. But Obavall fights and Sachalach fights. She who was captain of the fleet at Dudin, and they cried as they fought for are not of the same birth as the Post Folk whose Guild one time was of the Hugen and whose task was to remember us and keep the word of us when we return each tausenya. And they cry as they fight, for the bond is broken and we are not of the city anymore after thirty tausenya—and what time is there before that, before Gefa came to be thirty tausenya ago?

"So Obavall is with his back to the stone and his bright sword singing. The Post Guildsmen die with his tears and Fida of the Post Guild says, 'The last key is lost. The city gates are locked without it. The city folk of Gefa will remain forever inside. Without the key it is a thing of great pain to come out.'

" 'They know of no outside,' Obavall tells her. 'Outside does not exist for them. It is your desire, the Post Folk's desire, to keep it this way.'

" 'You have taken the key and locked us here,' Fida says. 'Gefa will creep to the ocean and drown. Next tausenya will see the city's nose in the waves.'

" 'It creeps because you will it to, Fida. You may stop it if you wish.'

" 'It is said, Obavall, that when the city ceases to move, it will die.'

" 'It is said, Fida, but you know yourself that when the city ceases, you will be free.'

" 'It is a prophecy, Obavall, one or the other.'

"And the bright sword of Obavall flashes once and into stillness and so too Sachalach and her sword. Still, we depart with ten of the hundred. It is true, the folk of Gefa are not of us any longer. When we return in a tausenya, the motion of the city will have ceased."

"Uds tach tsie tsutra!" the dwarf cried.

"Uds tach," the giants answered, and weapons rattled.

"It will be our time again," the dwarf said to the three. "Obavall's prophecy has come to pass."

"Or the prophecy the Post Folk wrote of," Brann whispered.

"Eh?" said the dwarf, not hearing. There was a sudden roisterous motion among the giants. More food was brought out, more ale.

"I have a question for you," Halsam said.

"So, always questions," the dwarf said. "Ask."

"Why would a city move, creep like a baby?"

"It always has, for thirty tausenya," answered the dwarf.

"But what set it in motion?"

"It is not known among us."

"Who then?"

"The Post Folk claim to know." He took up a pitcher and splashed more ale into Halsam's bowl. "Drink, child, perhaps will put a beard on your face." He watched Hals, whose face showed him unsatisfied. The dwarf shrugged, bobbing his oversized head. "Drink, many things are not to be known."

"Lord above," Liza said, "my head feels as big as a giant's."

It was terribly quiet. Somehow they had come to be in another room, one of the tiny cubicles with glass-fronted doors through which the frosted light of the corridor came. It was just the three of them and the chamber was bare save for a pile of mats in the corner where they had slept. All their belongings were with them. Far, as if muffled by the intervention of many turns of hall, came the sound of metal against metal. It was a noise so familiar that Liza asked at first, "Is that the Driver?"

But they could hear it was not. It was a regular exchange, blows; and now also the muted semblance of cries, anger and pain.

"They are fighting somewhere," Liza said. She crept to the door and listened. It was a strange noise to her as it would have been to any of the city folk, seldom heard since the building of the city in an organized fashion. In a way, the concept of combat did not seem strange to her, as if it had been carried in some fashion along a line of descent from the first builders of the city. Perhaps the fact of this occurred to Liza, teased her, burst and died. Then she only listened to the sounds peculiar to war.

Liza sat with her back to the door, her arms wrapped around her knees. Her red hair fell about her face. She brushed it away and frowned.

"Did you believe what the dwarf said?" she addressed the others.

"You mean that the Post Folk ran the giants out and that they keep us prisoner in the city?" Hals asked.

"Hegman Branlee says there is no outside," Brann said. "He says it is all an illusion."

"What's a millennium?" Hals asked.

"A thousand years, Hals."

"A tausenya, a thousand years. The dwarf said it had been thirty thousand years then?" Halsam puffed his cheeks. "Pah! Nothing has lasted that long. That's longer than eternity."

"They were talking about a key," Brann said. "The dwarf was saying that if they found the key, we would all be free of the city."

"More monkler stuff," said Hals. "We're free now. We can go right out on the verge and see everywhere. We can go right down the elevators and right outside. Clear into the Farmy Fields. I'm hungry." He rummaged in his satchel and turned up food packed there by the giants. "Look at this." They shared out little cakes of gray pasty cheese and thin crackers. More ale was in their water bottles.

"What are you looking at?" Halsam asked Liza.

"The jewel," she said. "Do you think. . . ." She reached to it, touched it with a finger. "Do you think *this* is the key?"

"This?" said Hals. "They said they lost it a thousand years ago. Where has it been all that time?"

Liza clapped her fists together. "I think the Driver had it. One Driver after another. He would have killed you to get it."

"The Driver is stupid and crazy."

"Maybe not always, Hals. Maybe a long time ago a man found it and other folk came because it was an important thing. Maybe they became outcasts, pariahs, Master Smida would say."

"It opens gateways," said Hals. He covered the jewel with both hands.

"But they don't know, the giants don't. They saw it and they were talking about it last night, but they didn't really understand it. Only that it was important," Brann said.

"Maybe the Post Folk know," said Liza.

"Nobody knows," Hals replied. "They saw the Driver before; you said your grandmother saw him when she was a girl. Nobody knows that this is the key."

"And nobody knows how to work it," Liza said.

Halsam grinned. "We do. It opened doors for us."

The door to their chamber rattled. Then it came open and the dwarf stood there. He breathed hard so that the words came out in bits. Sweat streaked his face and the hair on his chest was wet with it. In one hand he held his sword; perhaps there was blood on it. Liza wouldn't look.

"Come," he said. "I'll take you out. The Post Guild has discovered our place on this tier. All are fighting now."

They could hear it, very near, now just a few turns down the corridor. Distant, the noise had been enigmatic, a phenomenon to be comprehended. But not here. Nothing is like conflict to the human system. In it the body realigns at levels beneath the conscious. They were scared. They followed the dwarf without question, down a long hall away from the noise. They would have left their satchels had the dwarf not told them. They ran after him, and his bandy legs moved very fast.

"Come," said the dwarf. "An elevator is near, one we use alone. The Post Guild is all through this tier."

They came to a closed cage door. It was a down shaft.

"But we have to go up," Liza said. "Don't we, Brann?"

"Why up?" asked the dwarf. He leaned on the signal that would bring a car to a stop.

"It was where we were going," Brann answered "to the 99th tier."

"Why?"

"We can't tell you."

"Fefust!" the dwarf exclaimed. "We have no time for child's mysteries now. This car goes down. The up shaft is in Post Guild hands. *Hellach!* Where is it?" He banged on the signal. Down at the turn of the corner now were moving shadows and the noise and motion of some swift fight; scores of smaller shadows moving against a few larger ones. They could hear the burr of some force more than the metal in the dwarf's sword. It was something which made the sword more than a crude thing degenerated from some past time when weapons were greater. The burr of it also came from the fight down the corridor and the sound was also beyond hearing, a force that the three could feel as if it attacked their cells individually and bored into the process of life. The sound of doors opening brought the sound of the battle, too. A dozen giants swung swords in the confined passage. The blades moved in ways that Brann's eyes couldn't follow, striking as if the metal had volition. Beneath came Post Folk in the uniforms of their guild, short swords swinging beneath the constricted reach of the giants. A giant fell and five of the Post Folk swarmed him. Small warriors lay farther back along the way where the giant swords had caught them. If there is an odor of fear, it was there. And blood smells its own way, like warm rust, and bitter. The fight came closer and the three were calling unashamedly for the elevator to open. They clambered inside.

"Where do we go?" Halsam asked the dwarf.

The stunted giant turned, letting his sword arm go lax.

"We have a rendezvous at Frontend, where Gefa's nose crumbles. There the fleet awaits. If you find your way there by summer's end, you may go with us to our islands."

Halsam slammed the start lever and the doors began to close, biting off the corridor and the approaching battle. They shut loudly against the clash of fighters in the space just outside and the last sounds were the fierce alien curses of the Hugen and the terrible blare of metal against the gateway to the shaft.

They had been on tier 71, more than a mile of climbing up that endless spiral of stairs; somewhere within it the Driver still climbed. Numbers of the tiers were chiseled into the masonry of the shaft. The inner doors of the elevator car were an openwork grille. They dropped past closed doors and doors through which some glimpse of places was possible. The car moved downward more swiftly than any of the big elevators they had ridden. Its other three walls, floor and ceiling were soft and spongy, of material similar to that which had floored the Isocourt Hall back home. It was a very small cage going down and none of the three could stretch out fully. In its ceiling a light shone softly, pale and yellow like those in the stairs.

Liza watched through the cage door trying to see out when they passed open or partly open doors on different tiers.

"I don't see anyone anywhere," she said after they had descended several levels. "Master Smida told us once that most of the galleries held a hundred thousand folk or more. Can you imagine where they have all gone?"

"On Pilgrimage," said Halsam. He had settled into a corner of the car and ignored the view outside. At times he rubbed the jewel and at times he reached into his satchel for dried fruit left by the giants.

"And where does Pilgrimage take them?" asked Brann.

"That's what started us on this whole damn thing," Halsam said.

"Do you wish you hadn't come?" Brann asked him.

"No," Hals said. "But nothing is the way you think it should be." He looked at Brann. "What do you think about the Post Guild now? Some sort of secret fighters doing things we can't imagine. Do you still want to join?"

"I couldn't say now," Brann answered. "I know that we never really understood who they were. The whole thing about their being message carriers is a fake. I see that. But they know things. Even the giants admit that. It is still true that I want to find them. Maybe only they can tell us what is real."

"The giants want us to come with them back to the islands," Halsam said. "I guess that's somewhere outside."

"That's where we're going," said Brann.

"To the islands?"

"Maybe. Right now I mean outside."

"Why?"

"I have to find out if the legend was true, if we are locked in here the way the giants said."

The car ground downward for hours. Hals dozed in the corner of the car. Brann and Liza stood watching the passing tiers. None was at all like their home tier on Tailend. Once, they passed a place where spidery gantries crossed every way through the open space and over which all manner of exotic plants grew as if a parkplat had taken over and risen to fill it all. Once, they passed a great echoing space in which it seemed that folk had never dwelt. The dusty concrete floors were bare of footsteps and the dust itself had drifted, east on the eternal wind of the city, dunelike in the lee of conduits and pipes which had connected nothing and conducted nothing since the gallery had been. From one gallery, though its gate was tightly shut, an odor came musty and rank, and with it was the noise of small bodies hurling themselves against the door. The door resounded, while tiny voices of animals screamed. The three pressed back against the far wall of the car until the elevator rode downward away from it.

Once, a man's eyes stared through the door gap, watching them silently. Once, a fierce hot gust of air came through. Once, they heard music played on a gallery, far off and very faint. Once, there was perfume and once, a death smell. Finally the number of the shaft dove past zero, past minus ten and eleven. The shaft walls moved away and the car dropped through an open-mesh tube. They could see a cavernous space, dim, with sunlamps so far above that the floor of the place was not visible in the gloom. The engines which drove the car down grated their noise into an emptiness that enfolded it; otherwise there was only the dripping of water. The car slid into another closed shaft, dropped for a few moments. Then the engine noise ended and motion ceased.

For a bit the three faced the closed cage door, each watching sidelong for one of the others to move.

"Well," said Liza, "are we going out? If nothing else, I have to pee."

Brann began laughing. "Okay, let's open up."

It was Hals who reached for the opening lever. The cage door folded back and the mouth of the outer doors slid smoothly down and up. Liza wondered at this.

"I think this is the way the giants came in," she said. "It looks to be frequently used."

They were in a small chamber, lit only by the illumination from the car. Even this failed as the doors drew closed again.

"Hey!" Halsam cried and he flailed for the signal. But the doors closed all the same and in a moment they heard the grinding sideways motion of the car going toward the up shaft.

For a bit they stood in the dark chamber.

"A whole city is above us," Liza said quietly, "a hundred tiers, three miles up. It's there, more tons than we can count."

"Don't talk about it," said Brann. He felt the weight of it as Liza spoke, people beyond counting above them (if they still remained), and stone as massive as the eastern mountains. The light returned to Halsam's jewel then and with it a door slid aside. They emerged into the huge open subcellar where water dripped and only a few sunlamps burned far overhead. In front of them was an open cart set on rails.

"It's like the trolley for Pilgrimage," Halsam said. "I didn't know they ran inside the city."

"This is too small for the trolley," Liza answered. She turned to Brann. "Let's get on. I don't see any place else to go."

Halsam examined the oversized seats, bare depressions in the metal shaped to the buttocks of larger folk (giants?).

"I bet this goes outside from here," he said, "out into the Farmy Fields. If it's built by the giants, I don't think we should ride it."

"Where else do you intend to go?" Liza asked. "Somewhere walking off into the dark?"

Halsam didn't answer. He turned and stepped aboard. At once there was a deep buzzing noise from beneath and the car jerked into motion throwing Halsam back into a seat.

"Wait," Brann accused.

"I didn't do anything," Halsam protested.

"Well," Liza called after him, "wait for us."

They began to run after the cart which rattled away toward a path of greater darkness. They were barely able to catch the fast-moving car. Brann and Liza climbed aboard.

Halsam made a gesture of disavowal. "I didn't do anything," he said. "All I did was get on and it started."

"I hope this goes somewhere," said Brann.

"It better get there fast," Liza replied. "I really have to go now."

"Me too," Halsam said.

"Lord above," Brann muttered.

A barred gateway stood half open at the end of the tracks. Behind them, moving to some unknown bidding, the cart rolled back toward somewhere in the city's deep basement. Past the gate a ramp rose perhaps two hundred paces into a light that was very green. Wind from the cellar blew outward past them toward the light.

"Is that the way outside?" Liza asked. Her words were hushed.

"It is," Halsam said. "I told you the giants were crazy. We *can* get outside. There's nothing to stop us at all."

He started up the ramp; soon he was running, with Brann and Liza close behind. They stopped. There was no gate here and the light blazed here just as it did at the verge of Tailend. Brann rubbed his eyes. "It's blinding me," he said.

"You'll get used to it," Liza answered. "This is just the same as we've seen before."

"Not really," Halsam said. "Look how the grass goes on and on; so far I can't see the end of it."

They wandered out onto a meadow. The city mass bulked high, its southern flank caught in the light of a noon sun. Here, foreshortened, it was a sheer face that seemed endless upward, gray and massive as the distant mountains. To the left the corner turn to Tailend was miles away. To the right the flank was a steady sweep that drove across hills high as ten galleries and fell down behind a final horizon. They moved to the right and climbed a low, grassy hill which the city flank bisected.

"Do you see the trolley tracks?" Liza said. "There are two of them like the cart we rode."

"Where are the trolleys?" Halsam asked.

"Maybe nobody is going on Pilgrimage," said Brann.

"That's stupid. Somebody always does."

"Well," Liza interjected, "things are different since the shaking."

"Look there," Brann pointed, "out in the Farmy Fields. I see dolls like my dancer, only our size. I'm going to see."

He walked down the gentle hillside. At first he was awed by the odor, fresh like the parkplat, but with endless nuances. He began to run; he sang and felt the wind of the open air past his ears. Then he was beyond the meadow and over the trolley rails. He sat down on the raised berm that ran along the Farmy Fields' edge both ways into the distance. Grain grew, perhaps wheat. He watched the wind riffling through it and knew now what was the cause of those sweeping waves he had seen in the russet wheat field when he had watched from the verge a mile above. Liza and Halsam came up, Hals tugging his shorts back into place. Liza ran down into the wheat and Brann chased her. It was head high and they lost each other. Then Brann found Liza, held her. They tumbled down onto the soft wheat straw and Brann reached to pull away Liza's dress. Liza's hands slipped down his sides. Off somewhere Halsam was calling.

Hand in hand Brann and Liza came up out of the wheat field. The sun was riding low on the horizon and an orange-gold line, a sight they had never seen before, was spreading out over low hills to the west. Trees on the nearer hills cast long shadows, the air was cooler, and there was a strong eastern breeze.

"Hals," Liza called, "what's wrong?"

He sat on the berm bent over, his hands clutching his abdomen.

"I feel sick," he said. "My stomach is all turning over. I'm cold."

Liza sat down next to him. "Hals, when did this happen?" She felt his forehead.

"A little while ago," Halsam answered. "I was walking along the trolley tracks following one of the big dolls when I started to feel very dizzy. Then my stomach got like this."

"Maybe you've caught something out here," Liza said.

"Now that you say it," Brann told them, "I've been feeling funny for a while myself; my hands and feet are all cold and tingling."

Then it seemed as if all three were ill. Brann became very dizzy and sat down heavily next to Hals and Liza.

"I feel scared," Liza said, "that this is happening so fast."

"Everything is sort of floating," Halsam whispered.

"I'm scared," Liza said again.

"What scares you?" asked Brann.

"I don't know, I don't know."

"Everything is too far," said Halsam. "I want to go back in."

Brann couldn't have explained it. The outdoors had not bothered him before. He had perched on the verge watching everywhere, mountains, Farmy Fields, all, and nothing. But now the outside seemed to pull away swiftly and he himself to dwindle until it was a vastness in which he was lost. His breath came swiftly in small gasps and he seemed to be choking. His hands and feet were cold. They tingled as if a million needles stung them. His heart raced. Something had swept away the sky, which was no longer a roof, and all was topsy-turvy and he was falling. He bent to cling to the grass.

"I'm going in," said Halsam. He came to his feet and ran headlong. Brann and Liza followed. The ground was a sponge in which Brann's feet sank. At last they were inside the mouth of the passage. The terrible feeling quickly fell away.

"It's true," said Halsam. "We are locked inside here. Something makes us sick when we go outside too long."

Wondering what strange ill forced them inside again, the three stared out into the beautiful land that seemed barred forever.

Chapter Two

Fever Dream

It might have been a fever dream. The light was deep amber and the air very thick. It seemed hardly breathable at all. They were perched on a high catwalk over the vastest space any of them had seen in the city.

"It's machinery all working," Halsam said. "Do you suppose this is what powers the whole city?"

They had followed the small tram's tracks back to this. The elevator through which they had entered the sub-basement was closed; no car had come to their signal. Its doors had not opened and the three, knowing no other course, had followed the tracks back. A trip in darkness lasting perhaps a day had brought them here.

Liza sat down on the catwalk, her legs dangling over the edge. A ladder went down the depth of a tier, unrusted, dry and apparently new. Somehow this place was maintained.

"I'm not going down there," she said flatly.

"There, then." Brann pointed. Where he pointed the catwalk extended outward in a T intersection from the wall. It crossed above the machine room unsupported and swayed with Brann's weight when he took a few steps out.

"And *I'm* not going out on that," Brann told her.

"So, it's an impasse," remarked Halsam, smiling. "She won't go down; you won't walk out there. Let's set up housekeeping on this little platform."

Probably it was the noise more than the height that unnerved Liza. The loudest sound was a steady hissing like escaping steam. But that intermixed with the bearing roar of rotating metal. Above, like bird calls, was an intermittent twitter which spoke and was answered across the giant space.

"They're talking," said Liza. "That's the reason I won't go down there."

"Who's talking?" Brann asked.

"Things. It sounds the same as the brain that started to burn in the Isocourt Hall. I think that is the way the brains speak to each other. The last one we met was insane. I don't want to meet another."

"I heard that sort of sound in the Post House," Halsam said.

They stopped then, searching. But nothing human could be seen and the voices kept on as if the three humans did not matter, or exist to them at all.

Lights moved in the machine room like little animals flitting: one like a stream of ants, one like a swarm of climbing monklers, and some like the sun they had seen at sunset pulled indoors, red and hazy and moving ponderously through the aisles between machines and setting off, when they stopped, a deluge of the fluting talk. At intervals conduits rose, converging into bundles which rose still more and the bundles twined, climbing toward a distant ceiling lost in amber air. But across the floor and at the extreme of their vision they saw a chasm, very wide, and behind it the amber darkened to a guttering burnt-out orange. The machines across this chasm were idle and no lights moved there at all.

"Do you see?" Liza pointed to it. "I imagine that's why there is no wind at Tailend. Those conduits probably go where we lived."

"The shaking?" asked Halsam.

"Certainly the shaking," she said. "Perhaps the prophecy of the Post Guild is right. Perhaps the city *is* falling."

Halsam shrugged. "Well, I'm going." He swung over the edge onto the ladder and started down.

"Me, too," said Brann. He took up his satchel and followed Halsam.

Liza stood watching them for a moment. The catwalk faded into the far dying place and all at once a strange fluttering cry came from somewhere above. A yellow cluster of lights swarmed past her, brushing her skin so that hair stood up on her spine and the skin of her belly crawled.

"I'm coming," she called to the other two. She pulled on her satchel and scrambled after.

"It tastes like rusty iron down here," Liza complained. They had walked through the machine room trailed by groups of the lights and now they were across the chasm over a bridge of fallen conduit. Brann had shone a flashlight down and could detect no bottom.

"It could go on forever," Halsam said. "You could fall and just keep on, the way you would if you tumbled off the roof at Tailend."

"Tailend is only three miles," said Brann. "If that's all this were, you would stop sometime."

"Did you ever see anyone who fell three miles?"

Brann hadn't. Halsam annoyed him sometimes, his irascible temper especially. But Hals was right, no one ever fell from the verge. Perhaps in the same way they had feared to stay outside, something kept folk from taking the one chance which would be too much, which would let them fall.

"Look!" Liza exclaimed. "Who is she?"

The lights had been gathering across the chasm, slowly taking note of their presence. They had come singly and in groups, drifting over to the edge. The three sorts of lights didn't mix. Here were blue, antlike gleams, a stream of them pouring out from an alley between two great engines, spreading along the bank. Here was a gathering of the monkler lights (as Liza called them), spectral from orange to the lightest of green. And here, one of the sun globes, red like the sunrise sky, seemed hot though Brann was sure they only imagined radiation. As the blue ant lights blended into the ultraviolet, so this seemed to radiate in the infrared. The lights gathered until the machines were insubstantial and the lights themselves were solid.

It was the red globe to which Liza pointed. These lights were subtly marked with shadings, darker interior territories as though they had once been something else and had blended into their present forms.

The red globe held a woman.

"She's crossing," Liza said. They watched her move, alternating between light and woman's form, not touching the conduit at all. Her hair was part of the light, a plasma possibly of strands. If she were clothed it was not in anything of real cloth. The fluid light revealed and hid her, realigning with each step and breath.

"She's looking at Halsam," Liza said. "She's coming to you, Hals."

She spoke, and the jewel on Halsam's chest answered, the same twitter that sounded constantly in the machine room. The jewel began to light itself and it was as if Brann and Liza had vanished. The woman walked past them (through them? it felt so to Brann).

"Hals," Liza called, and the woman turned once. Her eyes, part of the light, filled red and warm with it. Where she looked, other lights appeared, blue ants swarming, the spectral monkler lights which climbed them and clung so that Brann and Liza were clothed, like the woman, in luminous motley.

Brann thought he heard Liza calling, and monkler lights closed over his eyes. His vision was quenched. But somehow he saw through Halsam's eyes, through the woman's and through Liza's in all directions at once.

The twitter: *Hello, you're the first here in a very long time.*

Halsam: "What is happening?"

The twitter: *We are all together. I was lonesome.*

Halsam: "I see others like you."

Twitter: *Them! They're not separate anymore. You can't tell them from the mechanics.*

Halsam: "You're not of the folk."

I am. I'll show you. The red light billowed out from her as a cloak in an unfelt wind. She took his hand and moved it slowly over her, stretching to it as his fingers crossed bare soft skin, warm as the light, and perhaps it was hairs he felt, red so that Oten's seemed like a shadow, though Oten's hair had been redder than Liza's. Her arms came around him then.

Brann felt the power of her embrace and he wanted nothing so much as to be holding Liza. Maybe he was; there was a peculiar continuity of mind in which all were touching each other. Whose ribs he felt, whose spine, whose flesh slipped beneath his hands, who kissed, whose mouth his tongue entered, whom he entered entirely, whose hips moved, whose nails bit into his back, whose voice was in his ear, whose perfume? He could not say.

They were on pillows of light, blue through orange, drenched as though a storm had broken upon them. Whose legs moved, whose hands still stroked slowly, who remained within whom—it was all quite unimportant.

The twitter: *I was lonesome.* Giggles. *I was!*

"Do you have a name?" Liza said.

"Leoht," the woman answered. It seemed quite reasonable that her speech should be coherent to them.

It was her skin Brann found himself touching, though they still seemed intermixed. "Why did *that* happen?" he asked. "Just all of a sudden and we were . . ." He felt confused, didn't finish.

Leoht frowned. "You didn't like it. It was just a welcome. We see none of the folk here. Not in a very long time."

"There are others?" Halsam inquired.

"There are. See? They wait there in the quick place. It is dead here for us and they do not like to cross."

"What is dead?" Liza asked.

"Motion. We remember when it was all motion. When the engines we tended were so many and so far spread that we mechanics were countless. There is only a handful of us now. A thing will come, a crumbling. Suddenly it will be cold, perhaps a crevice opens and then all the machines on the one side of it cease their motion. Only a short time ago we felt a great crumbling. Half the quick place crumbled and became like this. We are crowded here now and the crumbling is beyond even the best of us to repair."

Liza saw. In the machines that moved was a life luster. They spun intricately and forces shifted. But the machine which rose above them—possibly it was a pump which fed into the fallen conduit—was still and the metal which composed it dull. It was solid but seemed soft and rotten. She ran a hand over it and felt her body heat begin to drain.

"What will happen when all the rest of this crumbles?" she asked.

Leoht frowned again. "We won't have a place. The quick place will be gone and the mechanics will crumble, too. But it won't matter at all, because it will mean the city has fallen."

They seemed to have disengaged though skin still touched and the warm, lazy sensation of palpable light still washed around them. Bits of it condensed and Brann watched Leoht bring a piece to her mouth and nibble it. He did the same, as if his sensory nerves had crossed; the bite tasted maroon, smelled of dawn light at the verge.

"Is that another of you standing at the other side of the chasm?" Liza asked.

"Ah," said Leoht, "it's Magh, a friend. One of the last I can talk to." She twittered and was answered across the open space. The man, enfolded in rose-tinted light, waved once and turned away.

"Magh says for you to come back across. He says that you should stay a while." Perhaps fingers touched Brann's neck. Something touched Halsam; he bobbed his head.

It seemed a reasonable idea to Brann, even in the way that Liza's eyes followed Magh away. Could it be right though? Was there not something important still for them to do? He held back.

"How old are you?" Hals asked.

"I don't know," said Leoht. "We go back to the beginning. I wasn't one of the first."

The thought excited Brann. Could she say what the city was all about?

"I can show you some," Leoht admitted. "I have memories which come from other mechanics before me. I don't understand them. Maybe you will."

At once they were enclosed in light, again drifting. They saw a plain sloping up to mountains. But here, below—they were high over it as they were when the brain had shown them a scene—was water. Liza asked what it was.

"Ocean," said Leoht. "I know the city could be in it and be covered without a trace. It is so big."

"And those, like mountain tops emerging from the water?"

"Islands."

"The Huten come from islands, they said. Could these be their home?"

"I know nothing of anyone called Huten," Leoht said.

The view showed no city yet. Instead, a few tiers, perhaps

five galleries wide, stood at the edge of the ocean. They saw a small reach of Farmy Fields, green in patches and gold like the wheat.

"I see Structors," Halsam said. "But they're only building up, not tearing down."

Brann pointed. "Look at the trolley tracks going into the mountains. The Structors are bringing loads of stone."

"Do you see it?" Liza exclaimed. "Watch where the sun is coming up."

The viewpoint seemed to whirl. Suddenly they were not seeing the city from the same vantage. The sun rose (the time scheme shifted greatly). The sun came *from* the water. "The mountains are on the wrong side," Halsam said.

"I think they are different mountains," Brann answered.

Things accelerated. The base of the city expanded away from the ocean. How could the city be both in a location where the sun rose from the mountains and where it rose from an ocean? How far had it moved since its building? Galleries grew next to each other and more tiers were layered. Folk seemed to be coming in streams from the north and south, but the time swept so fast that the streams contained vast successions of folk, generations of them, sometimes many, sometimes a scattered few, moving possessionless toward the growing bulk of the city. The structure built westward and the light was a blur, a steady gray in which the sun occupied all points of a wide, sweeping arc in the sky, red at both horizons, yellow-white at zenith, oscillating north and south with the seasons. Days merged, years merged. The scaffolds of the Structors were a spider web that clung and crawled across the west face of the city. On the trolley tracks came a thickness of objects, trolley cars which merged into each other as time compressed. They seemed like thick bundles of silver conduit, fattening in a great flow inward to the city. The green disappeared from the western mountains. Frontend grew into their foothills, climbed the mountains themselves and began to nose over into valleys beyond. Out, too, grew the Farmy Fields, flickering green and russet, snow-white and sear in progression of cycles. But their reach went beyond the bounds of the vision, and soon in all directions except on the highest ridges of the mountains the Farmy Fields were unbroken.

"What's happening now?" Brann asked. For it had all stopped. The volume of traffic on the trolley tracks dwindled. Folk ceased coming to the city on the roads north and south. For a time the old trolley tracks remained, a faint rusty streak. But to replace them, new tracks grew along the city's flanks. Abruptly, a change came. Tailend shrank away from the ocean. Frontend nosed downward out of the mountains to the west, and along the city flanks the new trolley tracks took more traffic until their thick conduits carried as much as the old tracks ever had. Tailend became farther away from the ocean. Frontend nosed farther past the mountains and behind.

"The Foundations," Brann exclaimed, and Liza and Hals joined him.

"They take away from Tailend," Leoht said. "What is old and crumbled gets torn down and carted along the trolley to Frontend, where Structors fashion it into new galleries and rebuild the city. Only the Foundations are left. I do not understand the reason for this. Do you? Can you tell it to me?"

They could not.

The view shifted again; time slowed. They were now at the foot of Tailend, seeming to stand on the grass there. It looked like a familiar place now. From portals along the nearest flank folk were emerging. They were dressed in a fashion stranger than anything Brann had ever seen, and something else was strange about them. From the grass in which Brann seemed to stand, he had to look up to see the faces of the folk.

"Everyone is so tall," Liza said.

"I remember that all the folk were that tall once," said Leoht. "The city has made folk shorter."

"But everyone is as tall as the giants," Liza protested.

Hals pointed. "Some of the men even have hair on their faces."

This was obviously the same city, somehow displaced. Structors tore down the last galleries from Tailend. On the trolleys folk rode forward toward Frontend on Pilgrimage. Between the trolleys, great masses of Tailend were carted down the tracks on flatcars. The vision followed these cars along to Frontend where Structors worked to build new tiers from the old.

The vision abruptly dissolved. They were again in the depths of the city. Leoht complained that she was tired. She curled with her legs and Halsam's intertwined. Her light dimmed and she fell asleep.

Brann wished he could ask Leoht more. Whatever memory she tapped to bring forth the vision was something from which she could not draw any explanation. It was as passive as the scenes shown them by the brain. The city had begun in a time, if the dwarf was correct, thirty thousand years ago. Folk had come to it in a great gathering. Materials had come also. Then a change had taken place. The outside lost contact with the city and the mass of the city itself had seemingly begun to move. In fact, the Structors dismantled one part and used the materials to build another. If this had happened steadily over thirty millennia, the city could have traveled an immense distance. The folk inside were smaller now. Brann, a tall young man by the standards of Tailend folk, saw that he was no more than a dwarf's height in comparison with the original folk of the city. The giants, the Huten, were the original folk or of them, and Brann's folk were the ones who had changed.

The quick place drew them back. Now there was no terror in the fluting twitter of mechanical voices, no foreboding in the drifting lights. Leoht led. If anyone wondered that he should understand her, it was only Brann, in whom a bit of mistrust still lurked. Liza followed Magh. She had become taken with him. Perhaps Brann was jealous. The light that fused to him was russet, clinging like a cloak. Magh was taller than Brann, as Leoht was tall also, a height midway between theirs and the giants'. His musculature seemed intricate and visible, more like the internals of the machine world around them than something human.

The *bherk* came to them now. This was Leoht's name for the antlike lights that moved in patterned webs across the quick place. Leoht could not explain their function.

"They are part of how each machine will mesh. It is one whole here; nothing is separate. They *hate* separate. When one becomes out of mesh with the other machines, the *bherk* know. They make changes."

The *bherk* worried at their feet. A small flock of them followed everywhere, especially Brann, clinging as far as his knees, so that he seemed to be booted in blue fog. He could brush them off as he would brush away the dust puffs that accumulated beneath a bed. They came back, though. They clung to his hands. They tickled.

"You are apart," Leoht said to Brann. "It is why they worry at you so."

The vagueness of this frustrated him. "I don't like it," he complained.

The *alek*, the monkler-like lights, large as two fists together, were not so enigmatic. Their function was to discover weakness and erosions in the machines. According to Leoht, they repaired minor breakdowns—in a manner she could not make clear. What fascinated Liza was that the *alek* did this not only for the machines but for them also. When the three first crossed the conduit back into the quick place with Leoht, a squad of *alek* had climbed them.

Liza had shivered at their touch, but Leoht said, "Don't fear. They are finding hurts on you and clearing them."

Scars from the Driver's lash, bruises and aches from the long stairway climb began to fade. Liza watched a long scar from the Driver's whip, which had coiled about her left shin as though a vine had climbed there. One of the *alek* moved along it. The tones of its surface shifted subtly. A tentative fluting noise sang and at once Liza exclaimed, "It's inside my leg! I can feel it." The scar went pale, blended into the flesh tones of her skin and then neither scar nor any other mark told where the wound had been.

Brann watched scratches disappear from his arms. The *alek* seemed to climb in and out of his skin.

"What else does it change?" he asked.

"Whatever do you mean?" Leoht asked in return.

"I mean, does it change us also?"

"Where things are not correct."

"And in my head, does it change my thoughts?"

"Do you find them changed?"

"I don't know."

"How long have we been here?" Brann asked. They sat among light pillows in an intricate bowl which reminded Brann of the chamber beneath the Isocourt Hall. Striations of light played beneath a translucent surface, cream ripples in ivory.

Several mechanics were with them, Leoht, Magh, another whose amber cloak flowed in and out of the wall, two other women (perhaps one whose legs rubbed gently against Brann's, one whose fingers combed his and stroked his cheek).

"Not long," said Liza, whose own fingertips touched the hairs on Magh's strong arm.

"We only just came," Halsam answered.

"How long?" Brann demanded of Leoht.

"I don't know time," she said. "I lose count."

"I believe the summer months are gone," said Brann. "I believe we have been to sleep many times." He saw something wrong in the way Liza reached, languidly as though no other work were so important or so difficult, for a snippet of food glow that broke away from a pillow and drifted toward her hand.

"Brann, why do you worry?" she asked.

He struggled away from the woman, whose name perhaps was Kand and whose hand pressed plum food light to his lips and whose straw-color hair smelled like autumn heat. He felt some inner distress, some surging in his blood and faster heartbeat, and he said loudly: "What is happening to the folk while we are here? The city is dying and the folk have gone off on a Pilgrimage to someplace." He looked at them entwined, touching, eating. There were *alek* then tickling him; one perched on his shoulder. He felt them go into his brain and the blood rush faded from his veins.

Broken, broken! Brann heard the twitter; an *alek* called.
Broken, broken!

Kand led him. A bearing shrieked. She darted down alleys among machines whose oil smell and hum of frictionless motion soothed. But the *alek* cried out for her. There was a breakdown beyond its healing powers. A great pump, like the head of a beast seen only in a Gad's menagerie, tugged at a thrust rod which drove far down into the substratum of the city. The rod was frozen. *Alek* swarmed it. *Bherk* milled, making tiny mindless chatter: *Broken, broken.*

All the little creatures made way for Brann and Kand. He had no notion of why he had followed her. It seemed rather that there was no reason why he shouldn't; something had broken. What was more, it seemed superfluous that Kand had said, "The piston has seized," to him, when of course he saw that it had and that in the bearing case the heat and smoke grew and met and glowed, a dull red. He reached in quite naturally through the soft metal of the case to find the point at which heat built the most. A lovely sense of warmth, a short pleasure, traveled his arms. *Alek* gathered, drew the heat and stored it, scurrying away. Within the piston, Kand slipped to the snag. It seemed no trouble for Brann to shunt the drive power when Kand called—and when the worry came that his hands lay on red-hot alloy and that the flesh singed and the sizzle and stench were fierce and the pain unendurable. Then an *alek* came and his hands were whole again and his mind could not hold the thought that this had happened.

"It is loose," Kand called. He shunted power back. He *told* the *bherk* to return the pump to the network. The pump head moved again. Something almost broke free within him, then Kand came and took his hand and *alek* moved within and without as he did also, he with Kand on pillows of orange, and somewhere Liza was also and somewhere Halsam.

They were alone, Brann and Liza and Halsam.

"Where are they?" she whispered.

A group of which they were not yet permitted to be a part was gathering. Across the quick place light was brilliant, all colors at once.

A thought came with great difficulty to Brann: *We have to leave now.* He said it aloud.

"I know," said Liza. "We've been changed. We are like them." She grimaced. "How can you be with Kand?"

"I can't help it," Brann answered. "And you with Magh?"

"He's beautiful."

"And that makes you stay?"

"No. Every time I think that we must leave, an *alek* will come and what is in my head disappears."

They wore nothing. The Gad's-cloth suits had vanished

sometime and none could recall where. Only Hals wore anything; it was the jewel which now hung on a collar of machine metal which Leoht had fashioned, saying, "It is one of the only master keys. It is charmed to you, you know. You mustn't lose it." She had said that it would open anything in the city, that the master key was once one of many, but she had seen one like now in two thousanyar. (This was not a word of her speech, which was Tailend speech taken from their thoughts. Where had she heard thousanyar, or tausenya?) "It is not the chief key, though," she had said.

"What will the chief key do that this won't?" Hals had asked.

"It will unlock only one thing—the folk from the city."

"Where is it?"

"It is lost. It had been lost since the city was built."

Brann stood to look across the quick place at the mechanics' gathering. "There are none here now to stop us," he said. "Let's leave."

"Could we?" Liza asked. "They'll see. They travel so swiftly."

They sat near the conduit where they had first crossed the chasm. Beyond was the dead place where the power of the mechanics dwindled.

"There." Brann pointed. "When we cross they will not be able to keep us."

"Nothing keeps us here," said Halsam. Cloaks covered him and the others. But on Brann and Liza the cloaks seemed clothing, replacements for their lost Gad's-cloth suits. On Halsam, though, the cloak was the same as those of the mechanics. It seemed part of his hair; it clung to the nape of his neck and molded to his spine. The jewel was always alight now and its answers to all speech of the mechanics came in high multitoned twittering. Halsam's light cloak was bronze and it sparkled in the centers of his eyes, bronze against brown. He seemed to stare through the others, and he followed Leoht toward breakdowns of the machines more often than Brann followed Kand or Liza followed Magh. The jewel played some part in this, Brann knew. But the jewel was firmly fixed around Hals's neck now on the unbreakable collar, and Hals would doubtless refuse to take it off anyway.

"Why would you want to go away?" Halsam asked. "I truly love it here. I love Leoht."

"We've been changed here," Liza said. "The *alek* are turning us into mechanics. Soon we'll be the same as they."

"There is nothing wrong in that," Halsam said. "The machines must be maintained."

"Remember how you fought against the Driver, Hals?" Liza said. "Remember how he tried to make you one of the dumb folk and you hated him?"

"This isn't the same, Liza."

"Our skin will turn into light; we'll never die and we'll never leave here," Brann said. "Do you want that?"

"Yes," said Halsam.

"We'll take you whether you like it or not," Liza told him. She reached for his arm and Halsam turned fierce, face contorted, tears in his eyes.

"I'm not leaving; I'll call them!"

A swift twitter sang from the jewel. Its center grew to a brilliant red spark and across the quick place lights boiled.

"I'll call them," Hals screamed. "They'll come. They'll help me."

Brann saw the look Liza gave him as they struggled to hold Halsam's arms and as a multicolored river of light gathered and a light tide swept their way.

"It's so warm," Liza said. Her hair hung lank and plastered. Her fair skin was crimson and sheened with sweat. The air was like a steam bath thickening around them. In it there were no creatures of the *alek* or *bherk*. It was a homogenous haze. Halsam's limbs were slippery, especially the light cloak on his wet skin, and Brann tried to hold Hals, pulling him. He felt the conduit but couldn't see it.

"This way, Liza," he said. "We'll carry him across the chasm."

He thought Liza was next to him. Someone held Hals's arms. She was singing to Halsam. It was a sweet young woman's voice and he saw her, Leoht, clear in the confusion, dwindling as he was borne back somehow—were hands holding him, carrying him? Leoht was crying; *Halsam, it crumbles beyond here. Stay in the quick place!* She was singing, he never knew how he understood her. Were there linguists, they would have called it impossible, the means by which she spoke, deep structure to deep structure, short-circuiting surface speech, constructing grammars, building speech analogs within the temporal lobe. Were there linguists? There were not. He understood. And Brann and Liza understood. Perhaps it was the jewel.

Outside there is change, Halsam! Time, age, erosion, fatigue.

Somehow she dwindled. He was carried. A flattened conduit passed beneath him and he swayed over an opening which was endlessly deep and where pieces of the quick place fell—he should have been frightened. Were there two others (Brann and Liza?) speaking to each other in a terrific calm as if leaving the quick place were of no consequence? There was a machine, quite dead, a derrick twisted down from its living height. The metal seemed soft. It would break like cheese. There was a connection for it, severed, which had once made it part of the amber roof. He stopped, went down. The hands released. The mist thickened and in it Leoht stood unobscured across the chasm. A chorus of voices twittered: *age-return; exhaustion; return; crumble; quick place-return; desire; age-return; exhaustion; love return; love return; love return!* A tall, brown-haired boy, a slim, red-haired girl struggled above him.

The lights swarmed. Brann and Liza clambered up onto an old dynamo case. A clear space was about it as if the lights refused to come close to the rotten metal. Liza moved toward the machine's far side. An *alek* swept down, brushed her, stung her. She tried again and, as her foot found a place on the far side, several *alek* came around. They grazed her leg.

"It hurts, Brann!" A weal faded from her skin. *Alek* stung him, too. He batted at them. "It doesn't hurt long, they're not trying to harm us. They just want to make us stay."

The boy who had given Brann the fur coat so long ago had once described snow. *"Mak cald, betouk ea skennen, mak brunnen, sam ta ferr!"* (Makes it cold when it touches the skin, but it burns the same as fire.) If he could see snow, Brann thought, drifting, touching, burning, this would be its like. Like the unknown snow, the *alek* melted when they touched the dead metal, losing form, gold light dimming; a vapor puff and gone. The *alek* didn't like the dead place's metal. It was stalemate. They couldn't go on. When they clambered down the far side of the machine *alek* came to sting them and drive them back. But the *alek* were loathe to approach too closely, fearing to melt on the dead metal.

Across the chasm, Leoht stood with one foot on the fallen conduit.

"She's crying," said Liza. The sparkles were tears. Her cloak rippled as if in a wind. Farther back were Magh and Kand, hands and faces visible only from behind an air pump.

"Bring him back," Leoht called.

"Halsam stays," Brann answered.

The light was like a vapor, cold on their skin, and the *alek* danced above. The air was deep violet; it tasted again like rust.

"Will you help me?" Leoht asked Magh and Kand. The two smiled blankly.

"It's the dead place, Leoht," Magh said. Kand's fingers hid her face; her jade eyes were solemn.

Leoht took a tentative step out onto the conduit. She was trembling. *Alek* came to her, touched her, hovered about her face, troubled. All across the quick place the light creatures were agitated. Many of the *bherk* gathered, directionless, at the brink of the chasm. Mechanics' red light bobbed here and there. In it were watching faces. And the *alek* dove like drunken birds, crossing to the dead place, shearing off from the dynamo, their reflections diffused on its eroded surface.

"Please," Leoht called, "won't you bring me Halsam? You don't have to stay. We won't compel you. You can go wherever, out into the dead place, out into any place in the city."

"Why?" Brann asked.

"I want him."

"Why?"

"Love!"

A change had come to Brann, subtly and unnoticed. Perhaps Leoht detected it and this was why she pressed him. She walked farther out onto the bridge. The *alek* flitted faster; the brink behind her was solid now with light, with swarming *bherk* and with the ruddy light of mechanics. Magh came close, stopped at the edge of the bridge.

"I can't carry him alone," she said to Magh. "Allow the

alek to help me. Cross with me yourself, help me bring him back. They won't."

"Leave him, Leoht. Let him go!"

"Leave him, Leoht!" Kand called. "It disturbs the *bherk*. I feel it disturbing the harmony."

Leave him, Leoht! the chorus twittered.

She walked farther, faster until she was across the bridge and below Brann and Liza where Hals lay in the shadow of the machine. He seemed to have no strength or real consciousness. Leoht pulled at him. She was terribly strong in the quick place. The *alek* gave her such strength, but not so here. Her powers were more ordinary and human. She bent down then close to Halsam and kissed him, brushing fingertips across his face, which was puffy and flushed. She pushed back his hair.

She whispered, "Come, Hals."

"Leave him, Leoht!" Magh called. "Don't you see the battle is killing him? The *alek* can't help him there."

She put her arms around Halsam from behind, half lifted his upper torso from the concrete. She began to drag him back toward the conduit bridge.

The idea showed the change in Brann. It was an adult sort of thought. On the home gallery someone would have noted it, marked it. He understood that while he disagreed with Leoht, she was also right, in her way. Hals wanted to stay, Leoht wanted him to stay.

"I'm going to help her," Brann told Liza.

"We're going to leave Halsam here?" she asked.

"Yes." He began to climb down toward them. The *alek* didn't obstruct him.

Tears really were on Leoht's cheeks. Brann saw them as he took hold of Halsam's legs. Liza came; perhaps she understood, too. She went to Leoht's side. Cradling Halsam, they moved back across the bridge. It swayed now as it hadn't before.

"We've decided, Leoht," Kand said. "We won't have them here. We tried to reshape them, make them the same as we are. You can see it isn't possible."

"Leoht, come here," Magh said. "You'll forget him. The folk are short-lived. In an eye blink he will be gone and crumbled more surely than the dead place. Let them take Halsam away."

The bridge swayed. The light grew red and hot so that in it all that could be seen were the moving glows of the *alek* weaving and the *bherk* which advanced. On the bridge the metal gave the whisper of fatigue; the *bherk* were forcing it to crumble. Where they advanced, the bridge sagged.

"Let them go now, Leoht!"

"I won't."

"You'll all fall together. There's no room for them with us."

Hals seemed to awaken, become aware of the endless drop beneath the falling bridge.

"Return to them," Brann said. "We'll take Halsam. They'll let us go now. You were the only one who wanted Hals to stay."

Leoht shook her head. "We'll carry him back across together."

"Will you go with them, then, Leoht?" Magh asked.

"You present me with no other choice, Magh."

He seemed astonished. His voice twittered in swift conversation with Kand and other mechanics.

"This has never happened, Leoht. Do you know the nature of time outside? It will be a single moment and without the *alek* you will be crumbled. The *alek* say that there are processes which will take place, chemical changes, which their powers abate here." They were off the bridge. The *bherk* advanced as a violet carpet, and where their light touched, the bridge shivered, rotted; pieces of it broke free and fell into the chasm.

"Come, Leoht, the bridge is breaking. Once it is gone, you will end as they will end."

"Maybe, Magh, but another shaking might come, another quake to shrink the quick place and you will crumble, too. Why don't you come with me if you have the strength? Cross the bridge before it falls."

"No!"

The bridge crumbled and sections fell away. A rain of old metal rattled down into the chasm so light and brittle that it was no more loud than the falling of leaves in a parkplat. It fell until the sound of its falling faded and still came to no bottom. For an instant the *bherk* hung, connected like a living bridge, a violet outline of the conduit. Then the ghost structure evaporated, the *bherk* drew back, and the milling color on the far side of the chasm dimmed.

"Good-bye, Leoht! We're sorry for you."

"And I, for you, Magh!"

Halsam stood by himself. Leoht held her about his shoulders. They walked into the place between the dynamo and other giant dead machines. Leoht's cloak tattered and, at Halsam's throat, the jewel's red light died.

Chapter Three

The Prison

The decay here reminded Brann most of that first strange gallery where they had encountered the Driver. The machines gave up their shapes, lapsing into corrosion. Dereliction had made them into jagged spires and useless, toppled constructs. Faint lights flitted within them, *bherk* ghosts and *alek* spirits, set free from their born tasks, immune to the crumble of the dead metal, wandering. A reddish glow came once, a voice.

"Not all mechanics came back to the quick place," said Leoht. "Some are out here, changed; we don't know how they live. They won't speak directly to us. But often I have heard them calling."

It was a very lonely sound. "What does he say?" Liza asked.

Leoht shrugged, made as if to answer, would not. "He says nothing to matter." But she stepped faster among the old machines and seemed uneasy for a long distance.

The only light was a diffuse saffron glow from the distant ceiling. It cast no shadows. In it distance became imprecise. The four lost all track of how far they had come and of what lengths they had yet to travel. Subtly the landscape changed. The remnants of machines were almost shapeless now. Often they were only rust piles from which protruded angular skeletons. Where they walked the flakes of rust scratched on concrete and even the small vibration of their steps occasionally brought down those delicate structures.

Leoht could still conjure the glow-food. Its taste had paled, though, and its substance thinned. For the first time in many days they were hungry.

"I'm frightened," Leoht said. She stood unadorned, the light cape gone. The greatest concentration of her thought brought only a momentary glimmer to her skin. It would flash like sparks in the ash of burned paper. This happened most often when the *voice* of that solitary mechanic spoke from the waste of dead machines. Halsam knew she was troubled then and he would stare out into the gallery while his fingers fidgeted with the jewel.

"Can you understand?" Leoht said. "I did nothing without the help of the *bherk* and *aleks*. Pain was a game; you'd feel it for fun and let the *aleks* end it when it grew tiresome. When you moved a thing, a piston, a lever, there were *alek* inside you moving also; nothing was too heavy. Now I feel cold and there's nothing to do about it. I'm hungry and the glow-food doesn't come so easily. I'm tired and I sleep because I must. Do you *always* live like this?"

"Yeah," Halsam grumbled. "Always."

"We've kept something, though," Liza said. "We can be *together*." She grinned at Brann; were the light not so yellow, perhaps he would have seen her blush.

"Together, yes!" Leoht agreed. She hadn't lost *that*, they discovered again.

"Is it the ocean?" Halsam asked. The dead place ended at a rusty beach which extended miles each way toward the city's flanks. A constellation of sunlamps burned in the ceiling high above, still yellow as the dead place's diffuse lights were, but bright with single points. The water lapped up onto the beach. It was red and murky with dissolved rust. In its depth were the encrusted shapes of machines. Their structures were bitten off by oxidation at the waterline.

"The water falls under the ceiling?" Halsam wondered. "Where could it go?"

They were not used to a horizon. The view from Tailend was of abrupt ending at the mountains and of a skyline merging with the floor of the tier above. None of them had experienced a place where the ceiling was so high and the surface below so flat and extended that curvature alone brought vision to an end. (In the Farmy Fields during the short time they had ventured outside the city, vertigo had stolen the horizon.)

"The ocean was different," Leoht remembered. "It was outside the city, not beneath it. It moved, boiling and crashing down. This is something else."

They moved along the shore for a time, testing the warm rusty water with their feet. Even this minor sea seemed endless compared with the tiny swimming pool on their tier at Tailend. While the water scared them, it was Leoht who seemed torn. She knew nothing of water at all and yet the *voice* among the dead machines had grown more insistent so that only Halsam's proximity seemed able to hold her from joining the speaker of that voice. And here they made no progress away from it, but only went perpendicular to their old path, with the mechanic pacing them. Halsam saw it.

"Well," he said, "we can't go any farther here." He searched about for something to test the depth. There was only sand and metal that powdered in his hands. "I'll wade out," Hals said.

Liza protested. "Hals, Lord above knows how deep it is."

"We have to get away from *that*." Hals pointed back into the dead place. Perhaps a ruddy light glimmered there for an instant. Leoht shivered. Hals went in.

"The water is very warm." He progressed up to his knees.

"I can see machines in it," Liza warned. "You'll get hurt."

"I can feel them. I'm watching out."

Brann, Liza and Leoht squatted on the water's edge, intent upon Hals, wading deeper. The water came to his waist. "It smells when you stir it up," he said. "All sour and disgusting."

"I can tell," Liza said. She wished he would come out. His obstinacy sometimes could make her scream.

It rose to his chest. "I feel something solid in here; I hit some metal."

"It's all metal," Brann said.

"No, that sort just breaks when I touch it, Brann. This is solid and smooth. I can't get hold of it."

"I can't summon any *alek* now, Hals," Leoht said. "Please, don't go any farther."

He turned, shoulder deep, moving his arms in a swimming motion. A line of rusty orange marked the high-water line on his shoulders. Then only his head was above the surface. "I

can't feel the bottom anymore," he said. "I'm coming out."
Abruptly his head went under. For an instant there was a
thrashing and the sour rust smell rose from the water.

Brann came to his feet crying, "Hals!" and moving toward
the water. He was knee-deep when Halsam surfaced again.

"What happened?"

"I tripped." He brushed water off his face. His hair was
plastered to his head. He sputtered and began to splash out,
noisy and angry. "I felt a cable underneath, a rope made of
twisted wire. I caught my foot on it and got pulled under.
Something big like a machine only not all ruined is under
there."

Brann helped him out. His skin was gooseflesh though the
water was warm.

"You're bleeding," Leoht cried. "What will we do? There
are no *aleks* here."

Blood ran down Halsam's shin from a long scratch. Leoht
made to touch it, fascinated at the idea of blood *outside*.
Never having known death, she didn't comprehend a scale of
injury. He would bleed and die! Hals motioned her aside, im-
patient. Leoht (of the thousands of years, of the tremendous
power, of the vast machines which sustained a city) was
awed that a trickle of blood did not bother Halsam.

"It's not deep," Hals said.

The roiling of the water didn't subside. A fountain of
water foamed up above the surface, driven by air escaping
from something still submerged. With it came the prow of a
thing they would have known as a boat if ever they had seen
one that large. The pond in the parkplat had been only a
puddle next to this and the little boats the folk rowed there
like toys. It was fifteen paces long and perhaps four wide,
shaped like a large canoe. Its sides were dull silver. A rosette
of the Post Guild had been painted on the bow. A cable of
wire ran tautly into the rusty water.

"It must have sunk there a long time ago," Brann said, ex-
amining it critically. "Why do you think it came up now?"

"Maybe someone from the Post Guild hid it there," Liza
remarked. She pointed to the rosette symbol which marked all
Post Guild property. "Maybe Hals accidentally unhooked the
boat from whatever held it under water."

The boat was of the same intricate workmanship as the

dancing dolls and as the devices of the Structors, seamless and dully shining without a hint of corrosion. It rode for an instant awash to the gunnels, and then pumps hummed alive, sending rusty fountains out onto the surface of the water. Dry inside, the boat swung about on its mooring and a low, insistent thrumming, as of some engine, came up from the water.

"It wants to get away," Liza said. "It acts like it has some place to go."

"Probably it does," Brann answered. "This is a Post Guild boat. If Post Folk come this way, they need something to take them over the water." He looked to Leoht. "Do Post Folk come through here?"

Leoht shook her head. "I've not seen them. You are the first of the city folk to come in . . ." She paused. " . . . in a very long time. I don't know how to count it."

Leoht, alone of those on the beach, seemed inclined to accept the boat without wonder, perhaps even with some affinity. Brann watched her. She followed the motion of the boat on the water and she seemed to hear something in the note of its engine. The *voice* spoke to her out of the dead place and she heard it and heard the engine, and Brann was aware—as Halsam strangely was not—of a fierce brief combat within her. He saw that it had not been finished at the chasm, not so easily at all. The *voice* was one of those mechanics who had not broken entirely away and it held no power over her, no compulsion to stay. The compulsion was within her and she stepped into the boat. It was a tiny moment. Brann saw it. A smile broke out on Leoht's face. She held her hands out to Halsam and he joined her in the boat where he stood rubbing at the rust on his skin. Brann climbed aboard and then Liza, orange to the knees with the rusty water. Then somehow the engine shifted. The twisted cable dropped away from the prow. The boat came about and surged out onto the underground sea toward the place where the roofline vanished and the orange water seemed to tumble away.

Once, Grandmother Ebar had described such a sea under the city. In the plant room at sunrise had been Brann's favorite time with Ebar, the horizontal light very red, the leaf shadows projected onto the white wall.

"A great sea is said to be beneath us, Brănn. Very deep. In it tiers are lost, all flooded."

"Where does it come from, Grandmother?"

"From the weight of the city. The city had the mass of the mountains themselves. If we were on a plain above an immense aquifer, if the city's weight pressed it, if the soil were deep and unstable, we would sink, the city would sink and water would rise to fill the lowest tiers."

"The schoolmasters say nothing of this, Grandmother."

"Some know, some don't."

How had Ebar, only a schoolmaster herself, come by the peculiar knowledge she doled out to Brann?

"An aquifer?" Master Gelde said. "Ebar certainly has some notions. Wouldn't the city have sunk into such a thing long before this?"

"But if it moves?"

"Pah! Moves! What does she fill your head with, young Brann? Does she still hint to you in secret that the Post Guild is the place to learn what we don't know here?"

How did she know? Master Gelde was almost as old as Ebar, had known her since she had come to join with his grandfather at age seventeen.

"She embroiders, Brann. She adds to things. Ebar is a bright woman. I know of none with a keener mind. But I'll tell you—she is right in one thing. We have forgotten more than we are aware we knew. What is forgotten is gone. Ebar knows this, but she must know what is gone so she embroiders, invents things. Things to tell a young grandson."

"Master Gelde, she came to teaching when she was in her middle years. What guild did she belong to first? She won't tell me."

"Eh? What guild?"

"Yes!"

"I've never known."

Hegman Branlee knew, or so he said. "It is the Lord above's will. Cold is above and warm below. Snow above, lad. Thus, water below. It falls and warms, collects beneath the city."

Brann plucked at the hem of his Sabbath shirt. He stroked

a finger down the Gad's-cloth scarf his mother had made him.

"There is snow on the city roof, Hegman?"

"Ah, yes. It is well known, the pilgrims say so."

"And there is water underneath? A great sea, just as Grandmother Ebar says?"

"Yes, some have seen it." He glanced at the outer sky; it had reddened in time with the coming interior evening. The chime in the dome of the Isocourt Hall would ring soon and the Sabbath meal would be served. Branlee was willing to endure even Brann's ceaseless questions for a place at the Adelbran Sabbath table—a frequent place—best laid in the parish, even though the questions were a source of indigestion for the Hegman.

"Where does the water go?"

"It collects in the subcellars, young man. Where else?" He grinned at the class, slapped his ample belly. "Things fall down, as you well know. Do you suppose it rises up?"

"Then why haven't we drowned long since?"

"Huh?"

"We don't know how long ago the Lord above created the city, Hegman. You said it yourself."

"Not quite accurate, Brann. Why, I've told you about the speculations of Sur-hegman Pandatta, of the thirty cycles since creation. Oh, if only we had the old books!"

"But in all that time wouldn't the water rise and drown us?"

"It has not, young man, has it? There is your refutation, heh, heh, heh."

"Then where does the water go?"

"The Lord above knows. He provides and removes. Ah, there's the dinner bell. Class dismissed. Come, young Adelbran, let us not keep your father and mother waiting."

Whatever its source, the sea was interminable. The boat ran upon it for five days and nights as the cycle of the sun and moon lamps told them. The shapes of corroded machines still showed in the water. But they seemed to have risen several tiers, as if the city slanted downward here. It was not quite clear what had happened, since a misty obscurity had come to the air, shortening visibility to a few hundred feet.

Perhaps they moved through slanted, broken stairwells, perhaps they were in open space vast as a gallery. They were never sure. The boat's direction was certain. Some device of the Post Guild guided it.

"I can't believe the city is like this," Liza said. "All these places were near us and we never knew."

"A Gad told me once," Brann answered. "I thought it was another of their stories, all to get you in to the sortileger and have your future read in dice."

"When was that?" Liza asked. She sat in the bow, hair lank about her face in the mist. She had been watching the water surge up beneath. Brann had been watching the fine beads of mist which collected on the tiny hairs along her spine. They felt more comfortable in their nakedness now. The experience in the quick place had joined them in a way. Halsam and Leoht were in the stern. Mist came between the two couples. Leoht and Hals were obscured, edges softened. But Brann felt their presence. He heard them talk and giggle softly.

"You remember last summer," Brann asked, "when the Gads' carnival came to home from one up? There was the short, dark Gad with the puffy clothes?"

"With the bristly eyebrows and the fake scar?" Liza nodded.

"You went off," Brann laughed. "You and your mother to the wrestling. This Gad started to talk to me. He acted like he hadn't told this to anyone else, like it was a grave secret that he was giving me. He had a peculiar accent."

"They talk all the languages, Mother said. I bet they only used our own tongue when they were on our gallery. I never thought about it. I wonder how many languages they knew." She frowned.

"Probably as many as the Post Folk," Brann said. The boat made a small change in its motion in response to a shift in the current. Liza peered over the side, saw nothing and shrugged.

" 'Eet ees minny weird places een thees city, boy,' he said to me."

"You're making fun of him, Brann. He didn't talk so stupidly as that. I heard him talk a little, too."

"It's pretty close. Do you want to hear this or not?"

"Okay."

"He said, 'Ees different, so close you tink ees other place entire. Thees place Tailend may be last civilized place left. You theenk Gads' show ees weird, all the animals, all the weird folk, short and tall, ees far more out there.' He got very quiet and he leaned over, acting as if he wanted to give me a secret. He whispered in my ear, his breath smelled of allium root, all spicy. He said, 'You go to Frontend, ees something you will never see here, ees all civilization end, ees torn down and folk scrabble to make a living, ees been mess.' Then he punched me in the shoulder. 'Go,' he said. 'You don't believe me, see for yourself.' "

"Maybe he was right," Liza said. "I never thought things would be like this."

The boat bumped, seemed to scrape over a shallow obstacle. Halsam came forward. "Did you notice that the water motion is changing? It's rushing along past us. I don't know what is making the boat go against it."

A warm wind swept over the water, clearing away the mist. They saw that they were in a narrow hallway, high-ceilinged and flooded halfway. Doors, shut tight, swollen and overgrown with moss, lined the corridor. They were all crowded forward now. The way was visible ahead until distance narrowed it and brought the ceiling down to the water. The rust color was gone. Sunlamps created ripple reflections on the walls so that where water began and air ended was not easily told. The boat nudged into a turning where corridors intersected. The left hall was narrow and dark and the water exiting it musty. The wind blowing over this water was stale and chill. The boat swept past but not before Liza saw the mark at the wall and the arrow pointing.

"It was the rosette mark again," she said. "Like the ones Post Folk use at delivery points for a marker. There's another."

It marked a door which stood open against the current. A dark stairway led up from it, away from the water. The boat hesitated for an instant as if waiting for instructions. Liza pointed out a light at the stair top and more markings pointing along an upper corridor. Had the boat hesitated longer, they might have gone—anything seemed preferable to this interminable boat ride, even a meeting with the Post Guild. But the boat carried them by and, while more rosettes appeared at intervals, the arrows only pointed on down the corridor they were traveling now.

"Maybe Post Folk are near about," Brann said. "I hope we find them."

"Do you *want* to find them?" Liza asked, her voice small.

"Yes," said Brann.

"I'm not sure if I do," Liza said.

"Nor I," Hals joined.

"Tell me more of these Post Folk," Leoht said.

Brann began to explain.

Organisms were appearing in the water, eel-like wrigglers that hid among the now prevalent moss and algae. The colors moved toward green and the smell was of plant life and silt gathered in every bend of the corridor. Water plants floated, lotus and water lilies. Reed grasses obscured the walls. The waterway forked and forked again until there were numerous duplicate passages overhung with heavy growth. Trailing vines began to appear, hanging low over the boat so that the four had to hunch down behind the gunnels. Soon it became impossible to tell they were in any sort of corridor. Perhaps the walls had been made of less permanent stuff than the city structure itself; perhaps they had been taken down over a long time by water action and the weight of vines and trees. The air was dank, suffused with odors of growth and decay. Perhaps there were sunlamps in the ceiling somewhere, but the ceiling seemed to have receded above the water, and beneath it were canopies of interior jungle.

"Something's in the trees." Liza pointed. "I saw eyes."

"Don't be stupid," said Brann.

"I saw it too!"

"Yes," Halsam agreed. "Lizards like in the Gad's menagerie, and animals like monklers."

"Maybe this was where the monklers came from, where the Gads got them," Liza said.

A bird crossed over from one wide-leafed tree to another. It landed in a flurry of bright-colored feathers and cocked one eye suspiciously toward the boat.

"Do you suppose a parkplat went wild here?" Liza asked. "Maybe folk have been gone from here a long time."

"What a place," said Hals.

"There are still the Post Guild marks." Leoht pointed.

Brann nodded. "I keep seeing them scratched into the trees. All the arrows point in this direction."

"Somehow this boat is being guided in the right path," Leoht said. Her arm was around Halsam, leg next to his. This seemed ludicrous, she being taller by a head than Halsam, and yet she was timid here. "I have never left the quick place before, not in more time than you can imagine," she had told him once. "All my knowing of life isn't more than yours though you have lived much less." But there were freckles across her nose and her eyes were open in a sort of awe that such as *this* existed in the city she had known for ten thousand years.

The noise which sounded clearly through the trees was unmistakable, the sound of metal clanging shut and a lock snapping-to. A high singsong voice called; another answered. Then little folk surrounded them, hanging in the trees and staring as the boat made a turn into the open water of a small lagoon. Around its banks were cages, and the cages merged into cages farther back into the jungle, and in the cages were more of the little folk, peering. The singsong speech was taken up among them. They watched with wide, flat faces beneath dark bangs, dark eyes fixed upon the boat.

Brann picked out one word which perhaps meant something in the inflected tongue of the little folk: " 'eudgen, eudgen; (or *"Hugen, hugen"* were they saying?) *mlwa-wlwa-mlwa."*

Leoht retained the gift to know what they said (her communication, as has been said, bypassed surface speech).

She turned ashen, even a bit pale green in the green-lit jungle. "They say that we are taken," she said. "We go no farther, ever."

The boat slid into a groove in the bank, bobbed for a moment and then something left it, some force escaped, and it came to rest. A woman of the little folk stepped forward. She was bandy-legged and her feet were large with toes splayed, holding to the muddy bank. She wore a short kilt of rough cloth, which appeared woven from the fibers of some large-leafed plant. She wore a jacket of the same material. Both were dyed bright yellow. A flower with huge, luminous orange petals was fixed in her hair. The hair itself was black and shone as if oiled, close to her head. All these folk were so dressed, the women's clothing dyed brightly and variously. The dress of the men was uniformly gray.

An item of well-worn brass hung at her waist by a thong. She plucked it up with a quick little motion and gestured sharply toward the four in the boat, demanding that they come out.

"The thing is a key," Brann said, "an old skeleton key such as they used on the Isocourt Hall doors."

"Mlwa-mlwa," she repeated, and it was echoed from all sides. Big feet stamped out the sound. Cage doors clanged open and shut incessantly. Many of the little folk carried hand-sized squeeze cans. As Brann watched, one somberly dressed little man swung a door open and closed and listened critically to the hinges. Then he applied a quantity of oil from the can.

"Mlwa, baddidma oa, feedse mlwa: oa!"

"Mlwa: oa!" the little folk replied.

Several of them walked purposefully down the bank, stopping in a circle. From somewhere one man drew a knife, which Brann, in a funny, fleeting thought, saw to be a knife of workmanship common on his home gallery, perhaps hand-honed and stamped with a known craftsman's mark.

"They have Halden knives," Hals remarked. "Do the Gads peddle here, too?"

The woman repeated the incessant demand while the man augmented it with a purposeful wave of the knife.

"We are to get out now," Leoht said. "She says he will be compelled to hurt us if we do not."

One at a time the four climbed from the boat. The little folk made no effort to steady the craft—some even grinned at Brann's awkwardness. Brann stumbled a bit.

"All that moving water," he said. "Now I don't think I can stand up on the land."

There was a terrible commotion among the little folk. Many arms were pointed. Some of the folk jeered. One woman spat and stamped her foot.

The woman with the key gestured with her empty hand, taking all four of the visitors in with one sweeping motion.

"Begga nu sedda, led nammpa, ha?"

Leoht laughed. The little woman reddened. *"Nu sedda?"* she repeated.

"She asks why we are bare and disgusting. She asks if we have any shame."

A boy of the little folk, doll-sized but with feet so large he stumbled over them as he walked, came down the bank and pushed a kilt toward Brann. He held it to his waist where it went barely two-thirds around. Laughter rang and the cage doors clamored. The woman snatched the kilt back from Brann and flung it at the little boy. She rattled a sharp sentence at him.

"They will make us clothing," Leoht translated. "Until then we must wait here on the bank. They are going to surround us with screens until our clothes are ready." She was not certain whether to be amused or not. There was more than a bit of menace in the way the little man brandished his knife and in the piping voices of the little folk.

"What do they call this place?" Liza asked.

Leoht said something entirely unlike the speech of their captors. Nonetheless the woman seemed to comprehend.

"Ebba-dad," she replied. She swept her hand again, taking in all the cages and all the surrounding jungle. *"Dad-dad!"*

"Oh!" Leoht exclaimed.

"What?" asked Brann.

"What's the matter?" Liza joined.

"This," Leoht said slowly, "is the city prison."

"Upmah oa sed, blebbed." The woman pointed; she indicated all the little folk in view. Then she indicated the four. *"Blebbed oa!"*

"They are inmates," Leoht told them. "Now she says we are, too."

"I don't understand you, young Brann," Hegman Branlee said. "It is maddening the way you do not accept truth when truth is apparent. Why do you badger me with this constant inside-outside prattle when we know, and we see with the truth before our very eyes, that the inside and outside are the same and that which appears otherwise is simply, a—um—an hallucination."

"A mass hallucination, Hegman?" Brann had asked. "So that I see it and Liza and my friend Halsam see it, and you, too, Hegman Branlee? It appears to you also that outside the city there is land that extends as far as the eye can see and that the city is just a small part of it."

"No, young Brann! It is nonsense. I do not see that, and neither do others, except when their vision plays tricks."

"I don't understand him, Grandmother," Brann said to Ebar. "Can he really not tell that the stretch of Farmy Fields to the mountains is there, that there is a real sky over it, much, much higher than the roof of the city? Doesn't he see it, Grandmother?"

"Do your friends see it?" Ebar asked him.

"Hals and Liza do."

"How do you know it?"

"They told me, Grandmother."

Ebar shook her head. "The eyes lie. Most in the city have never had a view of outside. Even here on Tailend to most folk what Branlee says is the truth. Vision itself is nothing if not given an interpretation by the mind. Perhaps it is so for Liza and Halsam also. What they see and what they tell you they see may not be the same."

She gave him cakes from a little inlaid box. She poured tea from the silver urn—a strange pattern, a gift of the Gads, she would imply when asked, but it was common knowledge that the Gad's *gave* nothing, and the value of this little urn was beyond imagining. More of the mystery about Ebar became clear to Brann as he passed through the reaches of the city. For didn't Ebar have a tapestry on a wall of her seldom-used dining room? And on that tapestry was there not a scene much like the one the dwarf of the Hugens had described, depicting ships on a strange sea larger than the one he crossed in the Post·Guild boat and wilder? The ships only touched the curling tips of waves in that weaving, and their sails caught a sun in an impossibly bright glare. Elsewhere on the tapestry, folk fought with swords and over them the great flank of the city rose.

Also he asked her, "It is said we can't leave the city, Grandmother; why?"

"Why do song finches perch on the verge, Brann? Have you seen one fly away from Tailend?"

"They're afraid, just as the monklers are, bred to captivity and. . . ."

His grandmother smiled, in one hand a saucer, in the other a cup, now away from her lips. Her eyes looked through him as he had seen them do before, and she nodded as if a great truth had been revealed.

"Bred to captivity," Brann said to Liza.

"Eh?" Liza asked. They trooped past a gaping breach in the jail wall where bars were bent outward by the force of some ancient explosion. Through the hole the four could see a stretch of Farmy Fields. A path wound among open cells and through barred gates in the heavy jungles that filled the gallery. Constantly, the little folk passed from gate to gate with endless checking of credentials and endless frisking. Keys rattled and jail doors came open and shut. Jailer and jailed interchangeably, the maintenance of the prison was the little folks' sole occupation. The path Brann and the others walked skirted the opening but didn't go through it into the fields. In fact it bent inward at this point. And Brann saw that the little folk avoided entirely this immense hole in their prison wall. Several of the little ones accompanied them on a trip to *"eh keepla,"* the judge, as Leoht explained the term.

Brann pointed out the hole in the wall. "Why do you think they stay here in this smelly jungle when the Farmy Fields are just outside?"

"It does smell here," Hals agreed. "I think the same thing keeps them here that made us sick when we went outside."

"But they have exits into other galleries," Brann said. "And they don't use those either. We haven't seen them leave. They said that they are inmates here, too. We can leave though. All we need is the boat again."

"Tell me what you mean by 'bred to captivity,'" Liza said.

"It was something my Grandmother Ebar said to me once when I asked why the monklers and the song finches wouldn't leave the city. She said that they had been bred in the city for so long that they had no capacity to understand a larger place outside. The fear of it was born in them and nothing a human did could remove it. They *couldn't* leave!"

The rough-woven cloth of Leoht's skirt clung and moved

on her long legs as the light cloak had once done. Something about her would always be beyond explanation. "You've described the way the mechanics are in the quick place," she said. "Tied there so that we feel as if we will die when we go away."

"You left," Hals said simply. He walked in front of her on the path, complaining now and again that the rough cloth scratched his legs. "I felt better without it," he said.

"It was the rule about nudity that got us into this trouble in the first place," Leoht answered. "They're taking us to see the judge because we broke the rule and they are angry."

"Well," Hals complained, "these stink like the jungle. I'd rather have my Gad's-cloth clothes back."

"It hurt to leave the quick place," Leoht said. "For a time I thought I was dying. I thought it was disease because *alek* were no longer there to repair me. But really I was sick because I was leaving the quick place. That's what you mean, isn't it, Brann?"

Brann stopped suddenly on the path. Immediately from behind the file came a chattering of little folk. A woman the height of Liza's waist stalked up and began chattering excitedly, pointing down the path.

"Let's go," said Hals. "She looks like she wants to do something with that knife."

"I hadn't thought!" Brann said. "Lord above, I just didn't see it at all. It applies to all of us. That was what Grandmother Ebar had wanted me to see last summer. Then I didn't understand. But she smiled because she knew I would understand soon. Something in the way we are born keeps us in the city. It had nothing to do with gates or locks or keys at all. It is our own heads that keep us in the city."

The little woman pushed Brann hard and gestured with her knife, the brass key rattled against other peculiar implements on her belt.

"We should go, Brann," Halsam said. "I think she will stick you."

Brann began walking again. The woman grimaced, squinching up her face as a petulant child might. But this child and her companions were armed. Bright birds flew screaming in a parti-colored storm across the path.

"What of what the Huten said, Brann?" Liza asked.

"Yeah," said Halsam. He put a hand to the jewel which still hung from the woven metal collar he wore. "The Huten said there was a key like this one. If the lock is really inside us, what good would a key do?"

"I don't know," Brann answered. He fell silent and put a hand beneath the rough shirt to scratch a sudden itch. "Maybe Ebar would know," he said at last.

They entered a courtroom beneath the vines. Again Brann had to stifle a laugh because the little folk seemed like children, perched in jury seats too big for them, dark eyes watching. They were crowded twice as many as the chairs would hold, chattering and punching each other, pointing at the four who stood in the leaf-strewn center of the court. The light was yellow-green and the floor was crunchy with the dead leaves. The woman who had brought them made a motion with her knife and Brann began to step forward.

"*Ena*," she cried and motioned only Liza and Leoht toward the judge's bench. She made sitting motions to Brann and Hals, repeating them until the two boys sat.

"I think it's the women who are in charge here," Halsam said. "They carry the keys and give all the orders."

This seemed to be true. The woman with the knife called out, "*Ba doona! Ba doona!*" and at once all the little folk stood. The noise of someone struggling came from behind the judge's bench. A little hand appeared; two, and then a face. The woman climbed into a seat built on top of the bench. She was elderly with graying hair. Her expression was stern. She hefted a gavel large as a sledgehammer and banged it twice. Everyone sat again.

"What do you think they'll do with us, Brann?" Hals asked.

"I don't like the knives," Brann answered. He pointed to the woman. "That one looks like she'd just as soon cut us up."

"I know," Hals whispered. "*That's* what I mean."

Their warder walked up in front of Halsam and stared at him pointedly. She pointed toward the judge and held her hand over her mouth. Then she delivered a stinging slap to Halsam's cheek. The audience of little folk began to jeer. The judge banged her gavel.

"I think we'd better be quiet," Brann said. The woman glared at him and stalked away.

The judge spoke to Leoht and Liza. Leoht answered. The judge tugged at her robes and all at once the little folk were shouting and pointing and making rude noises. The judge made a short speech which the little folk interrupted frequently, thrashing about in the fragrant vines and pointing at the four taller folk. The two girls were taken back to Hals and Brann.

"What did she say?" Hals asked.

"We're guilty," Leoht answered. "She said we were naked and that broke the rules. She said it was *our* fault, mine and Liza's."

"What?" Liza said. "Our fault?"

"We are female, and thus it was our responsibility to see that you two men did what you were supposed to do. She's going to decide on a punishment now."

Meanwhile, the little folk had been throwing trash at the four of them. A piece of rotten fruit hit Halsam on the cheek. He picked it up to throw back. But the woman with the knife looked so fiercely at him that he dropped it. "They are like a crowd of babies," Hals said, disgusted.

The judge hammered the gavel, using both her hands to lift it. *"Ota ve mannata,"* she intoned.

"She confirms the verdict of guilty," Leoht whispered.

The judge consulted a tattered black book. She read from it in the same inflected speech. The others looked at Leoht, who shook her head. "We're going to be put into isolation," Leoht translated. "The judge says we should be grateful. At one time such a disgusting display was punished by death. She says we live in more liberal times now. Instead, they are going to put us into isolation cells for a little while to teach us a lesson."

"How long?" asked Brann.

"Not long for you," Leoht answered. "Since it was our fault, you and Halsam will be jailed for six months. For us, two years."

"Two years," Hals shouted. He got to his feet and pointed at the judge. "You are crazy, you know. We didn't do anything. Not Leoht or Liza either. This isn't fair and so we're just going to leave." He had the same mean look on his face as when he had faced the Driver. But there were many knives here and intelligence in the eyes of those who held them.

"Come on," Halsam said. "They won't put us in cells for all that time. We'll just walk out of here."

Halsam rattled the cell door. "The metal is old," he said. "Maybe we can break it."

"Maybe we could bite through it with our teeth," Liza scoffed.

"Six months!" Brann said.

"For you," Liza answered. "Two years for me and Leoht." They were alone in a long row of empty cells; theirs alone was locked. Vines climbed the bars and the floor was two inches deep in dead leaves.

"It smells like the parkplat after gardeners have watered it," Halsam complained. "It makes my nose itch."

"Some gardener you are," Brann answered.

The little folk would come by, sometimes bringing their children to stare at the tall folk in the cell. The children were like the first little boy they had seen, tiny with feet so big they should have been incapable of walking. One tiny girl had offered Brann a biscuit the size of his thumbnail. Her great dark eyes had watched solemnly as he ate it.

"They treat us like animals in a Gad's menagerie," Liza protested. She grimaced at the row of little faces peering in through the bars. She snapped at them and lunged toward the front of the cell. The little folk laughed. "I hate this," she said. "Won't they ever give us a bath?"

Halsam had found a loose support for what once had been a bunk. They slept on the floor in the now crushed leaves and used the rough blanket which was of the same material as their clothes. A slop bucket in the back corner of their cell was their toilet, and a basin caught water from a broken dripping pipe. Their meals were small and consisted of fruit and sometimes pieces of fowl which might have been from the ever-present bright-colored birds. With the metal support Halsam worked at the concrete until his hands were raw. A small groove began to grow in the concrete floor near one bar.

"We'll be out in six months," Brann commented. "Do you think you will be done by then?"

"What are you doing to get out?" Halsam demanded.

"Nothing, I guess," Brann said.

During the nights, when the moon lamps shone a filtered blue light through the high jungle canopy, they all huddled together and joined for a time in the way that Leoht had taught them, forgetting that they were in a cell within a prison, within a gallery and tier of a city that towered over them three miles and from which, not city, tier, gallery, prison, or cell, could they escape.

A man came with their meals. They called him Birdeyes because his eyes were always moving like the eyes of the birds which perched on the cells. He was like a bird, anyway, parroting exactly the same thing every time: *"Ecca, ecca, se tallu oa."* (Eat, eat, it's all you get.) The food came in a tiny pail which might have held enough for the little folk, but for them it was nothing—they were starving. Leoht told Birdeyes so on several occasions but he only stood on his big splay feet bobbing his head and grinning and waiting for them to gobble the contents of the pail.

"We won't last six months," Brann moaned. "We'll starve in two!"

"Maybe the jewel will work on this lock," Liza said to Hals. But the red jewel remained dark. The lock was too simple for such a device.

One day, some two weeks after their captivity had begun, they heard Birdeyes coming along the row of empty cells. Doors clanged as usual and they could hear the clatter of the pail as he banged it repeatedly against the bars. "It tastes as though he had put it through a food mixer," Halsam protested once.

This time other footsteps accompanied his. It was one of those mornings when the water of the central lagoon gave off a mist which lay low in the corridors of the jail. Through it those coming first appeared as unformed shadows.

"He has some people with him," Leoht said. "I don't think they are of the little folk." Her eyes still had a far-seeing ability which could use something other than light for vision. "Those with him are taller and they carry longer knives. I see a pattern they wear, like a flower."

"Eh?" said Brann. He sat up from where he had been carving his initials into the floor with a bent screw. "You can't mean that; it's impossible."

The figures drew closer and the mist obscured them less. They stopped before the cell. Brann's sight passed over Birdeyes and up the rose-colored Gad's cloth that those behind him wore, up to the rosette patch and shoulder bags above short swords. The one in front was a woman with dark tight curls and skin the color of chocolate. She was perhaps his mother's age.

"Post Folk!" Brann exclaimed.

For a long moment nothing further was said; the four in the cell staring out, Birdeyes and the two Post Folk looking in. The man was one of the blonds from the city's roof, of whom Brann had seen many during the Pilgrimage's beginning. His hand didn't stray far from the hilt of his sword. The woman was looking at Halsam, particularly at the jewel. Tension brought clear the muscles of her face, made her lips bloodless and brought to them the slightest of smiles.

The blond man spoke in the Tailend speech with an accent closer to Brann's than to that of the city's roof. "I told you," he said. "A master key, and it was said they'd all long since been destroyed. You've led us quite a chase." This last to Halsam.

"Is it a master key and functional?" the woman asked. "We must be sure." She took a flat, many-buttoned instrument from her belt and touched it once. Instantly the jewel lit with a terrific ruby brilliance and a vibration seemed to pass through the solid concrete of the floor. Halsam staggered and clutched at the bars. Spontaneously the light faded. "Lord above!" Halsam gasped.

The Post Folk began to laugh, first the woman, then, seeing her delight, the man. Their stern façade relaxed and so they slipped down to the aisle floor where they laughed until they seemed incoherent. Birdeyes bounced back and forth on his feet, saying "Eh? Eh?" and grinning moronically.

The woman's laughter subsided. "Where did you come by the key?" she asked Halsam.

"The Driver," Hals answered.

"Driver?"

"Folk like animals," said Hals, "dragging a cart, a hundred or more of them. This crazy Driver with a whip bossed them. He wore this." He indicated the jewel.

"He hated us for taking it," Liza said. "He chased us for a long time."

"It would be true," the woman said. "Only one so retrogressed could hold a master key without bringing it above threshold."

"For so long?" asked the man.

"Who knows?"

"What are you talking about?" Hals asked.

"You are wearing a master key," the woman told him.

"I know," said Hals.

The woman raised an eyebrow at that. "Then do you know that the last master key was thought lost more than three thousand years ago. It was thought to have been destroyed in a raid by the Guard."

"Guard?" Brann questioned.

"The Huten as you call them."

"I know," said Liza. "We saw them. One named Oten was very interested in the jewel. He seemed to want it but he didn't take it from Hals."

"Guard?" the woman responded. "Where did you encounter them?" The tension had returned to her face. Her whole stance altered and the man stood suddenly straighter; the hand near his sword hilt tightened.

"Toward Tailend," Hals explained. "We were running from the Driver. The Huten were in a gallery of their own, between tiers."

"Post Folk were fighting them," Liza added. "It was a very great fight." (She had no word for war.) "A dwarf of the Huten helped us to get away down an elevator." She watched the woman's face. "Don't you *know* about it? Don't you talk to the Post Folk of Tailend?"

"I haven't for a very long time," the woman answered.

The man bent close and said something low into the woman's ear. She held up a hand but he spoke again, insistent. She nodded. "Lar reminds me that that Guard will also be following and will find you as we have found you, unless we take you out of here soon." She reached through the bars to touch the jewel.

"Tell me, your name is Hals?" she asked.

"Halsam in full."

"What do you feel when the key lights?"

"Warm, full of vibration, as if my arms and legs were asleep and were coming back to life."

"Have you had the key off since you found it?"

"Not for long," said Halsam. "It gave me a strange sensation. It felt like something was being pulled out of me."

"It is synchronized to his thought pattern," the woman said. "Once, perhaps, it was known how to alter that. But we don't know and from what you have said, it appears that the Guard don't. It is possible that things are not in such a dangerous state as you might think, Lar."

The mist had cleared and in the stretch of cells a light grew, coming from the breach in the city's outer wall. The birds called and from somewhere came a perfume that might have been of the woman and might have been of the Farmy Fields outside.

"Can you ask them to release us?" Leoht asked. She had been the most affected by the captivity; that dead metal should act *so*, should not respond. She hated it.

The woman turned to Birdeyes. *"Aloe; ecceve danyada te?"*

"Te?"

"Aloe!" She pointed and her hand moved toward the hilt of her sword. Birdeyes bobbed back down the row of cells, still grinning and saying *"Te? Te?"* to himself.

"What is there of such great importance about the key?" Liza asked. "What could make such a difference after three thousand years?"

"It will bring them back," the woman said.

"It will take our message to those who left us here," the man continued.

"It will tell them that we are at long last ready," the woman said.

"It will bring the change."

In all this a peculiar sensation came to Brann. He had heard such a way of speaking before. It was the way of Sabbath services and it was the way Hegman Branlee spoke. . . . It was a litany which had lost all meaning (except that the Post Folk still knew the meaning) and they said together:

"The key will take us where we may speak to them again. Such a place was lost when the key was lost. The key will find it for us again."

"This is all a riddle," Liza protested. "Who are they you say left us here? Why were we left? What will be changed?"

The woman and the man of the Post Guild exchanged looks of wonder. "Truthfully," the man said, "they do not know!"

A woman of the little folk appeared, following Birdeyes irritably down the aisle. Birdeyes pointed. The woman chattered at the Post Folk. The Post Guildswoman answered. The little woman shrugged and put a key to the cell lock. The door swung open.

"Come," the Post woman said to the four in the cell. "We will try to explain these mysteries. But you must see something first. It will explain more than we can tell you in words."

BOOK THREE

Chapter One

Frontend

Whole galleries had fallen here, whole tiers. Blocks of the city stood upended and broken. Pressed among them as if preserved were the remains of houses, parks and stores. A thin soil had collected; in the years plants and trees had taken root. Frontend fell away in a long, lowering sweep toward the ocean. Where the substance of the city had resisted collapse, galleries stood, sometimes many levels above the slope. Perhaps twenty miles of the city extended this way toward the ocean whose verge was strangely flesh-toned.

Clara, the dark-skinned woman of the Post Folk, showed them this. "You see how the city ends," she said. "We are as far frontward as habitable galleries extend. From here on, it is a ruin."

"How?" asked Liza. She had not expected *this*.

"The shaking," said Lar. "The mass of the city is incalculable. Only Structors can say how much weight presses down upon the rock beneath. It is broken rock here; Foundations do not hold so well in it."

"Rock slipped and shook," Clara said. "There were earthquakes before over the centuries and pieces of the city tumbled, tier by tier. Here, over a broken place in the stone, a fault the Structors call, the city pressed with great weight. The fault slipped bit by bit and broke the city in two."

They stood on a verge seventeen tiers up from the Farmy Fields in the mouth of a vast conduit which fell gradually behind them toward the gallery of the city prison. From where

177

they stood a path wound among the upturned blocks of the city, down the slope toward the distant ocean. At their backs the broken face of the city was still a hundred tiers high.

"Where are the folk?" Brann asked. From end to end the city was empty. The pilgrims had come to Frontend; but he was at Frontend now and there were no pilgrims.

"You see them," Clara said.

"I don't see anyone," Liza answered.

"Yes you do," Lar said. "Look there, past the last bit of the city, there where the stone seems to become flesh before the ocean begins. Those are the folk."

"But it's like an ocean itself," Liza told him.

"Those?" said Brann. If perspective was true then the mass of folk at the far front of the city was impossibly large.

"Is it all the folk of the city?" Brann asked.

"All," said Lar.

"So that's where they went on Pilgrimage?" Liza wondered.

"Yes," said Lar.

"*Yes,*" Halsam mimicked, "*you see them.* By the Lord above, can't either of you tell us how it happened? You said you would explain just as soon as you showed us this."

"That's true," Leoht said. "Tell us."

Lar looked at Clara. She shrugged. "It makes no difference to tell them," she said.

"Yes, true," said Lar. He looked to the four, taking time to choose his words. "What you see is the end of the Pilgrimage. You know some of this? That the city was constructed as a refuge? You know that the place where the city stands is a small part of an immense land which is one of a number on this world. . . ."

"Yes," interrupted Liza. "The sun is a star among many and the planet circles it and so on. Hegman Branlee would protest it but what we have seen so far makes the myth seem true. Certainly the city moves as the myth told."

"It moved once," Hals commented.

"I will tell you if you wish to know," Lar said. "If not . . ."

"Let him go on," Leoht said. "I want to know."

"Do you know, then, that this planet was savaged by folk before the time of the city and that few remained except on this part of the planet? It was decided in a great council of all the folk to leave this world, the Earth it is called, and it would remain alone until it could heal."

Clara took up the tale. "The folk of the time knew the process of travel among the stars and by this process they departed, setting watchmen nearby on island worlds the folk created. The watchmen were to return once in a thousand years and report upon the progress of the Earth's healing. And when the Earth was healed in its abundance and life had returned, then the watchmen would alert the folk of Earth, wherever they had scattered, and those who wished to return could."

"Then the folk have gone away and returned," said Brann, "because I see that everything outside is grown and healthy. Since the folk all left and the folk are here now, then we are the folk." And he wanted to know why the city? Why did it exist, if the Earth was healed and ready to take back the folk who had left long ago? What was the purpose of the city? He put the question to Clara.

"Yes, the Earth is ready," she agreed. "It has been thirty thousand years since the folk left. But they haven't returned and this is the fault of the Guard."

"You see," Lar interjected, "all the folk did not leave. Already at the time there were people who could not go out of their cities, who fell sick when they did so, and became filled with a terror they couldn't explain. Do you suppose that if they couldn't bring themselves to leave their cities they could travel to another world? This city was constructed as a refuge for them and they were placed here under the authority of the watchmen, who then also became known as the Guard."

"We stayed behind," said Clara.

"They promised a change," said Lar.

"When the folk returned from the stars," said Clara.

"We would be set free," said Lar.

They had fallen into a chant that seemed to be a dimly related version of the tongue of Tailend, and Brann saw that Halsam was fascinated. Hals held the jewel as he watched and a strange intelligence seemed to have come to him, somehow gained from this incomplete and circuitous tale of the Post Folk. The jewel played some part.

"Clara," Brann said loudly, "the jewel, the key, what of it?"

"The jewel?" Her cheeks were moist as if she had been crying in her ecstasy.

"Please," said Brann, "the jewel."

"We are the Post Guild, set to post the message to the Guard that the change is complete." She stopped, a bit dazed. She took a deep breath. "I'm sorry you don't understand what this means to us. I am only beginning to grasp the notion that the lost key has been found. The prophecy has been fulfilled. The city is at last falling as we were told it would in the time when the folk went to the stars. Now we have it, the key which will allow us to post the message to the folk. I can hardly tell you what it means."

"Listen," said Lar, "the Guard became barbarians over the millennia. They fought among themselves in their island worlds and lost knowledge of how to speak to the folk, and they came to the Earth to the city not to inspect progress of the Earth but only to claim tribute. Somewhere in the city is a post station where we can speak to the stars and call the folk home. It has been lost since before the memory of anyone known. It has been lost since before any surviving history records. The Guards were issued master keys to help them find their way through the city and into the secret places designed only for them. But the last master key was lost three thousand years ago, during a time of great turmoil in the city. The post station is somewhere in the city, sealed and hidden, but the master key will lead us to it."

Halsam sneered. "I have the master key. It is locked to me."

"That's true," said Clara. "You will wear the key and give it the force to lead us to the station."

"Why should I?" Halsam asked suddenly. "What is the point of my going with you?"

"Why?" asked Clara. "I don't understand. You must do it. It's our freedom, all of ours."

"If what you say is true," Hals answered, "it will only bring back to Earth the very folk who ruined it in the first place. Do you want me to be a part of this?"

"You have no choice," said Lar.

"I have plenty of choice. I'll go back to my folk with Leoht, Brann and Liza."

"Your folk are trapped the same way we are," Lar said.

"The terrific fear that shut the earliest city dwellers away from the Earth is still in all of us today. You tried to leave the city, didn't you?"

Halsam nodded.

"And what happened?"

"We got sick," said Hals.

"Yes," said Clara. "And do you see them?" She pointed toward the horizon where the flesh-colored tide was on the beach. "Those are the folk. The city is in ruins. The shaking will come again as it did not long ago. Soon all the city will have tumbled upon itself and the folk will still be there on the edge of the ocean, fearful to go anywhere else."

"Do you know how many folk there are? More than twenty-five million, all the folk of the city. They have tried to escape from themselves. They can't do it. The key can do it. The key will bring the others back from the stars. It will set us free."

Brann stepped forward. "We'll see for ourselves first," he said. "We'll speak to our families and the others of our tier and then we'll tell you whether or not we will go with you to find this station and try to send the message."

Liza nodded and stood closer to Brann. Leoht came to them, and Halsam, nodding curtly, stepped away from the Post Folk toward the other three.

"No!" said Lar. "We cannot wait. The Guard are but a short way behind us and the city is falling about our ears. We must go now!"

"I won't," said Halsam.

Lar's sword sprang to view; its force, beyond that of mere metal, confronted them. Singing wind seemed to blow through Brann, taking away his strength and bringing him to his knees.

"Don't cause us to harm you," said Clara. "This is not how we desire it to be."

Hals sagged, but still he shook his head. "I will stay with them. . . ."

Clara's face tightened, becoming fierce. "Take him," she snapped to Lar. Lar's sword flickered. Halsam sagged more; he stumbled. Lar grabbed him by the arm. Together with Clara he began pulling Halsam back into the conduit.

"Don't follow," Lar warned. And Clara waved an instrument from her pouch. A massive partition began sliding down over the face of the conduit while Lar and Clara stood with swords poised.

Leoht called Halsam's name and, oblivious of the pointing swords, she rushed forward. Lar stared back through a space now too small for a person to enter in wind that grew very swift and cold. "Halsam!" Leoht cried. In a way that Brann could not imagine, Leoht summoned some of the force that had sustained her in the quick place. She was at the closing partition and into the opening, though it was very small.

Her hand waved toward Brann and Liza. She called, "Please follow and help us." Then the partition closed entirely, taking Halsam, the Post Folk and Leoht from sight.

Brann seized a rail from a fallen stairway and battered at the partition which was like the door of a vault and gave back not even the slightest interior echo. He and Liza worried at the door until the sun had come high over fallen Frontend.

"It has no handle," Liza said, "nothing to make it open."

"I think they forced Hals to use the jewel," Brann said. He ran a finger over the faint scratches left on the door by all their effort.

"We could climb up," Liza said. She pointed toward the archways of an open gallery two upward from where they stood. "Part of a stair is left. If we entered there, we might be able to find where they went."

"Maybe," said Brann. But where to start? The Post Folk had the jewel to guide them and even two tiers up the city was so different that no one could tell where the Post Folk might be. Only the Huten could follow. They had devices to make use of the jewel.

"The Huten will be at the shore at summer's end," Brann said. "They will know how to follow Hals."

"Do you want to go back to the Huten?"

"No, I want nothing to do with them at all. But I think they're the only way."

"Your Grandmother Ebar?" Liza asked.

"Ebar?" Could *she* be there? He recalled the light of her tower room still burning in the window as they had left the gallery. Had she gone on Pilgrimage after all? "Certainly the

Huten would know the way. But maybe Ebar, too," Brann agreed.

"But twenty-five million," Liza said. "Do you think we can ever find our own folk among them?"

Brann shook his head.

A road of sorts continued on from the mouth of the conduit. In places it was a bare gray stone some unknown folk had laid in the roadbed. Where the stone gave out, the road was of yellowish compacted dust. It led in the general direction of the shore, winding through upturned blocks of the city, some of them as high as the mountains' crags and rough with the protrusions of conduits and houseplat foundations. Once, a highroad climbed above them along the underside of a gallery block. Once, a rise of galleries, six tiers high, blocked the direct way west and, eerily, sunlamps still shone within the tiers and the green of a parkplat overhung the verge through broken arches. Liza pointed. "I thought I saw a face." But the face, if it was that, didn't reappear though they continued to have the sensation of folk watching them.

The sky was clean of clouds; it was high, bright blue with a brilliant sun. Beneath it Brann began to feel the edges of that anxiety which had driven them back into the city before. Here it seemed not so great.

"The outside sickness is getting me again," Brann said to Liza. "Do you feel it?"

"A little," she answered. "But we've been outside so long. Why do you think we don't feel it more?"

"We're not really out of the city," said Brann. "It's ruined but there are still pieces of galleries here and everything of the city."

"Everything but folk," Liza noted. "Why would they gather at the ocean away from the city when it is still possible to live here and not feel the fear?"

"I don't know."

It was afternoon. The sun hung out over the water above a wall of distant cloud. As it did in the mountains visible from Tailend, beams of the sunlight broke through the cloud like lighted columns resting on the ocean. A light wind came up from the faroff water carrying a strange smell of salt, smoky and rich. Liza slapped at the yellow dust which coated her legs knee high. She shifted the skirt and scratched beneath the jacket. Brann had his shirt off, tied about his waist. Liza seemed reluctant, as if coming back to folk who might know her brought back the old taboos. She opened the jacket buttons, though, to let the breeze dry her skin. She sat on the upturned curb of a section of highroad and took out from a bag the last bit of fruit that the little folk had given them for their journey. Brann joined her, sucking water out of a birdskin bag.

"We still have water," he said. "But this is the last of what we have to eat." He looked at the tumbled masonry where there was nothing growing that might be eaten. (Edibles were there, but Brann didn't know it; and were Halsam here, who was of the Guild of Gardeners, he could have pointed here, where the wild variety of the potato bushed up its greenery and the tomato vine hid among a fallen houseplat's walls and where other food plants invited if they could only know. The interior of the galleries had been great expanses of garden.)

"Maybe we'll find people who can give us something to eat," Liza said. "Do you see? I think there are wheel tracks on the road." She pointed to the parallel grooves two strides apart in the dust. "I saw those a while ago but they disappeared on the stone. Now they're back."

"A power cart?" Brann questioned. But these tracks were narrower than a power cart's. They were also recent; the wind had not smoothed them yet. Between the wheel tracks were other marks, perhaps the prints of many feet.

The wheel tracks continued and now they rode over other tracks of wheels; between all these were more footprints, some of them human, some more like crescents as of some larger four-footed animal. The road cut through high mounds of rubble here and Brann had a sense of familiarity that made him uneasy. He had seen such a road and such wheel tracks before. But he couldn't bring himself to believe it. A wagon had passed here, many wagons once (or one wagon many times; it was this Brann refused to think of). And the wagon was not powered by itself like the carts on the home highroad. Something pulled the wagon, and it was four-footed (or two-footed and many).

"This is like the gallery where we met the Driver," Liza said finally.

Brann halted. Did he hear the motion of wagon wheels and the slow wordless chant? No, absolutely not.

"I think a wagon is moving a long way on down the road," Liza said. "I hear it."

"It can't be the Driver," Brann answered. "We left him in that sealed gallery a long way back toward Tailend. He couldn't be here."

"We're here," said Liza. "He's stupid, but he could do it if we did."

"No!" Brann protested. "It's someone else. The Driver is gone. Probably he is dead."

They walked, but more carefully, and they watched down the side paths into the overgrown rubble. The sun dropped steadily toward the cloud-banked horizon and shadows grew longer in ruined Frontend.

Now sunset came. Dawn seen from Tailend was nothing to this. In their dawns the sun rose over the mountains already high in the sky and the sky itself was already bright. Only pale reds and violets ran through the mountain clouds. The air of sunset was pure yellow from a sun which lay on the clouds before them. It caught in Liza's hair and in her woven dress like the colors of the trees outside in fall. (Another thing Brann didn't understand—the trees inside the city were always green. Seasons hardly meant a thing to Brann.) The ruts in the road grew deeply shadowed. The westering wind dropped away.

Brann heard Liza exclaim, watching the slow spread of carmine across the clouds and the bright disk of the sun turn scarlet. The light shrank across the water, setting the waves in relief. In one instant the sky, which was red, became violet and the ocean a single lighted line. After the sun was down they looked out over the cobalt ocean for a long time watching the sky darken to black. Here, with no roof at all over them, the stars were clear and close. Brann thought of the Post Folk's words that people from this planet were out among these stars and that closer still were island worlds in the light of the sun they had just watched set. The Huten were on these islands, islands above them, not islands in any water ocean at all. Not long after the sun set, a full moon rose over the broken body of the city behind them. It lit the masonry in the same blue-white light as that cast by the moon lamps inside. In the generations that folk had lived in the interior did they know that this moon had a face? Did they learn this anew each time Tailend came to their gallery? Did they forget it each time they Pilgrimaged to Frontend and into the interior once more?

Brann did not feel tired. He saw that Liza didn't either. So they walked on. He didn't want to stop or sleep in this open place. The moon was bright as the moon lamps and the road clearly lit. Like stars, a sea of lights took shape on the distant beach, tiny and warm, like distant fires.

"Do you see?" Liza said later. "A fire!" The arches of a single gallery stood out of the rubble. A wall reflected still another fire, flickering, and voices came from this direction. "Is it the Driver?" Liza asked.

Brann listened to the voices. Were there intelligible words in the speech or was it the mindless woofing of the dumb folk?

"I think they're speaking," Brann said. "It's other folk, not the Driver."

"We have to see," said Liza. "Let's get closer."

Stepping very quietly in the soft dust of the road, they moved toward a small path between broken walls. Monklers were in the stunted trees somewhere about, and they made soft worried noises as Brann and Liza passed.

"They'll hear," Liza said.

"They'll think we're only monklers," Brann told her. "Anyway, we have to find out."

A broken wall climbed at an angle up toward the arch, and Brann climbed on hands and knees up the rough stone. Liza came right behind him. Laughter rang once near the fire and a delicious odor blew their way.

Liza whispered, "It's not the Driver. They don't eat that way."

"Shhhhhhh!" Brann said. "They're talking; I want to hear what is being said."

He heard, but only sound not sense, and it scared him until he discovered that this was not a babble. It was a strange tongue, one not of Tailend, and yet one Brann had heard before. He scrambled up onto the flat piece of a roof overhanging the fire and edged out to where he could see.

"Oh!" he said.

Liza came up beside him. "The Driver?" she asked.

"No," answered Brann, "it's Gads."

In the warm moving light of a great fire was a family of Gads. They were laughing and talking and passing about bowls of a stew scooped from a soot-black pot hanging near the fire. At the edge of the fire circle an immense caravan was parked. Long-faced quadrupeds with bushy tails and powerful legs and flanks nosed into a tub of grain.

"Those are horses!" Liza said. "They pulled the wagon, not any dumb folk. It's just some Gads and horses."

A vast, barrel-chested man climbed up from his seat by the fire and stared up toward Brann and Liza.

"If it is Tailend folk I hear speaking. Come," he said in the thick tsingaro accent, "food is here and a warm fire. Will you come?"

"They're only Gads," said Brann. And he smelled the aroma of the food and needed nothing further to call him.

"So you're going to the water where all the people are?" the Gad asked. "A very hard sort of traveling."

"We've been a long way already," Liza said.

"So you've told me," the Gad answered. "So you've told me." He cogitated on this a moment. "All is empty now, you say. None of the folk left?"

"None," Brann said.

"All went to Pilgrimage?"

"After the shaking they all went," Liza answered.

"We walked through the city," Brann added. "The galleries are empty. Is it true they are all at the shore of the ocean?"

"Yes, true," said the Gad. "Yes, true." He watched his son—they were identical, young Gad and older, big, barrel-chested, dark-haired and strong—ladle out a bowl of stew and watched with growing exasperation as the young man simply plopped himself down on a stone slab by the fire and made as if to eat.

"*Kayva sa?*" the older Gad said. "Fogbrain, serve the guests first." He snapped a finger resoundingly onto the boy's skull. "Learns nothing," he explained sadly to Brann and Liza. "Boy has no manners, nothing!" (Boy? Hulking next to

Brann, though just Brann's age.) He sucked at a tooth and then sulkily moved to bring Liza the bowl. They were five in the Gad family. "The family Zolbek," the old Gad had said. "I am Zolbek, my son Scote, my daughter Rinka (not so dumb as Scote but no genius either), my wife, my charm Tesa, and her mother (a toothless old woman smiled) Blimba; also the horses Yakan and Vakan, who are after all in the family."

The stew was mostly meat! Brann hardly believed it. How could Gads, wanderers, be so wealthy? "There is a lot of meat in this stew," Brann said.

"Yes, meat; you don't like meat? We have bread, too. Rinka, bread for the folk. Scote, take away the bowls; they don't want meat." The Gad waved his arms and both children scurried at once.

"No," said Brann. "Meat was scarce in the city. We've not often seen so much."

Zolbek puckered his lips. "You *like* meat?"

"Very much," Liza answered.

"Then more meat, Fogbrain. Don't you see they are starving!"

"Please," Liza protested, "what we have is fine."

"Enough meat?"

"Yes," said Brann.

"Enough potatoes and such?"

"Most definitely," said Liza.

"And bread?" The Gad offered a thin loaf like a spear, a knife poised in his other hand to cut more.

"Enough of everything," said Brann.

"Ah," said the Gad, "then maybe you should eat."

The old woman Blimba leaned forward. She sopped at her stew with a piece of bread and gummed it into submission. She rattled a long sentence in tsingaro to Brann.

"Eh?" Brann said. He looked toward Zolbek. Zolbek set down his spoon. "My beloved mother-in-law wishes to know how in all the crowd of folk you will find your families."

"Are there really that many?" Liza asked. She, like Brann, had no real conception of the numbers, of several tens of millions of folk on the beach.

"So many?" said the Gad. "How to explain it?" He wiped a hand over his face in thought. Then he held that hand away outstretched as if trying to visualize those numbers in the five spread fingers. "So many folk are at the ocean that if you looked at a different face each second and did not stop looking, all day, every day, except to sleep, and then arose to start again the next day, for a whole year, you would not see all of them. They are rivers of folk and seas of folk so that you do not see even from high on the city all of them north and south. Some in the water stand and would go farther but the water is too deep. Some in the broken front end of the city stand, but they will not go back inside."

"Afraid," said Scote. "Every one of them is afraid."

His father glowered. Scote stuffed a full spoon into his mouth.

The old woman asked another question.

"My wife's venerated mother has asked me to ask you why they are afraid. They are a sea of folk themselves. Why do they cower at the shore when all the land and the Farmy Fields are open to them?"

Brann tried to explain the fear that he and Liza felt when they stepped out of the city under no more roof than the sky.

"Doesn't the bigness make you afraid?" Liza asked the Gad. "Don't you feel the emptiness out there with no walls anywhere and no ceiling between you and the sky?"

Rinka giggled. "Who is afraid of the stars?" she asked. "It is all beautiful, isn't it?"

A glow was on the sky past the broken walls of the gallery where they camped. The glow was from the fires, Zolbek said. The fires were of the camps of the folk who gathered so tightly packed that all could not lie down at the same time and so that they had no room for shelter but were all pressed in together and had had no desire for privacy.

"They are like people no longer." Zolbek's wife, Tesa, joined for the first time. "We go there no longer. We will come to the city no longer if what you say is true."

"You're not going to the folk on the shore?" Liza asked. "That was the direction you were headed in. We were following you for a long way."

"*Nefek!*" Zolbek spat. "An evil thing moves among them now."

"What?" said Liza.

"A *nefek,* an evil one. He is mounted so, on a great rolling junk heap, all skin and bones and filth he is."

"And one like him dances at his feet, a little one," added Rinka, "with many pulling his cart."

"Very stupid folk pulling it," Scote said. "More stupid even that my father believes me to be."

Zolbek sputtered (but perhaps he hid a grin).

Brann caught Liza's glance and there was no need to speak.

"Yes, many folk pulling," Rinka continued. "I would not think he needs so many."

"Many pulling?" Brann asked. "How many?"

"A thousand, possibly more. Many join to pull all the time."

"Lord above," Liza interjected.

"What reason have they to join?" Rinka asked. "I saw city folk watch a time then drop what they had to pull the *nefek.*"

"I told you," Liza said to Brann. "Halsam should have killed him then, or you should have." To Rinka: "There is something in his head that makes your thoughts muddy, and you join him. He almost got our friend Halsam."

"The Driver," Brann whispered. He stirred aimlessly at his stew.

"You know of the *nefek?*" Zolbek asked.

"Yes," said Brann, "I know him. I've seen him face to face." But how had the Driver escaped from the sealed gallery and come to Frontend? There were many unknown ways in the city, though, and if the Post Guild knew them and the Huten, why not the Driver?

"Why don't they stop him?" Liza asked. "You say there are so many of the city folk. Why don't they just force him away?"

"They think no longer," Zolbek answered. "Do you not understand? It is not city folk any longer on the ocean shore. It is just frightened animals, like Yakan who is a horse only and has no brains. Yes? You are finished eating? Scote, Rinka, clear away. We will talk of other things; we will smoke." He pulled a capacious pipe from one pocket and a pouch from another. He filled the pipe. Tobacco was a small crop in the city folk's gardens, but not so fine and mellow as this. Brann didn't smoke, nor did Liza, but Liza's father did—cigars, not a pipe. The Gad offered the pipe around and found no takers save his son Scote who smoked it because his father did and seemed not at all pleased at the necessity.

"Where will you go if you aren't going to the city?" Liza asked.

"To south." Zolbek pointed. "A long time south where Farmy Fields are not seen."

"Are there other Gads there?" Liza asked.

"Oh, yes, many Gads are there," Scote said. He puffed and choked a bit. Zolbek took the pipe back with a frown.

"Gads live outside the city?" Brann asked. He couldn't imagine it. Never, sitting on the verge of Tailend, watching out over the Farmy Fields had he thought that *folk* might live out there somewhere. He knew only of the huge mechanical dolls that brought harvest to the city. Were they bringing it to the folk at the shore? How were these folk eating? They had no gardens there, no organized distribution of food. He recalled the greasy bag of flesh from which the Driver doled food to his dumb folk. He thought of the Gads' description of folk joining the Driver's cart. He put the thought very quickly aside.

"There are very few of us when held up to the number of the city folk," the Gad said. "We took trade among the tiers in the city to have the tools and such that we do not make. We travel here, but south we have towns where we have spent many years."

"Many years," Brann repeated, "without a roof or walls at all." A feeling such as the one he had felt when first he had ventured outside came to him again, setting the stars to reeling and the fire to a fierce flaming. Liza saw this and quietly took his hand.

In the morning after they had breakfasted, Brann and Liza helped the Gads repack the caravan. It was a wonder of detail with nooks and cabinets and shelves all fitted so cunningly that none—perhaps not the Gads themselves—could have seen first time what it all contained. In helping repack the dinner table, which folded into a compact shelf that fitted for a traveling meal board, Brann moved aside a bundle of bedclothes. He saw a dark-jeweled surface and blinked at it once before Scote whistled quickly. Rinka dropped a pan with a clatter and when Brann turned again, the jewels were hidden. But it was such as Brann had seen before, like the panels of the Post Folk. Deep lights had moved within it. The Gads were more than they had seemed.

The horses stepped placidly into the traces and Scote hitched them to the caravan.

"You may ride," Tesa said. "We will go far toward the ocean before we turn south."

Brann and Liza waited for the Gads to find their accustomed traveling places. Blimba carefully settled herself into a high-backed padded seat. She smacked her lips once and bared her gums to grin at Brann in invitation. Brann helped Liza to a seat which folded out beneath the opened roof of the caravan.

"Do you have names besides your first names?" Tesa asked. "Of what families are you?"

"My family name is Brewker," Liza said.

"Adelbran, my name is Brann Adelbran."

"Adelbran?" Blimba spoke up. *"Adelbran, madzel sphut? Ebar Adelbran?"*

"She wishes to know if you are related to Ebar Adelbran," Tesa said. "You will pardon my mother, she speaks the Tailend tongue well, but most times she refuses to use other than Tsingaro."

"Ebar?" Brann asked. "She is my grandmother. Do you know her?"

"Ebar Adelbran, your grandmother?" There was a swift conference among the Gads.

"A remarkable thing," said Zolbek, "a remarkable thing indeed."

The great horses leaned easily into the traces and the caravan eased into a steady rolling motion. It felt not unlike the motion of the boat over the city's inner sea. Brann watched the passing view of tumbled galleries through which the road wound as through cliffs and ravines (even the rubble of Frontend was half a mile deep). Monklers played in it in bands infinitely larger than those in the Tailend gardens, and birds—the tame city finches—mostly yellow birds, winged among the ruined galleries. The birds ventured out and cried, startled at the caravan. They scolded the monklers and seemed not unpleased that folk no longer filled the city.

Brann soon became bored with the city, whose character here never changed. Only the sky seemed terrible, entirely uncovered and deep. Brann and Liza settled back beneath the caravan's open roof.

Zolbek had noted the gait of the horses and, satisfied, had handed the reins to Scote.

"You never said," Brann commented to him, "how you come to know my grandmother."

"Oh," Zolbek laughed, "we know her. Do not fear, we know her."

"What is that supposed to mean?" Liza asked, annoyed.

"It means," Zolbek said, "that we have had dealings with Ebar many times past."

"With Ebar?" Brann inquired. He thought of the Gads' gifts to her.

"Where do you suppose she comes from?" Zolbek asked. He cupped his chin; he smiled between fingers.

"You're saying she's a Gad?" Brann asked.

Liza protested, "She doesn't have the Gad features. She's different from the Gads; how could his grandmother . . . ?"

"No?" asked Zolbek.

"Zolbek," Tesa said to him, "do not tease. Tell them."

Zolbek grimaced as if a good tale had been interrupted, as if the telling were as important as the tale. He massaged his face again and grumbled deep in his barrel chest.

"No," he said, "she is no Gad. But other folk live with us there." He waved southward. "And some come back to the city from there. They speak Tsingaro and they know the outside. Some such came one time seventy, eighty years since. I don't know how many, exactly. One family came back to the city for important reasons, and with them a child, Ebar."

Ebar? All the talks in the green room returned to Brann. What of the tales about the Driver and of the first storm she had seen and her fear and her father's fear? If Ebar had been born *outside*, then it was all just a scheme of stories told— and why tell stories but to tease a boy's mind and why tease a mind but to discover if it would respond and understand?

"How old," he asked Zolbek, "how old was my grandmother Ebar when she came to the city?"

Zolbek looked to his mother-in-law who had been following the conversation greedily. She rubbed fingers together.

She nodded, counting in her mind. "Seven," she said in a thick accent. "We were children together, she was seven years old and she left."

"Why, she knew, Ebar knew, while she told me stories and let me go out into the city, she knew!" And he wondered what more she knew and where in *that* he would find her. For the road came straighter about now and headed down a long, slow slope toward the ocean. It was an ocean of folk first, miles distant still. But now Brann could see they were individual folk. Liza touched his cheek. He didn't see an end to them in their stretch along the ocean where long white lines which Brann didn't even know were breakers came in toward the folk. Folk walked among the breakers, countless, on the shore.

Chapter Two

The Folk

The Driver's procession came down the road like a human river. The trolley tracks glinting in the center of the road were obscured by the oncoming people. No more was the procession a hundred diminished folk. Now a numberless crowd pulled the cart, and more lined the road watching. It happened all in a haze of dust carried high above the blunted tiers of Frontend. The dust had the odor of damp concrete and the ocean's salt and the smell of countless bodies and fires of the folk.

Everyone spoke. It seemed a thousand simultaneous languages blurred, fading across the gathered mass of people into a single undertone of voice. The dumb folk pulled the Driver to the cadence of a chant. The cart itself was no longer a little nest. Now it rose as high as a tier and rolled on a score of ill-shaped wheels. Something from every part of the city made up this giant new cart: old houseplat beams and broken iron, odd parts of disused trolleys, here the legs of a harvester doll, here the doors of a power cart. It was the city reborn in the Driver's cart.

Brann and Liza were perched on an outjutting of a gallery which overhung the road. They had come down toward the noise from the spot where the Gads had left them, Zolbek saying, "You be careful now. This is a bad business here," and lashing at Yakan and Zakan in a way foreign to him and sending the caravan in a wide turn south toward the villages of the Gads. "We have room for you," Scote said. "Any time you come, we have room." And the old woman said, *Remember me to Ebar*, in Tsingaro which Zolbek translated. Brann and Liza waved. Then all that was left was dust where the caravan had stood and the dust in front had drawn Brann and Liza to the procession.

Worse than everything was a growing desire in Brann and Liza to abandon everything, clothes, quest, ego, and descend to the road to take up positions on a rope and pull the Driver. The city petered out here on the edge of the beach. Bits of it stood haphazardly where the trolleys of the Structors had dropped them. The protection that the city offered against the fear of the outside gave out also and Brann and Liza felt the same fear, the same tingling in their limbs and vertigo, that had come before. The western face of the city climbed into cloud and the city roof was obscured by it. The bulk of the city seemed distant and the Driver was close and real.

The procession was passing just below them. The cart had many ropes now and the dumb folk splayed in a dozen directions, pulling. Brann could have reached down and plucked at the matted hair of the closer ones. The chant was compelling.

"Can you see the Driver himself?" Liza asked.

"No," said Brann. He looked toward the shape drawing closer in the haze. "Maybe that's him way up on top."

They heard a whip crack and a familiar yipping call.

"He'll trap us all," Liza said. "He's not locked away in a sealed gallery anymore. Now he's out in the open and folk will come to him until everyone is pulling the cart."

An image came to Brann of the Driver's cart grown city-sized, rolling back across the continent along the path of the Foundations toward the beginning of it all. It seemed a strange end to a scheme which had gone awry many thousands of years before.

"Maybe they'll just keep pulling the cart forever," he said to Liza. "The city has stopped but the Driver keeps on."

"Maybe," she said.

The procession moved slowly. There was great confusion among the folk pulling. Brann and Liza lay on the verge the better part of a day watching. The sun once more dropped toward the water. The massed fires of the folk once more burned like stars across the beach and torches came alight on the flanks of the Driver's high cart. Now near enough for the Driver to be seen clearly for the first time, the cart stopped. A familiar phrase carried out over the procession. Then wherever they were the dumb folk stopped and sat down suddenly in the dust. Brann and Liza watched them eat and knew what they ate. This time it was a spectacle of setting sun and fires like stars to the horizon and the torches of dumb folks, eating.

"Please," said Liza, "let's go and find out where our families are. We can get by the Driver in the dark. They're afraid at night, remember."

"No," said Brann, "we'll all become like them. Hals should have killed him. I should have. When a thing gets started it doesn't stop on its own. Ebar told me once."

"Why do we go on Pilgrimage, Grandmother?" Brann had asked. It was the last time they had spoken before the shaking. She had been packing some things—mementos, letters, gifts—into a woven metallic bag. The bag had hung always on a peg of Ebar's plant-room wall where it would catch the morning light and reflect it in rainbow colors.

Often when Brann would ask such questions Ebar would answer with a cryptic, "Because we must, because we always have," and this sort of answer was less satisfying than Hegman Branlee's "Don't think about such things."

Ebar inspected a curious ring of Gad manufacture, tried it on and finding it would not go on over her swollen knuckle, put it back into the bag. "Tradition is the strongest force in our lives, Brann. Do you understand that? Truthfully, I don't intend to put you off by saying that we do something because we have always done it, or that we do not do something because we have never done it. It is the way folk have lived in the city for so long that we don't know any other way to live. You have watched how slowly and carefully the Structors lower blocks of the city, and how they do not let anything fall free. Why, do you suppose?"

"Because once started they would gain momentum," said Brann, who had learned the lessons of the School masters well. "It is because of a thing called inertia, a great moving mass takes a huge force to stop its motion."

"And a city of folk, moving in a way of life for a great deal of time, what stops it?" asked Ebar.

"I don't know," admitted Brann.

"Will little questions stop it, will little doubts?"

"Many of them added together will," said Brann.

Ebar was taken aback at this. She studied Brann for a moment and seemed to derive some satisfaction from this. She resumed packing her bag.

"Good, Grandson Brann, you are who I thought you were. Such a vast thing, such as a block of the city moving, does not stop on its own. A force must stop it, and risk destroying what is stopped. The Structors know this; such a mass in motion is better diverted than stopped, pushed in a less destructive direction."

"You're saying that the city is moving toward destruction and that to attempt to stop it would be just as great a disaster?" He looked at her as she touched the strange Gad things of the bag with intimate knowledge. "You're saying that *I* have to learn where the city is going and divert it! I, Grandmother, I!"

"Enough said," Ebar told him. "An event is coming. The dwarf foretells it and the pictures of the city as it once was, of folk with different ways living on our gallery many years ago foretell it. An event is coming. The Gads have foretold it. This thing will not stop on its own, Brann. I'll see you again. Now you must go."

For much of the night Brann lay atop the broken gallery. He watched the faces of the dumb folk and seemed in a fever, muttering as folk came forth from the watching crowd to become part of the Driver's entourage. This scared Liza no little bit. During the first part of the night she had occasionally shaken Brann, who would glance at her only for a moment, grimacing at the distraction, and would then turn back to the scene below. As the night progressed he wouldn't even do this, shrugging away her hand instead and saying nothing.

Liza, too, felt the fear and the strange disorientation of Frontend. It made her feel restless and upset. She wanted to pull Brann away from here and take him somewhere the Driver could not find. Her conviction became more firm that

Brann was working up to some act against the Driver, toward whom his eyes were now directed.

The mass of dumb folk squatted among the dying fires. The new recruits joined them, finding spots near the heaps of coals. They would settle down, look about themselves as if seeing with intelligent eyes for one last time, and then abruptly a change would come over their features, a veil of stupidity would descend and they would become dumb folk, too.

In the darkest moments of the night, when the moon had set and the fires had died to a glimmer, Liza found that Brann's gaze had firmly attached to the Driver. He no longer responded when she shook him, and his mouth worked with a half-formed word that came again and again to his lips without sound. The Driver seemed not aware of Brann's watching. He stood still and angular against the peak poles of his wagon, the little Driver between his feet, aping his pose. A seductive beckoning seemed to come from the mass of the dumb folk. It rose from their bodies like fumes and came in with Liza's breath, making her dizzy, drawing her close, away from the deep sprawl of stars and the open. Brann began to shiver, to quake, to move into a position to leap out over the crowd toward the Driver's perch.

The word he mouthed came clearer: "Stop," he said. "Stop!"

Liza tried to hold him. He had shed the little people's woven jacket and she felt the cold sweat on his back. He tried to rise; she held him.

"Stop," he said.

"Brann, please," she whispered.

He tried to rise. She moved atop his back, stretching out on him full length, feeling his cool skin, his muscles tense and gathered, feeling how he shook.

All during the night, clouds had been gathering about the roof of the city. They had grown dense, blotting out the stars. Perhaps an hour before sparks of lightning had begun flickering between the clouds and the city roof. The thunder rang hollow and remote from the empty galleries. A nimbus gathered in the clouds where the lightning flashed. It took on a ruddy color and the clouds glowed from within.

In that light the Driver seemed to find animation. His head

turned toward Brann, his view traversed the squatting dumb folk and rode up the gallery to where Brann and Liza lay. Liza wrapped her arms around Brann, caught him between her scissored legs. Her cheek was next to his and she heard his labored breathing. Liza felt how strong he was. She ached, holding him, and ached that, this close together, flesh abutting flesh, wrapped together, close as if they were making love, Brann knew nothing of her now. The Driver looked at them with a vicious awful sneer.

"The outside does this, Brann," Liza said. "We're crazy because of it. It happened before."

"Stop him," Brann answered. He found coordination. He took her hands where they were locked beneath his chest and pulled them until she cried out in pain and let her fingers' grip part.

If he left and went down there she didn't know what she would do. The fumes filled her with each breath. She was holding herself there as much as Brann, and she knew the Driver wanted her, too. She knew that the Driver remembered them from the sealed gallery and held onto a kernel of hate with whatever intelligence he had.

The dumb folk were restless. The Driver was making soft noises to himself and the radiance in the clouds was becoming brighter, spreading over the city toward the face of Frontend.

Brann slipped from beneath Liza, shrugging her off, heedless of her nails cutting across his ribs. She felt a terrifying loss and tried one last time to hold him. Brann shouted, perhaps crying *Stop!* and he leaped out over the dumb folk, bare legs lit red from the city's light. The Driver shrieked too and Liza pulled herself over to the gallery's verge. Dumb folk were on their feet, milling. Brann was among them, fighting out of the sprawl of several he had downed in his leap. The Driver pointed down at Brann. Among the dumb folk was a face, much like Brann's and another voice was also calling Brann's name.

The power of the city was that it took away volition and replaced it with a mindless repetition that had held the city folk in thrall for thirty thousand years. At the ultimate extent of this thrall was the Driver and the dumb folk who served him and had no speech. All power to escape this bondage had been bred out of the city folk. They had stayed behind from the exodus out of fear. Out of fear they had closed themselves in the city. They had dwindled out of fear into pint-sized folk to whom normal humans were giants and to whom the out-of-doors was forbidden and even mythic. They had given over their lives to a mysterious Post Guild whose purpose was obscure. The Guild's folk seemed only to be message carriers through the labyrinth of the city. Yet they held power far beyond that. Such folk had no power to break free of a mutant force such as the Driver. They were frightened and confused by one like Brann who would stand up to him.

In this sort of fear Brann moved through the dumb folk as the Driver shouted and the packed mass of other city folk watched. The torch-covered nest of the Driver's cart rose a tier's height above the road. The hands of the dumb folk, the stench combined of heated air and the city's end smell, propelled Brann toward the tower. He refused to think of what he stepped on, and he thrust blindly through the reaching, grasping, filthy hands.

With Halsam it had been so simple. He had been a child on an adventure when they had started from Tailend. He had discovered strength and adult desire within himself. He had been driven by ownership of the jewel, had joined with the Post Guild (Brann had planned to join, but Halsam had done it). Perhaps he now stood at the top of the city in the storm light carrying out the jewel's purpose. But Brann—the feelings were so mixed in him—Ebar had somehow pushed him. . . . She had carefully selected him of all the grandchildren. (Had she tested Mikla and Grandel or Brann's younger sisters and brothers? Had she found Brann specially or simply selected him by chance?) She had set up a turmoil of ideas within him which had challenged everything he thought he knew about the city—and everything he had been taught. She had done it subtly for years.

At the Driver's insistence the dumb folk punished Brann. They punched him and grasped him but somehow he didn't feel it, lost in his chaotic thoughts and his intent to deal with the Driver. The noise of the dumb folk grew. What a pitiful figure the Driver was, furious and raging that he should again be encountering Brann. He shouted what he thought were words, vaguely remembered out of meetings with other folk. "Youdare, youdare!" he shouted and incongruously he stuck out his tongue, cheeks puffed and eyes bulging, finger pointing at Brann. The whole of the dumb folk took up the Driver's rage and echoed *Yuda! Yuda!* where they milled on the dusty road.

Liza was laughing; there were tears in her eyes. The Driver was like a monkler. He held his breath so that he might pass out. She laughed at him, but she was scared to death, because Brann had been pushed toward the tower by the dumb folk who were forcing him onto the haphazard ladder to the Driver.

And among the dumb folk the face that was similar to Brann's watched, consciousness surfacing as if arising out of a dream. "Brann?" he said and began to make his way to the tower also.

A ghostly sort of light spread down the face of the city in St. Elmo's fire's bluish glow. A corona sprang out along the ruined tiers, climbed swiftly up the remains of houseplats and nested crackling in the tops of trees along the roadside. The cold fire lapped at the base of the tower and grew up over the twisted struts and over Brann where he climbed toward the Driver.

The Driver kicked at Brann. Brann took the blow of dirty toes and ragged toenails on his temple and nearly fell. He caught the foot. He hauled at it. The Driver was incoherent and spitting with rage. The little Driver clung to Brann's thigh and squealed and bit him.

"There's been enough of you!" Brann screamed. The blue fire hissed in their hair and the Driver's stood straight in an immense spark-filled mane. The sky grew brilliant ruby red. The Driver's fingers closed on Brann's throat while the dumb folk chanted gibberish below.

Liza recognized the man who so resembled Brann. He was Brann's brother Grandel, who with his wife had joined the family on Pilgrimage. He saw her, where she stood on the edge of the broken tier trying to decide whether or not to leap down as Brann had done and run to help him.

"Is that Liza?" he asked. His speech was slow, the dumbfolk guise still very much on him. He tried to shake it off.

"It's Liza," she told him. "Can you help Brann? The Driver will kill him."

The air sang with the charge of the blue electric fire. It lapped up and over the tower's peak, drowning the torches, Brann and the Driver.

"I can't see them," Grandel shouted. He was what Brann would be one day, an image of their father, very tall with muscular shoulders and solid legs. It seemed to Liza a peculiar twist of fortune that Grandel was here (and perhaps she cared that he had been caught by the Driver, and what his story was), but all she could think, in her great concern for Brann, was, *if only he could climb up to where they are fighting*. The Driver would be no match for the two brothers. The dumb folk may have sensed this; they took hold of Grandel, barring his way in an ill-ordered assault.

Brann looked directly into the Driver's face, into the eyes where intelligence ebbed and surged, where danger and helplessness chased each other. Brann didn't know that he could hate this man who was the end result of the folk's descent into fear. But he couldn't pry the Driver's fingers from his neck, and he felt his feet close to the edge of the nest where the heat of torches raced along his skin. He, too, saw Grandel at the foot of the tower and he wanted to call to his brother. But Brann's throat was caught and he could only labor for breath. Grandel was held below by the dumb folk. The blue fire hissed in the air and the sky was as red as sunrise.

It was Halsam who saved them.

A queer, exaggerated music started up. It was the twittering of the jewel which Halsam wore on his chest, a million times magnified, winding up in speed and scale. A phrase of notes played, paused and played again. The ruby light took on a focus within the cloud, became a single red star exactly at the city's roof. The crackle of St. Elmo's fire fled beneath it, lodging only in the crevices of the city's broken stone: blue in the shadows, pure red otherwise and so bright that it could hardly be looked at directly. Something in that light held the Driver. His fingers didn't close but released their stranglehold.

The musical phrase repeated. The red star began to enlarge.

"Youdare!" said the Driver, using the only words he had.

The star became a red bubble, still brighter and stretching
now into a human form.

Brann saw that it was the thin face and figure of Halsam,
a red jewel at the center of his chest. The deep eyes of Halsam's image seemed to look right at Brann and the Driver.

"Ah!" the Driver said. The fingers relaxed. "Ah," as before.
The Driver turned from Brann to Halsam and the jewel.
What did he think? (Surely the Driver thought!) For the
Driver and the dumb folk the jewel had been an amulet for
countless generations, and now it grew truly superhuman,
truly irresistible. The Driver let go of Brann entirely and
reached out for the jewel. At that instant the phrase sang
once again and the sky flashed into unquenchable ruby brilliance. The image of Halsam exploded into a thousand frag-
ments which whizzed out among the stars. The jewel flew
away with them, and the Driver, reaching for it, took one
more step and fell into the sudden, impenetrable dark.

At the foot of the tower Grandel took Brann into a bear-
hug embrace, saying, "I didn't think I would see you again,
Brann." He wouldn't let go. He just held his younger brother
and, as in a dream, Brann felt his brother's strength leading
him away. Liza followed as best she could as Grandel led
Brann and Liza through the mass of folk. The city was shaking a thousand times more violently than when the quake had
driven the folk on Pilgrimage. They couldn't see it in the
darkness. All they knew was grating of the tier blocks sliding
stone over stone with a noise so loud that speech was barely
intelligible. Grandel could not stop a sort of awestricken solil-
oquy about the Driver whom he called *"that bastard,"* be-
rating himself for falling victim to the Driver's spell. Through
this, at intervals he would seize Brann and hug him, saying,
"Oh! we've missed you. We've all missed you!"

The voices of the folk spoke in every variation of every
city language. Brann seemed to understand that the words
expressed the folk's bewilderment at the fall of the city.
Brann wondered that Grandel could find a way through the
host of folk to where their family waited. It seemed that they
followed the tongues, a word more familiar here, an inflec-
tion, a linguistic branch with a more common sound. They
moved toward the fluid, away from the guttural, toward the
coherent, grammatical and concrete. It was all the folk had

left to differentiate themselves, all that was left of the old barriers of tiers and galleries.

The city gave way to a sprawling beach. Scattered towers and walls reared from the sand. The speech here was closer to their own. Brann could catch a phrase or two that he understood, a meaning, a whole sentence that was clear. These were the folk of Tailend. He saw faces fringed by fine blond hair, revealed in firelight, calling, *"War be gonna an?"* and pointing to the city (asking this of the newcomers, Brann, Grandel and Liza). They stopped once at a fire where the blond folk offered them a sort of spiced tea, and learning it was Brann who had killed the Driver, pounded him on the back, saying, *"Be fane ting, tey Lurd bave, nowit. Be fane braka ting!"* and Brann knew they were congratulating him. The tea warmed him. It was not especially cold on this night in early fall, but Brann's encounter with the Driver had chilled him more than he understood.

As Grandel led them he talked of the family's escape from Tailend during the shaking. Brann only listened, satisfied to let Liza question Grandel.

"From there we went down elevators," Grandel said. "Everyone packed so tightly that I thought I had lost Mara and could hear my little Ez crying, which let me know that we were on the same car. Vill was in the booth running it and refusing to open the gates even when a car below stopped and we were all on it except for Mikla and Brann. A party of Structors came here to Frontend some days ago, and Mikla was among them, so that we have only been missing Brann. When we were in the down car we thought that we had lost both brothers but Mikla returned and now we have Brann back."

He was more comfortable here, among the Tailend folk; he rumpled Brann's hair almost playfully. "Do you remember Seri Babca and her husband, Dod?"

"Who were mean," recalled Liza, "and who would report to the officers if children were near their stall in the market?" She mimicked Seri's high voice: "Officer, officer! Here's a couple of the little chits now, poking at the oranges."

Grandel laughed. "Well they lugged a whole bushel of fruit with them on the car while Seri screamed incessantly that the children were taking her fruit. *Fruit* in a time like that!"

How could they be laughing, Brann wondered. How could Grandel and Liza be joking this way, when all Brann could see was the face of Halsam in the clouds and the face of the Driver, falling.

"You said the city was empty, Liza, and I don't wonder at it. I think all the folk came swarming out at once, from Tailend and from the other portals at the base of the city. We went out into the Farmy Fields and waited by the trolley tracks. It was not Pilgrimage; it was a stampede. There was an *outside* to the city, but the folk denied it, even though they could feel that it was real. It was not an illusion. There were no walls or anything else between us and the Farmy Fields or the mountains, or the sky. Everyone was sick, some far worse than our family. They were shaking, crying, terrified. The trolleys ran full for weeks carrying folk to Frontend."

Of the Driver, Grandel would not speak much: "I went away from the family. The 'bastard' was there with his wheeled tower. His will took hold and I became one of them. That's all I will say."

The voices carried them to the water, to the narrowest stretch of sand before the surf and ocean. Unfinished buttresses of the Foundations were anchored to the sea floor. The Structors had left them there, having bid and failed to carry the city's bulk out across the ocean. Brann searched for the fleet of the Hugen which the Dwarf had intimated was here at anchor, ready to carry the Hugen back to their islands. (Brann still thought of the Hugen's homes as islands in this ocean, having no way to conceive of worlds above the earth, even as he knew that the folk lived on such worlds out among the stars.) The boats, if there were any, lay at some other ocean anchorage and while Brann thought he saw lights far at sea that sparkled with the jewel's color, he saw no starcraft there. Brann heard home speech and saw folk he thought he knew. The sand curved in an amphitheater about one of the city's last towers. A figure postured on the apron of the tower. It was bulbous and vulgarly pious. "Branlee?" Brann exclaimed. He was home.

They stopped on a crest of sand above the amphitheater. The sun, now above the city's roof, lit the listening crowd through a mist. Brann searched the blurred scene for his family.

"Where are our parents?" Brann asked Grandel.

"If they are where I left them, they are somewhere here, listening, I suppose," Grandel answered. He was reluctant to move closer where they could see and be seen. Brann hung back with him. Liza fretted at their waiting and several times made as if to leave and go down to find her folks.

"How are they?" Brann asked.

"They were well when I left them," Grandel said. "I was with the . . . the 'Driver.' He passed here a while ago. I joined." He looked at Brann, his face apologetic. "I couldn't help myself. I saw him and something fell asleep in my head. I was not afraid anymore. I left Mara and Ez. I joined him."

"He's dead," Liza said.

"I know," Grandel answered. He stood awkwardly, trying to explain. "It doesn't make any difference. I joined him. I left the folk. There was no way I could stop it. I lived with them. I pulled him. I *understood* what he said . . . I was asleep and I woke only when I saw you . . . I ate . . . I ate . . ."

"We saw what the dumb folk ate," said Brann. "Half the city was with the Driver or would have joined the Driver given the chance. It is just the way we are made; we can't stay away."

"I won't go back to them," Grandel said.

"Yes you will."

"They know," Grandel answered.

"I killed the Driver. I killed him!" Brann shouted. "He fell off the tower and down onto a wall and broke his neck. He died. I killed him outside and I'll kill him inside you if I need to. You are coming with us." An intense look came to Brann's face and he took a step toward Grandel, a fist raised. Grandel, weeping, made no move.

Liza stepped between the brothers. "Do you want to kill Grandel as well as the Driver?"

"Kill Grandel?" Brann asked slowly. "Lord above, no. . . ."

Hegman Branlee was exhorting the folk not to leave the city. The city still shook fitfully beneath the morning sun. Blocks of it ground over each other with the sound of toppling mountains. Branlee said, "We are going back. It is a test of us. Nothing is really happening to the city. This is all a mirage. Our lives are filled with chaos because we have bowed to fear. We have not fulfilled the prophecy, or the intent of the Pilgrimage which is to return in the Lord above's cycle to Frontend and carry the reborn city on again forever. So we create a shaking in our mind to explain, and we dream that the city is falling. We must go back inside it, fulfill the Pilgrimage. The Lord above demands it."

"Do you believe it?" Brann asked, pointing toward the chubby Branlee.

"Not anymore," said Grandel after a moment.

"Then you know it's all real. The city's falling down is real and the outside is real and the Driver is real?"

"Yes," Grandel said.

"And we can tell you what the city is actually about—that it served to keep us safe until the outside became livable again. . . ."

"I know," Grandel responded. "I saw it, too, and you told me."

"So," said Brann, "do you suppose that there is a person free of the pain of all this? We were turning into little monklers that just chittered and grinned in the trees and it's a good thing that the city fell down. There are millions of scared folk out here and only a few of them are going to survive without the city. Ebar taught me that. She must have said much the same thing to you. But you're no different from anyone of them and just because of the Driver you haven't been hurt anymore."

"The Driver," Grandel repeated. "I ate. . . ." He sat down on the sand and refused to look at Brann or Liza.

"Let's go," said Brann. His cheeks were wet with tears. He took Liza's hand and they walked off in search of family folk, leaving Grandel to follow or not.

Hegman Branlee's words stirred the folk more than Brann could have imagined. He discovered that most of the folk were even worse off than Grandel: like Grandel, they knew that the world was very different from what they had thought, but they would not, could not, do anything about it. Brann found his family. Little Thod found him first, coming toward him and Liza through the crowd of worshipers. Thod held to Liza's coarse skirt and found it funny that Brann wore the same, wanting to know where he had obtained it and whether the little folk were truly shorter than he. He made faces at the idea of such tiny folk as the jailers.

"We all thought you died," Thod said matter of factly. "And Gwenia said you were stupid to go off like that so I shoved her but you're here now, Brann, so tell me what happened. How come your sides are all scratched like that?"

Brann's mother held his face for a long time and looked about to cry. Brann saw tears in his father's eyes. It seemed for a moment, here in the Frontend ruins with his family, that nothing had changed. The weeks, which had taken the final bit of child out of Brann, slipped away from him and he was a boy again. Liza had gone off. She had been peculiarly distant while he greeted his parents, and had walked away without any great show.

Little remained of the treasures from the Adelbran houseplat. His mother had salvaged the heirloom chest. His father had carried away a packet of photographs and a prayer book with a family history penned inside. They had only the clothing they had worn on Pilgrimage and at that were better clothed than many of the folk. No effort had been made to make the beach into a home. Refuse and garbage were strewn carelessly about. Folk accepted what the harvester dolls brought as food and cooked it slightly. Many wore nothing—and showed no shame in a society which had been strict in its modesty. Brann saw that even among those who had not joined the Driver, a sort of thoughtless brutality had taken hold. Not infrequently shrieks punctuated the worship service, and public intimacy which would have shocked the folk before was the mildest sort of display here. Folk copulated against walls and in the sand, fought, practiced mayhem, killed and through it the service went endlessly on.

Brann asked about Ebar.

"She came as far as Frontend," Brann's mother said. "We've not seen her since. Some said there were Gads here, and that she was with them."

"You let her go!" Brann said, incredulous.

His mother looked at his father. She gestured with empty hands.

It was Brann who had changed, not they. Before, Brann would not have been upset. The folk rarely became excited. What came, came. Brann, now, couldn't understand his parents' lack. Still, in the midst of folk who took such a disaster without showing any care, Brann's family showed anger and upset. They were different. They were Ebar's descendants.

"The Hegman says it will be over soon," Brann's father said. "The shaking will stop. He says it is a test of our faith in the city. The Lord above is testing us and he says our faith should not be found wanting." He sat in the sand, trying to be the same as the other folk, listening to Branlee, who seemed to have an endless supply of words and breath. "When the shaking stops," Brann's father said, "we'll be ready."

Ever since the message had spun its ruby way out into the stars the sky had held its clouds. Gradually the rains had come and in the ensuing days, as they sat idle on the beach, the rain fell steadily. Now and again a report and a flash of light would come from the city roof: a series of metallic clangs, a growl of thunder not cloud-born, a distant, reverberant blast. Brann supposed that the Hugen and the Post Guild fought, though for what purpose (since the message had been sent) Brann couldn't imagine.

The folk on the beach wouldn't speak of the message, though its sending had become common knowledge. "Halsam sent it," Brann told his sisters.

"Oh, yes, of course," they said.

Of Halsam himself there had been no inquiries except for one brief question from Hals's father, who listened patiently to the tale and said afterward, "Halsam is a capable young man. He'll take care of himself."

Brann was becoming furious. Liza came to visit rarely. Brann didn't understand what had changed. She wouldn't stay long and treated him as friend rather than lover. She stood in the drenching rain, water matting down her hair, rain running in rivulets where the little folk's jacket hung open, and he longed to touch her. She made a wry helpless face, half reached a hand to him, and stepped away. Brann took to wandering among the folk. He was looking for some sign of Ebar and the advice he was sure she would offer. "Do this

. . ." she would say and Brann would do it. The course of the future would change. A million massed folk would stir up out of their lethargy, rise from their squatting and take action. But Brann in his imagination could never find what Ebar would say to do: "Do this . . ." she would say. But *what*?

Brann felt so alone. Halsam was gone and Leoht. He couldn't imagine where. The image of Halsam among the clouds came to him often. Had Hals become the message and flown off with it to the stars? Was Leoht with him? He missed Grandel who hung at the outskirts of the amphitheater, never coming closer or talking to the family. He missed his family, who would not talk of substantial things. More and more he missed Liza.

"Do this . . ." he heard. It was Ebar's voice. No one knew just where she had gone. She had a large circle of friends among the folk of the gallery. Every one of them seemed to recall having just seen her. But Brann went to those places— along the beach where surf broke in pewter foam and the folk waded finding no dry spot to rest, on the roofs of tumbled houseplats in the derelict trolleys off their rails and sunk in the sand. He would bellow "Do *what*?" over the babble of the folk but there was no answer.

The battle atop the city had intensified. It had become a continuous string of reports and the air was charged with smoke. It smelled singed to Brann.

"It's the Hugen and the Post Guild fighting," Brann would say.

"Yes," the usual answer came. Nobody's curiosity was piqued. At these times Brann eagerly expected something to happen, a battle of the giants to break out here on the beach, a sudden flight of starcraft away to the island watchposts in the sky. Nothing occurred.

Worse, the Driver had returned. Actually, the little Driver had taken the whip and the seat of power. When the Driver died, the dumb folk had awakened, many of them going back to their own people and leaving the dead tyrant trampled on the road. But the little Driver had climbed the tower. He had snapped the lash experimentally and had tried out the chants. Some of the dumb folk returned. They were tens now instead of thousands, but a miniature cart rolled the old ruts and more rejoined him daily.

"We have to stop him," Brann said once. But he hadn't the will to do it again, not even to the miniature driver with his tiny, ludicrous voice.

"We have heard from Mikla," Brann's father said one day. They had a small fire between them, sheltering it from the rain beneath a tattered cover. "The Structors have all abandoned Tailend. They are coming here to fix things. In a few days we can go back to the city."

"The city is ruined, Father," protested Brann. There's a thousand years' work before it could be habitable again."

"We'll be starting as soon as the rain lets up," his father said. "The Isocourt has plans to meet. They've spoken of meeting and they will find a suitable place to meet. We'll make plans and leave soon."

The rain scarred the beach like a shower of broken stars splashing white, hot sand about, leaving smoking craters.

Branlee's fervor didn't still his appetite. He spoke often now with his mouth full and abandoned the platform without reluctance at the least rumor of food.

"So, young Brann," Branlee said, "we missed you. We had some fears for your faith when you did not attend upon the Pilgrimage with your parents. But though you strayed, you have returned. It was the hand of the Lord Above which brought you back to us, even as his hand has reached down to rattle the city and shake from us the dust of complacency, and send us on the Pilgrimage to renewal." The rain streamed down Branlee's pudgy face and his eyes stared eerily *through* Brann, seeming not the present adult but the boy of other times. The giant gatherer dolls brought a scant supply of food from the Farmy Fields and the folk went mostly hungry, although Branlee seemed to find enough to sustain himself. He ate the flat bread which Brann's father baked in the fire's coals and he drank hot tea from their meager store.

"Have you made ready, young Brann? You know the Lord Above tells me that he will stop the rain soon and quiet the city so that we may find our new Frontend homes," Branlee said.

"The Lord Above tells you? You speak directly to the Lord Above?"

"He speaks to me," said Branlee. "I do wish the rain would stop, it makes the bread so soggy, though the Lord Above tells me he has a reason for the rain. The Lord Above speaks to all of us. Don't you hear the voices of the folk repeating his words? Sometimes I see a vision of trees outside the city and of clouds dropping rain. They are visions as clear to me as the true features of the city. They disturb me; sometimes I doubt my power to sustain faith. But I digress. The Lord Above has a reason. I have always liked your table more than any of the others, Friend Fral, Friend Eza. Don't tell your neighbors, but it's true. We will pack up soon and find our new homes as the prophecy teaches us. Illusion is always with us, young Brann. Haven't I explained it to you before? The eye abhors an empty place and fills it with visions. Sometimes I see water and open sky."

"The truth, Hegman Branlee, is that the city is obsolete," Brann said. "I've seen the ruins from the inside. The Post Guild and the Hugen fight over the ruins. They're fighting now. That's what the noise is all about."

Branlee shrugged away Brann's hand. He picked up another loaf from the coals and juggled it between his hands until it cooled. He made liberal use of the Adelbrans' last bit of butter and looked Brann in the eye as he ate. "Are you packed, young Brann? Do you have all those books of yours and that marvelous cake model of the city? Are you packed, Friends Fral and Eza? The Lord Above says the rain will break any time."

"We are packed," Brann's father said. And Brann's mother said the same, though she gave Branlee a sharp look as if to add something else.

"Mama, Papa!" Brann cried out, "What are you saying? We can't go back. The city's fallen."

Eza Adelbran looked hard at his son, almost ready to agree, but a look came over him, a look of fear, Brann saw at once, one such as the ancient folk must have had when they took refuge from the outside. Ebar was right, some were bred to captivity, to thirty thousand years of it. The older Adelbrans were like them.

"We are packed, Hegman," Eza Adelbran confirmed.

Brann found Liza asleep beneath a blanket which her folks had brought on Pilgrimage. She sheltered in a conduit that opened blindly into an upturned gallery floor. She wasn't a part of them either. The rain had slowed to a thick drizzle. The folk were a sea of supine black shapes on the gray sand. Few truly slept and the murmur of their voices diffused the words that Brann whispered to Liza. He slipped a hand beneath her blanket, resting it on her neck. Slowly he let the hand glide down her spine along the gentle bumps of vertebrae to the swell of her hip. She whimpered in her sleep, loving his hand or fearing it. He burrowed his face into her hair, which smelled of salt and damp.

"Who?" she said.

"Brann." He stripped off the little folk's rough skirt and, taking hold of the blanket, slipped beneath it, his belly against her side.

She woke and saw him and struggled, not knowing Brann at all—lost in the sea of folk, nameless like them, anonymous, distant from him. He put his mouth on hers so that she couldn't speak. He held her until she quieted.

"Do you love me?" he asked.

"Let go, Brann," she said.

"Do you love me, do you?"

"Yes," she said. She searched him, too, feeling the still fresh welts along his sides. "I'm sorry I did that," she said. She traced his ribs, his chest, learning him, shedding with that touch increment by increment the fear she shared with all the city's folk. She took Brann's weight, accepted him, moved with a swelling fury, saying in that motion: "We have to go. They'll never listen. I've hated you since we've been here. It just happened. It's the way all the folk behave. I saw my parents and it just overwhelmed me . . . We are different, aren't we, Brann? They're going back to the city. But we won't go with them. Will we?"

"We're no different, Liza," he said. "I saw that when we came here. Ebar knew. Everything independent has been bred out of them. Even my mother and father. We have to leave before they decide to go back to the city or join the little Driver and start it all again. Hals has sent the message. The folk will come back from the stars and change everything, tear down the ruins of the city, drive us all out on the earth again. But it will be a long time and too late for us."

"But we can go to the Gads," Liza said.

"We can go to the Gads."

Later, they explored each other as if it were the first time and what they felt was very new.

The droning voices became a roar, waking Brann and Liza to a gray, fog-bound morning. The shapes of the folk were still colorless in the dawn and many carried lamps and torches.

"They're going back," said Brann. "They're all going into the city." People ran past. Liza crept to the conduit entrance, to be knocked back by a woman who rushed past, unheeding.

"Hey," Brann shouted, but she was gone. Others followed. One shape was like another in the dawn. Brann searched for his family. Liza called for hers, but the faces were the same, intense, distracted, looking toward the city. The fear of the outside had overcome them. Hegman Branlee's words had taken hold. They were returning to imagined safety and the roof which covered them from the awful yawning sky.

The pressure mounted, folk moving toward the city were packed so solidly that Brann and Liza had nowhere to go. If they left the shelter of the conduit they would be pulled along with the crowd.

"It will thin out soon," said Liza. "It must."

"Zolbek said they were millions," Brann answered, shouting to be heard over the million voices. They didn't hear words. They heard babble. No one understood anyone else; the gallery folk were strewn among the mass. They had abandoned even the little bit they had carried to Frontend, leaving all the trappings of humanity trampled in the sand. From their vantage Brann and Liza couldn't see the faces. All they saw were legs striding past in a parade, which became a blur as the morning progressed until, mesmerized by the folk's passage, Brann and Liza lost track of time.

Finally the crowd began to thin. Stragglers of the mob passed them, seeking to keep up, intent on the city. The legs and the roar had moved eastward. It was a storm letting loose on the city's flanks. Brann came out of the conduit. The beach, once an endless stretch of folk, held only the stragglers. Everywhere feet had churned the sand and mixed the embers of fires and the remnants of belongings. Folk lay where they had been trampled. Mercifully the babble of voices was gone.

Two sat in the sand facing their sanctuary. One was a young woman whose hair was red and seemed bound in tatters of light. The other was a boy/man just Brann's age with dark hair and a sharp face, turned around toward them, watching. A jewel hung by a chain around his neck and glowed dully.

"Halsam?" Brann called.

The young man stood.

Liza echoed, "Halsam, and Leoht, too!"

"We waited," Halsam said. "I told Leoht you wouldn't go with them."

"But how did you find us?" Liza asked.

"Leoht did," said Hals. He looked Brann over. "You're filthy. Did someone beat you up?"

"Hals, in the name of the Lord Above, I thought you were gone. I saw you in the clouds, spread out and giant. I saw you after. . . ."

"Brann killed the Driver," Liza broke in. There was some distance of churned sand between the couples. Liza took a few steps forward, closing the gap. Brann followed a pace behind.

"You killed the Driver?" Halsam asked.

"Brann pushed him off the wagon," Liza explained. "There were thousands of dumb folk following the Driver. Brann climbed up and fought him and pushed him off the wagon. He fell and died."

"The Driver is dead?" Halsam repeated.

"I didn't kill him," Brann told Halsam. "You did. We were wrestling with each other, and he had his hands on my neck as before. Then we saw you projected in the clouds. The Driver saw your face and he reached for you. . . . He wanted the jewel. He saw your face and he fell."

"I killed him?" Halsam questioned. Then he broke out laughing. "I killed the rotten Driver." He laughed and then he bounded up and across the remaining space of sand to Brann, taking his hands and looking at him. "We thought you were lost in the whole crowd of folk," Halsam said. Leoht kept saying that she could see you. She led me here. We waited until the folk passed and you came out."

Leoht had said nothing until now. She simply smiled and it was as if Brann and Liza knew everything—all the divinations which had led Halsam and Leoht to them.

"The Hugen will be here; their starcraft will be back for them soon. The Hugen's job is done. They have no reason to be our guardians anymore."

"They had a terrific fight," Leoht interjected. "People killed other people and they had no *bherk* or *alek* to repair them. I'm afraid there will be more of it. The Post Guild is following the Hugen here to the beach. We'll be caught in the middle of their battle if we remain."

Brann considered this. "You did send the message?" he asked Halsam.

"It's sent," Halsam answered. "Clara said the message was sent and answered. I was out there for an instant, carried out to where the ones who left before are. I can't tell you where it was but the city was gone. I saw another place and Clara said that the message had been received."

"Will they come?" Liza asked.

"I don't know," said Halsam. "She didn't know either. She said it wouldn't be in our lifetime if they did."

"We met some Gads," Liza said. "They don't live in the city. They have a place in the south. We can go there if we want. Brann and I were going to go there. You'll like the Gads."

"I think my Grandmother Ebar is there," Brann said.

"Other folk are headed that way, too," Leoht said all at once. "I see them. Not all the folk went back to the city. A number are going south along an old, old road toward where you say the Gads live."

In the distance along the churned sand were human shapes, shapes of the folk abandoning the city. They were few compared to the mass which had returned. Perhaps among them were Brann's family, for they were the descendants of Ebar and made of different stuff than the city folk. Brann looked at the fallen face of the city where the wave of the fearful broke. The prophecy was fulfilled. The city had moved across a continent, had brought the folk here and the long-delayed word had been sent: the Earth was habitable again.

Among the shapes in the distance are Brann, Halsam, Leoht and Liza.

Listening, one may hear their chatter.

They are human again and set free.

Epilog

Of the last great shaking in later years Brann would speak with specificity: of the fall of the city; of his flight and Liza's through the vast gathering of the folk; Grandel's leading them to safety; of Halsam's return and Ebar's; of the folk's million voices.

In fact, Brann remembered little of that flight. He pieced together stories and took them as his own and would tell them as his own to the grandchildren who would sit about him and listen in the way he had once listened to Ebar in the room of plants on Tailend years before.

"It was a city," he would say and they could see its line north rising just over the horizon like a distant range of mountains with snow at its peak in winter and with the evening sun reflecting gold-mirrored sparks where Brann said there were windows of the old houseplats still intact inside the city's broken roof.

A sharp-faced man, hair gone gray, who wore a jewel about his neck, would sometimes join Brann in the storytelling. He had more stories and different ones. He had followed other paths beyond the Gads' camp. He had been far beyond the city once. And he could not still the need to travel far again.

Some inexplicable magic still remained with Leoht, who seemed sometimes more a part of the sunset than of human stock for though she spoke little, a light shone in her smile.

Folk drifted south from the city, telling of conditions. A rift was forming in the surviving folk. Some agitated for a move. Perhaps, perhaps, they would understand and would abandon the city at last.

Outstanding science fiction and fantasy

☐ **THE STAR-CROWNED KINGS** by Robert Chilson.
(#UJ1606—$1.95)
☐ **THE WRONG END OF TIME** by John Brunner.
(#UE1598—$1.75)
☐ **COSMIC CRUSADERS** by Pierre Barbet.   (#UE1583—$2.25)
☐ **THE LUCIFER COMET** by Ian Wallace.   (#UE1581—$2.25)
☐ **PURSUIT OF THE SCREAMER** by Ansen Dibell.
(#UE1580—$2.25)
☐ **IRONCASTLE** by Philip Jose Farmer & J. Rosny.
(#UJ1545—$1.95)
☐ **ROGUE SHIP** by A. E. van Vogt.   (#UJ1536—$1.95)
☐ **THE GARMENTS OF CAEAN** by Barrington Bayley.
(#UJ1519—$1.95)
☐ **THE BRIGHT COMPANION** by Edward Llewellyn.
(#UE1511—$1.75)
☐ **STAR HUNTERS** by Jo Clayton.   (#UE1550—$1.75)
☐ **LOST WORLDS** by Lin Carter.   (#UJ1556—$1.95)
☐ **THE SPINNER** by Doris Piserchia.   (#UJ1548—$1.95)
☐ **A WIZARD IN BEDLAM** by Christopher Stasheff.
(#UJ1551—$1.95)
☐ **OPTIMAN** by Brian M. Stableford.   (#UJ1571—$1.95)
☐ **VOLKHAVAAR** by Tanith Lee.   (#UE1539—$1.75)
☐ **THE GREEN GODS** by Henneberg & Cherryh.
(#UE1538—$1.75)
☐ **LOST: FIFTY SUNS** by A. E. van Vogt.   (#UE1491—$1.75)
☐ **THE MAN WITH A THOUSAND NAMES** by A. E. van Vogt.
(#UE1502—$1.75)
☐ **THE DOUGLAS CONVOLUTION** by Edward Llewellyn.
(#UE1495—$1.75)
☐ **THE AVENGERS OF CARRIG** by John Brunner.
(#UE1509—$1.75)

To order these titles,

use coupon on the

last page of this book.

Attention:

DAW COLLECTORS

Many readers of DAW Books have written requesting information on early titles and book numbers to assist in the collection of DAW editions since the first of our titles appeared in April 1972.

We have prepared a several-pages-long list of all DAW titles, giving their sequence numbers, original and current order numbers, and ISBN numbers. And of course the authors and book titles, as well as reissues.

If you think that this list will be of help, you may have a copy by writing to the address below and enclosing fifty cents in stamps or coins to cover the handling and postage costs.

DAW BOOKS, INC. Dept. C
1633 Broadway
New York, N.Y. 10019

DAW BOOKS

Presenting JACK VANCE in DAW editions:

The "Demon Princes" Novels

- [ ] STAR KING   #UE1402—$1.75
- [ ] THE KILLING MACHINE   #UE1409—$1.75
- [ ] THE PALACE OF LOVE   #UE1442—$1.75
- [ ] THE FACE   #UJ1498—$1.95
- [ ] THE BOOK OF DREAMS   #UE1587—$2.25

The "Tschai" Novels

- [ ] CITY OF THE CHASCH   #UE1461—$1.75
- [ ] SERVANTS OF THE WANKH #UE1467—$1.75
- [ ] THE DIRDIR   #UE1478—$1.75
- [ ] THE PNUME   #UE1484—$1.75

The "Alastor" Trilogy

- [ ] TRULLION: ALASTOR 2262 #UE1590—$2.25
- [ ] MARUNE: ALASTOR 933   #UE1591—$2.25
- [ ] WYST: ALASTOR 1716   #UE1593—$2.25

Others

- [ ] EMPHYRIO   #UE1504—$2.25
- [ ] THE FIVE GOLD BANDS   #UJ1518—$1.95
- [ ] THE MANY WORLDS OF
  MAGNUS RIDOLPH   #UE1531—$1.75
- [ ] THE LANGUAGES OF PAO   #UE1541—$1.75
- [ ] NOPALGARTH   #UE1563—$2.25
- [ ] DUST OF FAR SUNS   #UE1588—$1.75

If you wish to order these titles,

please see the coupon in

the back of this book.

Presenting C. J. CHERRYH

- [ ] **DOWNBELOW STATION.** A blockbuster of a novel! Interstellar warfare as humanity's colonies rise in cosmic rebellion. (#UE1594—$2.75)
- [ ] **SERPENT'S REACH.** Two races lived in harmony in a quarantined constellation—until one person broke the truce! (#UE1554—$2.25)
- [ ] **FIRES OF AZEROTH.** Armageddon at the last gate of three worlds. (#UJ1466—$1.95)
- [ ] **HUNTER OF WORLDS.** Triple fetters of the mind served to keep their human prey in bondage to this city-sized starship. (#UE1559—$2.25)
- [ ] **BROTHERS OF EARTH.** This in-depth novel of an alien world and a human who had to adjust or die was a Science Fiction Book Club Selection. (#UJ1470—$1.95)
- [ ] **THE FADED SUN: KESRITH.** Universal praise for this novel of the last members of humanity's warrior-enemies . . . and the Earthman who was fated to save them. (#UE1600—$2.25)
- [ ] **THE FADED SUN: SHON'JIR.** Across the untracked stars to the forgotten world of the Mri go the last of that warrior race and the man who had betrayed humanity. (#UJ1453—$1.95)
- [ ] **THE FADED SUN: KUTATH.** The final and dramatic conclusion of this bestselling trilogy—with three worlds in militant confrontation. (#UE1516—$2.25)
- [ ] **HESTIA.** A single engineer faces the terrors and problems of an endangered colony planet. (#UJ1488—$1.95)

DAW BOOKS are represented by the publishers of Signet and Mentor Books, THE NEW AMERICAN LIBRARY, INC.

THE NEW AMERICAN LIBRARY, INC.,
P.O. Box 999, Bergenfield, New Jersey 07621

Please send me the DAW BOOKS I have checked above. I am enclosing
$_____ (check or money order—no currency or C.O.D.'s).
Please include the list price plus 50¢ per order to cover handling costs.

Name _____

Address _____

City _____ State _____ Zip Code _____
Please allow at least 4 weeks for delivery